Praise for Sally Gunning's
DEEP WATER

"*Deep Water* is a good place to be when Miss Gunning's Bartholomew is at the helm."

—*The Washington Times*

"[A] great read that'll make a great movie. . . ."

—*New York Post*

. . . and cheers for the rest of the
Peter Bartholomew mysteries

"A great series. . . ."

—*Mystery Lovers Bookshop*

"Gunning brings a deep understanding of small-town life . . . and an unforgettable cast of characters. . . ."

—*Mystery News*

"A masterful job of weaving red herrings throughout the plot. . . . A very good read."

—*Rendezvous*

"Fascinating people, a setting that leaps to life. . . . Marvelous."

—*The Armchair Detective*

"This series is one of those rare gems that keeps improving with each new title."

—*Kate's Mystery Books*

"Gunning does a wonderful job with her locale and many characters [and] delivers a dandy mystery puzzle at the same time."

—*Wilson Library Bulletin*

"A kind of Cape Cod *Death on the Nile*—don't miss it."

—*Bookbeat*

Books by Sally Gunning

Hot Water
Under Water
Ice Water
Troubled Water
Rough Water
Still Water
Deep Water
Muddy Water

Published by POCKET BOOKS

MUDDY WATER

A PETER BARTHOLOMEW MYSTERY

SALLY GUNNING

POCKET BOOKS

New York   London   Toronto   Sydney   Tokyo   Singapore

This book is a work of fiction. Names, characters, places and incidents are products of the author's imagination or are used fictitiously. Any resemblance to actual events or locales or persons, living or dead, is entirely coincidental.

An *Original* Publication of POCKET BOOKS

POCKET BOOKS, a division of Simon & Schuster Inc.
1230 Avenue of the Americas, New York, NY 10020

ISBN: 0-671-56314-9

First Pocket Books printing December 1997

10 9 8 7 6 5 4 3 2 1

POCKET and colophon are registered trademarks of Simon & Schuster Inc.

Cover art by Jeff Fitz-Maurice

Printed in the U.S.A.

For Tom.
Thanks for marrying me.
(But I still say we should have eloped.)

ACKNOWLEDGMENTS

Pretentiousness in a letter of thanks or sympathy is an infallible sign of insincerity and lack of taste.

The above quotation was gleaned from Emily Post's 1942 edition of *Etiquette*, as were the quotations that head each of the chapters in this book.

The first batch of love and thanks goes to my mother, who, among other things, handed down (and thankfully ignored) the Emily Post. More heartfelt thanks to my agent, Andrea Cirillo, for the continued care and feeding, and to my new editor, Kate Collins, for her revitalizing enthusiasm. I'd also like to thank dressmaker Cathy Thompson for useful terminology and insightful reflections, Ray and Susan Gannon for the cafe latte, Marilyn Whitelaw for digging out nursery rhymes and good witches, and Bill Whitelaw for retiring before either of us croaked.

MUDDY WATER

CHAPTER

1

Invitations to a big church wedding are always sent to the entire visiting list, and often to the business acquaintances of both families, no matter how large the combined number may be, or whether they can by any chance be present or not.

Peter Bartholomew looked at the clock next to the bed and picked up speed. With one hand he reached for the shirt he'd just ironed, with the other he checked his jawbone for rough spots after the hasty shave. He still wasn't used to sharing a bathroom. Or rather, he hadn't counted on Connie spending half the morning in there. Pete's jaw felt plenty smooth, but the shirt was still hot from the iron and he shrugged into it reluctantly, leaving the top button undone. He grabbed the better of his two ties off the doorknob, but as he glanced sideways and saw Connie still at the underwear stage, he tossed the tie onto his bed. According to the radio it was the hottest day on Nashtoba Island since August 2, 1917. He'd batten down at the church door.

"Will you look at me?" said Connie. "I just got out of the shower and I'm sweating like a sumo wrestler. I hate this weather."

"I know that. Come on. It's ten to."

"I don't think I've ever been to a single wedding that wasn't exactly like this—stinking hot and me trying to cram myself into some tight, prickly dress that cost me a week's salary and will rot in the back of my closet for the next ten years." She yanked the dress off its hanger. It was a lime green, soft, cottony thing with straps. Standing there in long pants and long sleeves, soon to be faced with three pounds of suit jacket and a noose around his neck, Pete found it hard to sympathize.

Connie shrugged the dress over her head and turned her back to Pete. He zipped her up and kissed her on the back of the neck, where the freshly dried hairs were already beginning to dampen and curl. Despite the heat and the haste Connie's body drifted against him, but the move was tentative, as if she didn't trust him to hold his ground. And she didn't stay there long. She dove for the closet, and when she spoke again it was from somewhere among the shoes. "By the way, do you know what the odds are on this? Three to two against."

"Against what?"

Connie emerged from the closet with a straw-colored sandal in each hand. "Against Aggie and Walt. I read it in the paper—sixty percent of all marriages fail. Look at us. One day we're married, the next day I open my door and there they are."

"There who are?"

"The divorce papers. Your big solution to our little problem."

Little problem. That Connie had run off with another man. But now Pete glanced with some concern at his ex-wife. They'd supposedly gotten over this blame-game long ago. What brought on the reprise? The wedding, he supposed. He cupped her bare shoulder in his hand and gave it an encouraging squeeze. "Calm down. This time it's somebody else's mistake, not ours."

But the flesh under his fingers went taut as piano wire.

And there'd been no need to rush after all. Pete shifted uncomfortably on the hard pew in the First Parish Church and looked around. It seemed as if the whole island was there—all except the people who should be. There were no relatives at all on the bride's side, and the groom's side wasn't much better—a lone aunt and uncle who looked like they'd last smiled when Eisenhower got elected. Not that Pete could blame them for looking a tad run-down—he remembered the sullen sixteen-year-old they'd inherited after Walt's parents had died. For the bride's sake, Pete could only hope he'd managed to lighten up some.

A sound similar to the buzzing of bees broke out in the church behind Pete. He turned around. The same red-headed, pimply teen who'd led them to their seats walked by with a corsaged woman on his arm. Her makeup hadn't quite tamped down the evidence of either a rough night or a rocky morning, but her ensemble was straight out of the Jackie O school. Most of it, anyway. The well-put-together effect was countered by the crust of mud on the shoes. "Maybe that's why we're late."

Connie's head whipped around. "What?"

"That must be Aggie's mother. They'd have to wait for her, wouldn't they? Maybe she had a flat tire. Look at those shoes."

Connie looked at the shoes and then skeptically at Pete. And it was true, a good ten more minutes dragged by without further activity from the front of the church.

Finally Connie snatched a hymn book out of the rack and began to fan herself. "Honest to Christ, I'm so hot I

3

could throw up. What's wrong with these people, don't they believe in air-conditioning?"

"Not us New England Puritans. We believe in suffering." But as Pete spoke he cast another worried look at Connie. Her normal peach-blush complexion had turned the color of old wax. "Maybe you should get some air."

"Right. I traipse up the aisle as the war party traipses down it."

"You'd rather sit here and barf on the hymnals?"

But Connie didn't move. At least not out of the pew. She stayed where she was and fidgeted like a two-year-old. Finally she slammed the hymn book into the rack and swung around. "Look. What you said before—" She stopped. She faced front again.

"What I said about what?"

Connie rounded on him. "What you said back at the house. I want to know if you meant it."

"If I mean what?"

"You know. That it was a mistake."

Ah. Aggie and Walt. Pete considered. "I don't know, it's not like Walt's still a screwed-up kid. He's twenty-five. And look what he's done. He's fixed up that farm and practically cornered the produce market around here. Aggie's young, I know, but they've been living together since last summer. If they don't know by now—"

Pete looked up. Connie looked away. She looked even worse than she had a minute ago. This was more than just heat. "Do you want to go home?"

Connie shook her head violently and went back to the hymn book.

Pete went back to shifting his rear end on the bench.

It got later.

The buzz in the church got louder.

Every few seconds the glass face of someone's watch flashed in the light as the time got checked.

4

Finally there was some movement at the front of the church, but it wasn't the movement Pete had been waiting for. Andy Oatley, Walt's cousin and best man, leaned out the vestry door and beckoned to Pete.

In a moment of mutual weakness Pete and his partner Rita had hired the twenty-three-year-old Andy Oatley to work for their odd-job company, Factotum. He was, as their logo said, "a person employed to do all kinds of work," but whether Andy would ever actually do any of the said work was at this point up for grabs. Pete had been impressed by his muscles. Rita had been impressed by his cherubic pink cheeks, blond hair, blue eyes. The only trouble was, Andy had no idea what to do with either the muscles or the looks. He spent most of his time following, or running from, Rita's seventeen-year-old daughter, Maxine.

Pete tried to duck inconspicuously into the vestry, but the buzz in the church swelled after him. There were four other people besides Andy in the tiny room—the Reverend Rydell, the usher, and two women of roughly Andy's age who looked like they were wrapped in blue cellophane. It was hot in the vestry, hotter than it was in the church, and they all looked half-steamed.

"We can't find them," said Andy.

"Who?"

"Aggie and Walt. They aren't here. They were supposed to come together and they haven't shown up. We keep calling the farmhouse."

"And?"

"And no one answers."

"So go out and see what's up."

Andy lowered his voice. "I was going to, but the Reverend's kind of nervous. He doesn't want to lose track of the wedding party, he says. So I told him I'd see if you could run out and check. Just in case."

"Just in case what? Just in case they're throwing dinner plates at each other's heads?"

The blue cellophane with the red hair stepped up. Once she got closer Pete recognized the frail girl underneath—Ginny Turkle, an old friend of Aggie Scott's. "They won't be throwing any plates," said Ginny. "Not Aggie and Walt. It must be something to do with the car, something like that."

Now the Reverend Rydell approached. He had the kind of face that you didn't notice even when you stared straight into it, the kind of voice that carried whether he wanted it to or not. He gave Pete a smile that was meant to be reassuring and therefore set all Pete's alarm bells clanging.

"I'm sure it's nothing," said the Reverend. "I'm sure it's purely a matter of a torn hem, a missing cuff link. Still, I'd prefer not to scatter the wedding party in case they do suddenly appear on our doorstep." He glanced at his watch. "You see, I have another service at one o'clock. If you could run out to the farm, it would be a help."

Sure, Pete could run out to the farm. The question was, did he want to? Cars, cuff links, hems, any of those things and someone would have answered the phone, or called the church to say they'd be late. Pete suspected his dinner plate theory was closer to the truth. He also suspected he was better off staying where he was, watching Connie throw up. He tried to think of an alternative course of action, or at least an alternative person to take the course. He glanced without hope at the remaining blue-cellophaned woman and the usher, but they remained at the back of the room with their heads bent. Besides, the Reverend was right. Everyone else in the room was a member of the wedding party. They would have to appear front and center if Aggie and Walt suddenly showed up. And who else was there? Walt's aunt and uncle? Aggie's mother? In the entire congregation Pete had seen plenty of casual acquaintances and a whole lot of total strangers. He was stuck.

Pete gave Andy a grudging nod of assent and returned to the pew to collect Connie. She still looked like hell. Once they were outside Pete had the advantage, at least psychologically, of shedding his jacket, loosening his tie, unbuttoning the top button of his shirt. All Connie could do was to climb into the truck and sag against the seat with her eyes closed. But once they got under way, the wind through the open window seemed to do her some good. She opened her eyes and sat up.

"Keep an eye out," said Pete.

"For what?"

"Breakdown, accident."

But they saw nothing along the road except a lot of people in a lot of porch rockers, trying to manufacture enough breeze to dispel the heat. When they crested the last hill Pete could see Hay Farm below them, a white shoe box set down in the middle of a green and brown quilt. As they descended the hill the variations in the quilt leaped to life—the slick green of the corn stalks, the chocolate brown of turned earth, the feathery green of the carrot tops. As they swung around the last turn the shoe box itself sprouted details—gabled roof, new shutters, enclosed porch . . . and that was as far as Pete got.

Every windowpane on the porch was smashed.

CHAPTER
2

> First of all, the ones in sorrow should be urged if possible
> to sit in a sunny room . . . Occasional offerings of food
> should be taken to them on a tray, such as: a cup of tea or
> coffee or bouillon, with thin toast, a poached egg, milk if
> they like it hot, or milk toast . . .

Don't go in there," said Connie. "I'm not going in there."

Pete turned, surprised. When did Connie not go in anywhere? When did she not try to drag him in with her?

"It's okay," he said as he got out of the truck, a stupid enough remark in its own right. "You wait here, I'll be back."

But Connie's door opened behind him. He had just turned to discourage her from following when he caught sight of a face through the broken glass on the porch.

Pete bolted over the lawn and through the porch door. Walt Westerman sat on the porch, slumped in a webbed aluminum lawn chair, legs splayed in front of him, eyes wide and unfocused, skin like city snow—white with a gray cast. His hands, black with crusted blood, were cradled in his lap. Only when the hands twitched and fresh blood spurted did it dawn on Pete that Walt was alive.

MUDDY WATER

Pete heard Connie behind him. "I'll call the doctor."
She went inside.

Pete knelt in front of Walt. Most of the bleeding
appeared to be coming from the left wrist. Pete looked
around for something to staunch it, but when nothing
came immediately to hand, he yanked out his shirttail
and ripped. The rip went all the way to the armpit. He
shrugged out of the shirt, tore off a good strip, and
wrapped up Walt's wrist. "What happened?" he asked.

Walt didn't answer.

Pete looked around. Broken windows. Glass on the
floor. Cuts on Walt's hands.

"You broke these windows?"

Nothing.

Connie came back out. "Hardy's on his way."

"Did you see Aggie in there?"

"No."

Walt's eyes closed once and opened.

Pete looked at Connie. She looked better. Or, at least,
better than Walt. "Stay here?"

She nodded.

Pete went inside. The house was a typical turn-of-the-
century farmhouse, the first floor mostly kitchen, but
also small living room, mud room, bathroom, pantry.
Pete called first, then looked. Aggie was in none of these
rooms. On the second floor were three bedrooms and
another bath, but only one of the bedrooms looked like it
had been occupied in recent history. Very recent history.
A large four-poster bed had been slept in and was still
unmade. A blue suit jacket hung over the back of a
straight chair, a pair of gray pants and a tie lay across the
seat. At first Pete thought they were Walt's wedding
clothes, but the pants were wrinkled, and so was the blue
shirt that hung on the closet doorknob. Pete opened the
closet. Hanging inside the door on a separate hook was a

9

gray suit and a crisp, white shirt. Pete decided the clothes strewn around the room were from the night before.

But Aggie wasn't there.

Pete went back downstairs and out to the porch.

"She's gone," said Connie.

"Apparently."

"No, really. Read this."

Connie handed Pete a piece of plain blue linen stationery. It was nice paper—Pete could see the watermark. The handwriting was childishly rounded. *It's finally sunk in, we just plain don't see eye to eye on this. I've decided I have to go. I'm sorry if this hurts you, but I have to do what I think is best.* The note seemed to have been written under some emotional strain: the signature bobbled, the first *g* begun wrong, corrected. But after the false start it finished strongly, and there was no question whose name it was. *Aggie.*

"Walt?" asked Pete. "Aggie's gone? She's left?"

Again Walt said nothing.

Pete asked him a few more times, in several different forms, but with the same result. Nothing.

"Maybe he's in shock," said Connie.

Shock. Pete surfed his brain for his old Boy Scout first aid training and came up with two things. Lay him down. Cover him to keep him warm. Well, the *warm* shouldn't be a factor on a day like today. But Pete supposed he should get him to lie down. There was an old iron cot propped with pillows that seemed to serve as a makeshift couch, and Pete prodded Walt onto it.

When the doctor arrived it seemed to Pete that Walt's color, at least, had picked up some.

Hardy Rogers was not young, but it seemed to Pete he aged ten years each time he saw him. Of course, each time he saw him there was a dead, or a half-dead, body around. As Hardy stooped over the current specimen

Pete noticed his hair looked thinner, the shoulders bonier.

"Christ on a bloody raft, Walt, now what'd you go and do?"

At least the bedside manner hadn't changed. But Walt didn't answer Hardy either. The doctor unwound Pete's makeshift bandage and examined the wrist. He hooked long fingers under Walt's arm, pulled him to his feet, and led him into the house. Pete and Connie followed. Hardy steered Walt to the kitchen table, and as he set to work cleaning him up he asked Pete and Connie questions. Pete told him what little he knew. Connie didn't say anything. She wasn't usually squeamish about blood, but Pete noticed she kept her face turned away. Pete touched her arm, pointed to the phone in the hall. "Maybe we should get Andy."

Connie looked glad enough to leave the room. By the time she got back Walt's hands were encased in professional bandages, Hardy had peeled back Walt's sleeve and was poised over his shoulder with a needle. Pete hated needles. This time he looked away while Connie peered at it curiously. "A sedative?" she asked.

Hardy snorted. "He's no Queen Victoria. It's a tetanus shot. Make him some tea and call me in an hour if he doesn't snap to."

"And I'm no Florence Nightingale," muttered Connie, but she went to the sink and filled the kettle. Hardy moved toward the door, also muttering, something about damned fools. Pete was pretty sure he meant Walt.

The kettle had just started to boil when the first visitor came through the door.

Pete had expected Andy. What he got was the Reverend. He was still draped in his black robe, and it had to be hot in there—his face was beaded with sweat, not only in the usual places, but on his nose and his chin, and either his hair was full of grease or the sweat had soaked through. He walked up to Walt and laid a hand on his arm, smack on the site of the tetanus shot. Walt jerked away. The Reverend looked crushed. "Walt," he boomed in his ear. "I know what you must feel. Times like these are sent to test us. You must find strength in faith."

Connie handed him a hot cup. "Or tea."

The door behind them blew open. This time it was Andy, with his parents in tow. The resemblance was not striking. Andy's daily trips to the gym had made him as solid as the years of care and worry had made his parents ethereal, but ethereal or not, Estelle Oatley managed to push the Reverend aside as if he weren't there.

"Well, Walt," she said, "I suppose I could have told you. I suppose I did tell you. And I've never wanted to be more wrong in my life. But there you have it. You can't build a strong house on a cracked foundation, now, can you? Well, buck up, my boy. Why don't you move on home, or go away someplace for a while?"

"For the love of God," said Henry. "You think he can walk away this time of year? He's got corn to pick, and tomatoes, and the beans and the squash coming on. Then he's got to transplant the cabbage and the cauliflower."

Still, Walt said nothing.

The door banged again, this time behind the remaining members of the wedding party. The red-haired usher came first, pushed from behind by Ginny Turkle, and with the push and the red hair it finally dawned on Pete that the usher was Ginny's little brother, Duncan Turkle. The other blue-cellophaned woman Pete didn't recognize, but she seemed to recognize him. The minute she walked in she pinned her eyes on him in a way that made him suddenly and uncomfortably aware of his missing shirt. She was taller than Ginny, and prettier if you used

Hollywood as your guide. Eventually she removed her eyes from Pete's naked flesh and landed them on Walt, adjusting their expression accordingly. She slid into the chair across from him.

"Is it true, Walt? She's left you?"

Everyone seemed surprised when Walt spoke. "What'd you expect?"

"I know. But just the same. Oh, Walt. *Damn* that Aggie."

Behind her, the Reverend Rydell clucked.

Pete left the crowded kitchen and went outside to his truck. He was sure there was an old T-shirt under the seat someplace. Finally his fingers made contact with soft cloth. It was a T-shirt all right, but shrunk, faded, and streaked with rust. He pulled it over his head, swung his arms to loosen the shoulders, and jammed the hem into his pants.

The porch door slammed. The maid of honor, Ginny Turkle, steamed across the lawn in his direction, head down, muttering to herself.

" 'What'd you expect?' 'What'd you expect?' 'Damn that Aggie?' Well, damn you, Walt Westerman. And you, too, Patrice Fielding."

"Hi," said Pete.

Ginny Turkle stopped short. She saw Pete and blushed all the way down to her chest and up to her roots. "Oh, jeez, I didn't see you. I'm sorry. I didn't mean it, you know. He just, like, makes me so mad sometimes. I wanted to smack him one, I really did. And her, too. Damn that Aggie? Well, let me tell you something, even if Aggie did leave him, which I don't believe for one single solitary minute, but if she did, I wouldn't blame her one bit. Ooooh, I could just—" But she never said just what. She stood in front of Pete, legs spread, hands on hips, red hair glinting in the sun.

"Why don't you think she left him?" asked Pete.

"Because she didn't. She wouldn't. She loves Walt. And Walt loves her. He's, like, crazy about her. So they had a fight. So he said something dumb. So maybe she, like, walked off to calm down and lost track of how late it was. That doesn't mean——"

"Did you see the note?"

For the first time the shadow of a doubt crossed Ginny Turkle's face. "I saw it."

"But you don't think she meant it?"

"Of course she didn't mean it. She couldn't have meant it. That they don't see eye to eye? Of course they see eye to eye. They're in love."

Pete decided not to challenge this twenty-something definition. "So what do you think happened?"

Ginny Turkle shook her head. "I don't know what happened."

"Or where she is?"

Again, a shake of the head.

"Could she be at her mother's?"

"No. I talked to her mother right after Connie called the church. She was, like, clueless."

"Surprised?"

"Well, yeah, I guess. I mean, who isn't?"

Lots of people, thought Pete. Walt's aunt and uncle. Patrice Fielding. The Reverend.

And Walt.

"Maybe Aggie went looking for you. You're her maid of honor, aren't you? She could be at your house."

"No. I went straight there from the church. Then I came here and, like, there was Walt, being a moron, smashing windows and feeling sorry for himself. And Patrice, sitting there, damning Aggie to his face." Ginny straightened. "Hey, I'd better get back in there. Who knows what she'll say next." She turned on her heel and returned to the house.

Pete didn't follow. He leaned against the hot, faded paint of the old Jeep truck and looked around.

The broken windows made a sharp contrast to the scene around him. There were no shadows. The noonday sun had beaten them into the ground and everything stood out sharp and clean—the green of the fields, the red of the barn, the white of the house, even the wooden canopy over the old well looked new. Yes, thought Pete, Walt had put a lot of work into the place, not only turning it into a productive farm, but also making it a nice home. But not for Aggie. Not now. Pete wondered what the fight had been about. He wondered when it had taken place, when Walt had found that note. It had to be recent, or someone would surely have called and told the wedding guests. What could have happened to make Aggie change her mind at this late date? Something that made her decide they didn't see eye to eye. Something that made her drive off in such a hurry she forgot to call off her own wedding. . . .

Something that made her drive off.

Of course somebody must have looked, but for some reason Pete found himself walking across the lawn toward the barn. Half the barn was used as a barn—Pete made quick casual note of wheelbarrows, empty crates, and bushel baskets, ropes, hoses, chicken wire. The other half of the building was used as a garage, and Walt's rusty red Ford truck and Aggie's white Ford Escort were both there. Pete peered into the Escort. Empty. So somebody had picked her up? Another man? Probably. It had been Pete's experience that there was always another man. But they'd left it a little late, hadn't they? Wedding at eleven, escape at dawn . . .

Pete left the barn. It was so stinking hot outside his throat felt cooked. He moved toward the well, hoping for a drink, but when he got closer he found the new superstructure was deceiving. It was missing the bucket and the rope and most of its water. At the bottom of the shaft there was nothing but a plastic tarpaulin half-submerged in a pool of black mud. And a shoe. Pete could see a white shoe, or what had once been a white shoe. Now it was covered with mud.

And so was the ankle attached to it.

CHAPTER

3

If the death be sudden, or the nurse unsympathetic or for other reasons unavailable, then a relative or near friend of practical sympathy is the ideal attendant in charge.

The first person Pete found was Duncan Turkle, looking out of place, pacing back and forth on the porch, apparently oblivious to the crunch of broken glass. How to do this without bringing out the whole house? Pete gave Duncan a quick once-over. Sixteen? Knock off a year for the new suit. Fifteen. It would do.

"Duncan." He clipped it off short like a drill sergeant and it seemed to work. Duncan's head came up, eyes alert. "Go upstairs. I saw a phone in the second room off the hall to the right. Call the police station. Tell them to get the ambulance out to Hay Farm. There's been an accident. Someone's fallen in the well."

Pete waited a split second, braced for a rash of questions. Who? What? When? But Duncan—beautiful, pimply Duncan—bolted through the door and up the stairs without a word. Pete ran through the hall and into the kitchen. He saw at a glance things were much the same as they had been before—Patrice still sitting at the

17

table with Walt, Ginny standing on the other side of him, the Reverend and the Oatleys hovering in the middle of the room, Connie leaning against the refrigerator as if she was afraid she'd fall down. Well, it couldn't be helped. He'd need her, too. Their eyes met over the crowd and he jerked his head. He connected with Andy bodily—a hook under the arm and a pull into the hall.

"Andy, get the ladder from the barn. And a rope. Connie, do what you can to keep these people indoors. Whatever you do, don't let Walt loose. There's a body in the well."

Strange that her color suddenly returned. Adrenaline, he supposed. "Is it—?" She didn't finish. It was plain enough who she thought it was. Pete supposed it was plain enough who he thought it was.

Pete raced back to the well and looked down. Had something moved? He looked toward the barn where Andy was only just now disappearing inside. Pete looked again at the well, gauging the drop. Minus his own six feet, add an arm's length to it, factor in the mud . . . What the hell, he'd live. And he'd never much liked this suit anyway. He ducked under the canopy, scrambled over the stone lip, lowered himself until he was suspended full-length in the air, and let go.

He sunk in up to his calves, canted sideways, crashed into the wall, and came up on all fours. He pawed away the tarp. Patches of white skin and yellow cloth gleamed through the mud. Black hair. Aggie Scott, all right. But nothing moved now and nothing could possibly have moved before. She was stiff as a board and cold as a stone.

Pete pulled the tarp over Aggie. It was the only thing he could think to do for her, but maybe, probably, he was doing it for him. He stood up and looked at the white rectangles of light on either side of the well's canopy. "Hello!"

No one answered. A lot of time went by. Or at least it seemed like it. An old nursery rhyme began to run around inside his head and he couldn't get rid of it— *Ding, dong, bell, pussy's in the well! Who put her in? Little Tommy Lin. Who pulled her out?*

The police chief, Will McOwat.

Pete heard him first, his voice like a strange echo from an alien world, ordering people back into the house. Then several heads blocked out the rectangles of light and the chief's voice reeled into the stone tunnel around him. "All right down there?"

"One of us is," said Pete. "No rush on the other one."

The heads disappeared. The next voice he heard was Ernie Ball's, one of the volunteer firemen, ordering Andy to get the hell away from him with that ladder. Ted Ball, Ernie's son and the newest, youngest member of the two-man police department, could be heard from various points, asking what he should do, where he should go. There was the sound of a truck engine. The fire truck, Pete guessed. And more voices. The roar of a lawn mower. A lawn mower? No, a chain saw. The canopy disappeared. The sky opened, then darkened again as Willy's head and massive shoulders appeared.

"Heads up."

The foot of an official fire department ladder appeared over the stone lip and was lowered to meet him. Pete caught it, anchored it in the mud, took a last look at the immobile form under the tarp, and climbed. When he emerged he was surprised at how good the sun felt. He'd hardly scrambled off the ladder before the police chief swung onto it and down.

Connie pushed through the clutter of people that neither she nor the chief had managed to keep inside. He put an arm around her, or maybe she put an arm around him, he wasn't sure.

"Aggie?" she asked.

Pete nodded.

Connie's face went back to greenish-white, but, then again, so did a few others—the Oatleys, the brides-maids, Duncan Turkle.

"Where's Walt?" asked Pete.

"In the house. Andy's with him. I told him to stick close, but Walt's not going anywhere."

Ted Ball appeared beside Pete with a notebook and pen and a look that was half young rooster and half plucked chicken. "You better tell me what's going on."

"It's Aggie Scott. I saw her shoe when I looked in. I thought I saw something move, so I went down. But nothing was moving. She's dead, and has been for a while. That's all I know."

Ted nodded solemnly, as if the Ripper case had just been solved. He closed the notebook and turned to the crowd. "All right, everybody, let's move."

To Pete's surprise, everybody moved. Ginny Turkle, her face now streaming with tears, grabbed Duncan's arm and pulled him out of his trance toward the cars. Patrice Fielding followed, dry-eyed but somber. Henry Oatley dashed at his eyes with the back of his hand and said, "Come along, Estelle, we'd best tell the boy."

Pete caught Connie's eye and knew right off she could tell what he was thinking.

The odds were pretty good the boy already knew.

CHAPTER

4

Five o'clock is the informal hour when people are "at home" to friends. The correct hour for leaving cards and paying formal visits is between 3:30 and 4:30.

They sat on the screened porch in the dark, Pete and the police chief in rockers, Connie curled up on the slider at the far end, as far away as she could get and still remain part of the conversation. The question was, of course, why did she feel the need to be a part of this conversation? God only knew what time it was, and God only knew how long the talk would go on. True, the porch was the coolest place to be, and the soft air wafting over her from the water had done much to calm her down. Still, she could get up, walk out the door, cross the marsh, and sit on the beach. The night sand would feel cool on her feet, the breeze would be undiluted by screens, the sound of the waves running up the beach would heal her raw nerves.

But Connie didn't move.

"Hardy's sure?" asked Pete.

"He's sure," said Will McOwat. "Aggie Scott was strangled. He found the contusions on her neck. The marks were faint, she wasn't cyanosed. It happened fast. Possibly vagal shock."

"Cyanosed?" asked Connie, just as Pete asked, "Vagal shock?"

The chief answered Connie first. "Cyanosed. Suffused with blood. Vagal shock happens when the hand clamps down on the vagus nerve. It stops the heart cold, often before the usual symptoms, like cyanosis, appear."

"And it happened some time last night?" That question was Pete's.

"She'd been dead at least twelve hours when she came out of that well. That puts it before midnight. And she was seen alive at ten-thirty last night."

"So what are you doing here?" That question was Connie's. She hadn't meant it to come out so snottily. At least she didn't think she had. She could hear the creak of the weave in the nearest porch chair as the chief swiveled his bulk in her direction. There had been a time, after Connie had come back to the island but before she and Pete had sorted themselves out, when the chief had cast an interested eye her way. Connie had liked him for that. She'd liked him for other things since. For one thing, he'd saved Pete's life. For another, he'd gone out of his way a time or two to get Pete and Connie back on track. So why didn't she like him now? Why didn't she want him here? Because she knew why he was here. Because she knew what he was going to say.

Eventually.

"I came here to listen to your version one more time," the chief said now. "What happened at the house. What he said when you got there."

"He didn't say a damned thing," said Connie. "I found the note on the floor. I take it you've got the note."

"I've got the note. What did you do, pass it around the kitchen? There were more prints on it than—"

"If you recall, when we found the note, we didn't

know it was a murder. And if you also recall, I was pouring tea and serving cookies while you were—"

"What cookies?" said Pete. "Nobody gave me any cookies." The tone was the light one she knew well. She also knew that other tone behind it, the one that would ask, later, when they were upstairs, what was wrong. Okay, so later she'd tell him.

Maybe.

Suddenly Connie realized she'd lost track of the talk. The chief seemed to be recapping. "So there you have his version. Walt wakes up this morning to find the note saying Aggie has left him. He flies into a rage so intense he smashes twelve windows with his bare fist. Then he sits down to mope, forgetting all about the fact that he has a church full of wedding guests waiting for him. When you two arrive you find Walt in a semicomatose, presumably shock-induced state on the porch, and Aggie Scott dead at the bottom of the well. Walt's lack of surprise at the news that Aggie is dead we're, of course, expected to attribute to his state of shock. So what are we left to assume with this version? That in the course of the previous night a party or parties unknown arrives at the farm, apparently without Walt's knowledge, strangles Aggie Scott, also apparently without Walt's knowledge, and chucks her body in the well. In this version the note and Aggie's intended flight appear to be some sort of extraneous coincidence."

"Hold it," said Connie, but the chief stopped her with a raised hand.

"Let me get to the second version. It goes like this. Sometime during the course of the previous night, the night before Walt Westerman and Aggie Scott are to be married, Walt Westerman finds the note stating that Aggie is leaving him. He also finds Aggie. Either he tracks her down after he finds the note or he catches her in the act of writing it. Since the car and her belongings

are still on the premises, and since the signature is
botched, I favor the act-of-writing theory. Again, Walt
flies into a rage, but this time, instead of attacking the
windows, he attacks Aggie. He puts his hands around her
neck and intentionally, or even unintentionally given the
possibility of vagal shock, strangles her unto death and
dumps her body in the well. But that's only the prologue.
The first big act takes place this morning at the farmhouse. You and Connie walk in and find him sitting on
the porch, reading the note, looking despondent."

"And covered with blood," said Connie.

"So he punched out the windows before you got there
to make it look good."

"Oh, it looked good all right."

The porch chair creaked again. The police chief got
up. He came to the slider. A large hand cupped Connie's
knee and moved it over. He sat beside her. "Look. I'm
only going by the facts. Ginny Turkle tells us Aggie Scott
left her place at ten-thirty Friday night, heading for
Walt's. Her car is seen on the road to the farm at ten-
forty-five. Aggie isn't seen alive again. Her body is found
in Walt's well the next morning. His fingerprints are all
over the tarp. He admits he was home alone at the time
of her death. Add to that the fact that Aggie Scott has
just dumped him. Add to that Walt's long history of . . .
shall we call them impulse-control problems? Now if you
know something I don't—"

"I know this. I know I don't believe it."

"You don't want to believe it. Nobody wants to believe
it."

"You do," said Connie. "I can hear it in your voice. If
Walt did kill Aggie your work is over. You get a 'job well
done' from the entire community and a nice fat raise
from the selectmen." But the minute the words were out
of Connie's mouth she was sorry she'd said them. It
wasn't fair and she knew it. The chief knew it. She could

almost feel him struggling to keep his 230-odd pounds of flesh and gristle in his seat.

"If that's what you think you heard," he said quietly, "you'd better get your hearing checked."

Pete stood up. "Okay, Will, enough. It's two o'clock in the morning and none of us is hearing straight. We told you what we saw and what we did. Time for you to get lost." He held out a hand to Connie and she let him pull her to her feet.

"Look, Willy—" she began.

"No, Pete's right. It's too late for this. I suppose I needed to lay it out for somebody, see how it looked when I did."

And of course he'd come here. Where else could he go? The entire police department was composed of the young recruit Ted Ball, whose expertise ran to traffic tickets and crossing guard, and the dispatcher, Jean Martell, whose expertise ran to dispatching gossip. The minute the chief had arrived on Nashtoba he'd recognized the need for an insider's edge from an outside source, and Connie had always admired the instinct that had led him to Pete's door. But right now she admired the instinct that was backing him through it.

"Who knows," said Willy. "Maybe it'll look different in the morning."

But it wouldn't. Connie knew it wouldn't. Not to the chief, and not, she guessed, to Pete. What had he said at the farm almost the minute he'd seen Aggie's body in the well? *Whatever you do, don't let Walt loose.* Pete had no trouble believing Walt chucked Aggie in the well. Why did Connie? She supposed the chief was right about her. She didn't believe it because she didn't want to believe it. She was tired of believing in the mistakes. For once in her life she wanted to believe in . . . what? True love? Fairy tales? Happy endings? She snorted.

"I'll need you to stop by the station in the morning,"

the chief said to Pete. "Look over the junk we pulled out of the mud, make sure it didn't fall out of your pockets." He said good night to them both and left.

Pete and Connie headed for the stairs, still hand in hand. "Bad day," said Pete.

"Yeah."

"And not all Aggie Scott."

It was one of those statements he sometimes made that was really a question. Or maybe it wasn't a question after all. Either way, Connie didn't answer him. She couldn't. It was all too ridiculous. Too impossible. But of course that was the trouble, wasn't it? It wasn't impossible at all.

"The chief was right, you know. Sometimes it helps to lay things out in front of somebody."

Sure it did. But now? At two o'clock in the morning when nobody was hearing straight?

No. She let go of his hand and moved up the stairs ahead of him.

Besides, maybe in her case it would look different in the morning.

CHAPTER

5

---

*When receiving dinner or lunch guests, your husband
opens the front door, greets them, and helps the women
take off their wraps in the hall. Or perhaps they take them
off in your bedroom.*

Pete woke at eight, already hot and out of sorts. He
looked toward the windows. There were four of them, all
wide open, two facing the water, two facing the prevailing southwest summer wind, but there had been no
prevailing wind yesterday or last night and there was
none this morning. Pete wasn't used to this kind of
weather on Nashtoba, and he supposed Connie wasn't.
Maybe that was the extent of the trouble with her, but
somehow he doubted it. Right now, despite their damp
flesh, she was pressed against the back of him with an
arm locked around his chest and a thigh between his.
Pete removed her arm gently, slid out of bed, and hit the
shower. When he got out he felt just as hot and damp but
less out of sorts.

Then he remembered Willy and the requested trip to
the police station. He put on shorts and a T-shirt and
sneakers and felt hotter. Connie was still asleep when he
tiptoed out of the bedroom. He decided to hold on

breakfast. He'd feel more like eating once he'd finished with the business of Aggie Scott. He left a note for Connie on the kitchen table and went out.

The Nashtoba police station looked like somebody's summer cottage except for the two cars with the odd-looking blue lights out front. As Pete approached the door he wracked his brain for a means of reaching Willy's office at the end of the short hall without getting drained dry by the dispatcher, Jean Martell, up front. He pushed open the door and strode purposefully forward. Jean was on the phone. His ear was directly across from her mouth when she hung up the phone and said, "Oh, boy, oh, boy, oh, boy, is the chief ever up the creek now. Good morning. Don't you look all fresh-faced and squeaky clean. Come on. I'll break the news and you can pick up the pieces."

Pete followed Jean down the hall. It wasn't like her to make him ask. "News?"

"Ted Ball. He's in the hospital having his appendix out. And as you know, the chief's got his hands full with this Aggie Scott case. Wait a minute."

Jean knocked on the chief's door, opened it, and closed it. Pete heard her higher decibels through it. He heard the chief's low rumble. The door re-opened. Jean reappeared, looking slightly miffed. Pete suspected the chief hadn't fallen to pieces as much as she'd hoped.

"Go in, if you still want to," she said.

Pete went in. The chief sat behind the desk, looking the same as he had not too many hours ago, only with a darker stubble. If he gave it another few days, thought Pete, the hair on his face would be as long as the hair on his head. Spread out on a sheet of plastic on the desk in front of the chief was a pile of mud-stained refuse. Or some of it was refuse. Some of it was a gun. Pete pointed to it.

"What's that?"

"Colt Python .357."

It wasn't exactly what Pete meant. "It was in the well?"

Willy nodded.

Pete was afraid to ask, but he did anyway. "Walt's?"

"He says not. Both yesterday and this morning. That's about all he will say, as a matter of fact. 'Not mine.' But he'd have to say that. He's got no permit and he's got no title. It was reported stolen from the home of a Mr. Paul Francis in August ninety-four."

"So he told you the truth. It *wasn't* his."

Willy shot Pete a withering look.

Pete decided it was time to examine the rest of the junk and get out of there. A bunch of rocks. Some rusty nails. A rusted bucket. A plastic doll with no arms. A piece of chain. Some frayed rope. A ring, gold, with three small amethysts. A tin cup. A pencil. A screwdriver. And what looked like a few hundred pennies.

"Any of this belong to you?" asked Willy.

Pete shook his head. None of it had come out of his pockets. He pointed to the ring. "Aggie's?"

"Her engagement ring. Or so Westerman says. And it was in the mud at the bottom of the well, not on her finger."

"So what are you saying? She dumped the ring in the well when she decided to dump Walt?"

"She wouldn't keep wearing it, would she? She could have hocked it, I suppose."

"No," said Pete. From what little he knew of Aggie, she wasn't the type. He turned his attention to the pile of pennies. "Somebody seems to have emptied their piggy bank."

"Into the well. What do you make of that?"

Pete thought. "Nothing to say they did it all at once. Maybe it went in a penny at a time."

"A wish at a time?"

"Something like that."

Pete surveyed the litter on the desk a while longer. "You haven't arrested him."

"No, not yet. But he's lying about the gun. And something about that doll shook him up."

The two men looked at each other.

"What are you going to do without Ted?"

"The same thing I do with him," said Willy. "Only faster."

When Pete got back to the house Andy's truck was in the driveway, but he saw no sign of him until he opened his bedroom door and found him sitting on the foot of his bed. The bathroom door opened and Connie came out. Pete was relieved to notice that since he'd last seen her she'd thrown on a T-shirt, even if it was one of his. Connie had an unnerving habit of not seeming to notice when she was undressed. She still looked like hell, he decided, and he wasn't surprised when she climbed back into bed.

Andy bounced off it and came toward Pete. Pete stepped back to give him a wide berth. He'd been bounced at by Andy before and had ended up with three stitches in his head.

"Well?" said Andy. "What did he say?"

"Who?"

"The chief. I saw your note and I've been waiting for you to get back. He had Walt down there for hours and Walt won't say anything. I kept bugging him until he kicked me out. So what's happening? Is the chief going to arrest him?"

Pete and Connie exchanged a look.

"I don't know," said Pete. "But Walt's got a few problems."

"Like what?"

"Like Aggie's note. And like, according to Ginny

Turkle, Aggie left her house for Walt's around ten-thirty Friday, and the next time anyone saw her she was dead."

"Ginny Turkle said she went to Walt's? Well it's a lie. It's a—" Andy's voice trailed off. The muscles in his neck began to work like the gills in a fish.

"I'm just telling you what the chief's working with. First, there's a pretty good motive supplied by that note. Second, Walt admits he was home alone when Aggie died. Third, they found his prints on that tarp. Fourth, there's his record."

"What record? You mean when he flipped over drunk on the bridge? What's that got to do with it?"

"I think there's more to it than that. Some other episodes—"

"What *episodes?* You mean the time he pounded out that creep who was hitting on Patrice? No, wait. You're talking about the fifty bucks. Not fair. Dicky Trent stole it first. Walt just busted into his—" Andy slowed to a stop. He returned to the bed and sat down. "He's going to arrest him. The chief's going to arrest Walt. And if he does, that's it."

"Not necessarily. Walt will hire a lawyer."

"Oh, yeah? With what?"

"If he can't afford one, they'll appoint one."

"Yeah. He should be a real ace. You think I don't know how these things work? You think I don't watch TV?" Andy slid off the bed, walked to the nearest window, and pressed his face into the screen. When he turned around the tracks of the mesh were embedded in his forehead. "Aah, it's all over anyway. Walt doesn't care what happens. He won't tell the chief anything. He won't tell me anything."

Pete looked at Connie again. It was a mistake. She sat cross-legged under the sheet, pale hair as rumpled as the bedclothes, sea green eyes pinned on his face, eyes that said as clearly as if she'd shouted it, *do something.* Pete turned back to Andy, but it didn't help much. Andy was rubbing his forehead as if he could rub out not just the marks left by the screen but the thoughts underneath.

"Would you like me to try to talk to him?" asked Pete.

Four eyes lit up, two blue, two green.

So now what? thought Pete. He supposed other than filling out his own commitment papers, the next best thing was to get some background, so he could show up at Walt's armed with as much information as possible. He crossed to the bed and sat. "Why don't you tell me what happened Friday night."

"I don't know what happened. That's the whole point. I don't know and Walt won't talk. I didn't see Aggie after we left Martelli's. I didn't see Walt after we left Lupo's."

"Back up. Friday night. First you did what?"

Andy took a deep breath. "All right. We had the rehearsal. You know. You go to the church and you march up and down a few times. Then my folks took us to Martelli's to eat."

"Who was at the rehearsal?"

"The Reverend, me and Walt, Aggie and her mother, Ginny Turkle, Patrice Fielding and the kid, Ginny's brother. What's his name?"

"Duncan."

"That's it."

"Wasn't Aggie's father there?"

"No. Couldn't make it. I forget why not."

"And then?"

"Me and a couple friends of mine took Walt over to Lupo's. We wanted to bring the kid along, but Ginny wouldn't let us. We wouldn't have let him drink anything, but she said no anyway. He made this big fuss, you know, the kind you do when you want people to think you're okay but your sister was abducted by aliens. Anyway, he shut up fast enough when Aggie said something to him. He went home with them and the rest of us went to Lupo's. But Walt wasn't in the mood. He was all wound up. He left around nine-thirty, said he was going home to bed."

"What do you mean he was all wound up?" asked Connie.

Andy ran the back of his hand over his waffled forehead. "I don't know, the pre-wedding creeps, I guess. He kept thinking something was going to go wrong. And he was real tired. He'd been slaving all week trying to fix the farm up nice. I think he wanted to go home, go to sleep, wake up, and get it over with." Andy looked at them sheepishly. "You know what I mean. Get the wedding over with. Get going on the marriage part."

"You say you and your friends took Walt out. Your friends, not Walt's friends?"

"Walt doesn't have any friends. Not anymore. Once he and Aggie got together he kind of walked out on that crowd, the ones he kept getting in trouble with. It's pretty much me and—" he stopped. "I guess it's pretty much me now."

"And his aunt and uncle. Your mother and father."

"Yeah," said Andy, but not like he meant it much.

Connie shot Pete a look.

"So after ten o'clock Friday night you didn't see Walt? Isn't the best man supposed to bring the groom to the church?"

"Nah. At first Walt was going to ride with Aggie, but there was some big stink about that. You know, bad luck. Then Aggie was supposed to come with Ginny Turkle. But Walt told me don't bother going out to the farm, just meet him at the church. So I go to the church and Ginny shows up alone and I say 'where's Aggie?' And she says 'Aggie's coming with Walt.' Well, Aggie didn't come with Walt."

And there they were, back where the whole thing had started.

"What was Aggie wearing at dinner Friday night?" asked Connie.

"A yellow dress. With this big, white belt and white shoes. She looked great." He lapsed into morose silence.

"One more question," said Pete. "Did you ever know Walt to have a gun?"

"Sure, he had a gun. We both did. Shotguns. Me and Dad and Walt used to hunt."

"Not that kind of gun. A handgun. A Colt .357. They found it in the well. It was reported stolen a few years ago."

"You mean—"

"I mean did Walt have an illegal handgun."

Andy shook his head violently. "No. Not Walt. Nothing like that." Then he did something he seldom did. Those big, blue cherub's eyes that Rita had put so much faith in skated away from Pete's.

"What else did they find?" asked Connie.

"The usual junk. And Aggie's engagement ring. Some pennies. A doll with no arms."

Andy's eyes shot back. "Aggie's doll? The one she always kept on her bureau?"

"I don't know whose doll it was."

"About this big." Andy held his hands apart twelve inches. "And weird-looking. No arms. White dress."

"That size. And no arms, I remember that. I don't know about any dress. By the time I saw it it had been sitting in mud for a while."

"It's Aggie's doll, it has to be. She'd kept it from when she was a kid. I joked about it once, it having no arms, and Walt told me to shut the—" Andy glanced at Connie. "He told me to shut up. Later he told me it was some special doll that somebody gave her when she was little. How'd it get in the well?"

"Who knows?" said Pete. "But Walt seemed rattled to see it. He wouldn't say anything about it to the chief."

"That's what I'm trying to tell you. He won't talk."
Suddenly Andy seemed to droop. He yawned. "Sorry,
I've been up all night trying to get Walt to talk. Or sleep.
Or eat." He said the last word longingly.

"Go downstairs and put on the coffee," said Connie.
"I'll catch up with you in a minute, make you some
eggs."

Pete peered at her. Connie, making eggs? She scrambled out of the covers and headed for the bathroom
again.

Andy left. Pete stayed where he was, thinking. He
heard the faucet full force, then the toilet, then the
shower. When Connie came out she looked better and
sounded worse. "You know perfectly well Willy's going
to arrest Walt."

"Probably," said Pete.

"It's more than a probably. You heard him last night.
He thinks Walt did it. All he's going to do now is follow
that thought and collect what he needs to make the
arrest."

"Not fair," said Pete, but as he said it he wondered if
maybe, practically speaking, it was. With Ted out of
commission there was only one cop on this case. He
could head in only one direction at a time. And right
now that direction was Walt.

"And tell me this. What was Aggie wearing when you
found her yesterday?"

Pete thought. At first glimpse he'd seen the filthy tarp,
the foot . . . "White shoes," he said. And when he
dropped down he'd seen more mud and some pale flesh
and . . . "Yellow. Yellow cloth. I guess it was the yellow
dress."

"So she died before she'd changed out of the clothes
she was wearing at dinner Friday night."

"So what?"

"So where's the dress?"

"What dress?" said Pete testily.

"The wedding dress. Is it at Walt's or Ginny's or someplace else? Where did she really spend the night? Where did she plan to get dressed for her wedding? That's the place for us to start."

"The place for *who* to start?"

Connie didn't seem to hear him. She pulled underwear, shorts, and tank top out of the dresser and tossed them on the bed.

"Look," said Pete. "We've already lost a whole day's work yesterday. Did you see the list on Rita's desk? There must be six dump runs on there, four lawns, a couple of cars, more swimming lessons, a slew of mainland trips. Okay, so I've promised to talk to Walt, to try to get him to grow some sense, to get him to talk to the police. That's it."

"Oh, come on, you're going out to the farm anyway, you can ask about the dress. What can it hurt?"

Oh, it could hurt something, Pete was sure of it. The trouble was, as usual, he couldn't think just what.

CHAPTER
6

Persons under the shock of genuine affliction are not only upset mentally but are all unbalanced physically. No matter how calm and controlled they seemingly may be, no one can under such circumstances be normal.

Maybe it was because they were sitting at the same kitchen table they'd sat at on Saturday, but it seemed to Pete that Walt Westerman didn't look much different than he had the day before. Granted, it would have been hard for Walt to have looked worse. Still, he didn't seem particularly disturbed by the fact that he'd spent the morning at the police station, or, Pete amended, Walt didn't seem particularly *surprised* that he'd spent the morning at the police station.

"How are the hands?"

Walt looked down at his hands and up at Pete. Now he looked surprised, but something told Pete it wasn't over the state of his hands, it was over the imbecility of the question. Walt's fiancee was dead, he'd just been questioned in connection with her murder, and Pete was asking him how his hands were?

"What are you doing here?" asked Walt.

"Andy. He's worried about you. And so's Connie."

"Connie?"

"She seems to think Willy McOwat isn't looking in the right direction about Aggie."

"He isn't."

"So where should he look?"

Walt didn't answer.

"What are you thinking, Walt? If Aggie's dead you might as well be locked up?"

"I'll be locked up anyway."

"Who says?"

Again, Walt didn't answer.

"All right. If you don't care, I don't. I told you, I only came because of Andy. And the thing about the dress. But that wasn't my idea either, that was Connie's."

Walt raised his eyes. Pete saw a flicker of something like curiosity before he shuttered them.

Pete decided to act like Walt had actually asked the question. "Aggie's wedding dress. Connie wants to know if it's here. If it is, it might mean something."

"Like what?"

"Like who was the last one to see her—" Pete had been going to say "alive." It was the look on Walt's face that stopped him. And it showed him how much he'd been assuming a few things about Walt. What little there had been that was still alive in Walt's face drained out of it.

"I'm sorry, Walt," said Pete. "About all of this. About Aggie."

"Yeah," said Walt.

Connie struggled through the eggs-for-Andy episode, wondering what had ever possessed her to open her big mouth. Cooking, and eggs in particular, had never been high on her list, and this morning, what with Aggie and all, the very smell of them was enough to make her want to throw up. She turned her back as Andy ate and left him to his thoughts. They seemed to be deep enough. But then again, so were hers. And of the various things she could have chosen to think about, she didn't much surprise herself when she settled on Aggie and Walt. First, of course, was the wedding dress. If it wasn't at Walt's, it would probably be at Ginny Turkle's. Somebody should definitely check that. She doubted the chief had thought about the dress. He'd have been too busy collecting the usual information. Fingerprints. Tire tracks. Who was where doing what when Aggie bit the dust.

After Andy cleared out, Connie made herself some toast. Pretty soon she felt more like herself. She fired up her old TR 6 and drove out to the Turkle place.

The Turkle house was small and boxy and uninteresting. The only landscaping was a row of overgrown foundation plants. Connie sidestepped a renegade yew branch and climbed the concrete steps to the house.

Ginny Turkle's mother both opened and blocked the door in one efficient motion, hips billowing from doorjamb to doorjamb. Despite a measly half-dozen years between them, Connie couldn't help notice the contrast—she could have encased her own hips in one of the other woman's pant legs. But she doubted she could have pulled off her lion-guarding-cub routine if she'd practiced for a month.

When Connie asked to speak to Ginny, Faye Turkle planted her feet and took hold of the doorjamb. "Ginny's used up. She's in no state to talk to anybody."

Feet clattered on the stairs. Connie got a glimpse of scrawny legs, then baggy shorts, then a T-shirt hanging loose from bony shoulders. The whole was topped by Duncan Turkle's mix of freckles, pimples, and red curls that flopped forward as he ducked to see who it was. The minute he identified Connie he reversed.

Connie returned her attention to Faye Turkle. "Maybe

you could help me. It's about Aggie Scott's wedding dress. Did she leave it here? I'm told she was supposed to change here for her wedding."

More feet on the stairs and a surprisingly similar initial view of the lower extremities, but this time the face had no pimples and the red curls stayed put when their owner ducked. And when Ginny recognized Connie, she kept on coming. She yanked unceremoniously at her mother's elbow. Faye Turkle stepped backward with a meek, "Now, Ginny." The lion cub was in charge here, Connie guessed.

"Aggie didn't change at my house," said Ginny. "She was going to, but she didn't. I told them that."

"Yes, you did," said Faye Turkle from behind her. "And there's no need for you to do it twice."

"I'm sorry," said Connie for the second time. "It's just that we're trying to help Walt."

Ginny's eyes widened. "Help Walt?"

"He appears to be under suspicion."

For a few long, hot seconds Ginny did nothing but blink. Finally she blasted through the door, beckoning over her shoulder for Connie to follow her. They crossed the lawn to a picnic table under a semicircle of scrub pines.

At least it was cooler under the trees than it had been on the front step.

"They think Walt did it?" asked Ginny. "Why?"

"Because you told them Aggie left here Friday night for his place, and that was the last anyone saw of her."

Ginny took another good, long minute with that one. "He didn't do it," she said finally. "He couldn't have."

"Why not? Didn't Aggie go back to Walt's Friday night?"

"No. I mean, like, not right away. She was going to. I mean the first time. Then she wasn't. Then she did, but she didn't exactly—"

Connie held up a hand. "This all started at the dinner Friday night?"

"No, at the church. When Reverend Rydell asked Aggie where her father was, why he wasn't there to practice walking her down the aisle. Aggie said he wasn't going to be able to make it to the wedding. So the Reverend asked was there someone else who could give her away." Ginny's eyes went dreamy. "And that's when Walt spoke up. He said nobody was giving him Aggie but Aggie, and they'd walk down the aisle together, the same way they'd walk back up. Then Aggie's mom jumped up and said no, no, no, the groom can't see the bride before the wedding ceremony, it's bad luck. And Walt said baloney, they were living together, weren't they? They were going to ride together to the church, weren't they? Then Mrs. Scott went, like, nuts. So the Reverend kind of skipped over that part and moved on to the ceremony. Afterward, at the dinner, Aggie tried to talk to her mother, but Mrs. Scott just couldn't take it, thinking about Aggie and Walt getting out of the same bed on Saturday morning, coming to the church in the same car, blah, blah, blah. She said it was bad luck. She even said there was, like, no romance to it. Can you believe it? Like, what could be more romantic than that? But Mrs. Scott said Aggie should stay at the hotel with her the night before, and change up there in the morning and go with her mother to the church."

"And what did Aggie say to that?"

"Not much. But she shot me this look, like the whole idea was as romantic as—" Connie waited while Ginny cast about for a suitably unromantic image. "Toilet paper," she finished. "The trouble was, here her dad couldn't come. I think she wanted to make sure her mother would show up. So I chimed in and said, like, why didn't Aggie stay overnight with me, and Mrs. Scott could come by in the morning and help her get dressed."

"And?"

"Oh, they acted like it was this brilliant idea. All except Walt. He just sat there glaring at me like a gargoyle."

"But Aggie didn't stay overnight at your house."

Ginny swatted at some damp, red frizz on her forehead. "Of course she didn't. This is what I'm trying to tell everybody. They loved each other. At first Aggie figured, oh, all right. After the dinner she went home to pick up her dress, Patrice and I went back to my house—"

"What time?"

"I don't know. Wait, we left the restaurant at nine-thirty. The Reverend nabbed Aggie and he was talking to her in the parking lot. I remember looking at my watch, it was taking them so long, and it was, like, nine-thirty on the dot. Then we stopped off and bought a bottle of wine. We knew Andy was taking Walt out for a drink, so we figured Aggie should have some fun, too. But she didn't. Have fun, I mean. She showed up a few minutes after Patrice and I got back—"

"With the dress?"

"With the dress. We opened the wine and sat around talking, but it seemed, like, kind of mopey."

"Aggie seemed mopey? Why? Second thoughts?"

Ginny shook her head emphatically back and forth. "I know, I know, I know. You're thinking about that note, right? Well I've been thinking about it and thinking about it. I couldn't believe it when I saw it. And, like, I don't know. Okay, Aggie might not have been all bubbly Friday night, but I know why she wasn't. She wanted to be with Walt."

"So she left."

"Sure, she left. She might not have left if Patrice hadn't opened her big mouth. But Patrice is always opening her mouth. She's got some degree in computer science and thinks it's, like, the Nobel prize, she's working in New York, the big supposedly center of the universe. So she told Aggie this was her last chance or she'd be stuck with a cabbage farmer for life. Dropped her little bomb and left. And right after that Aggie jumped up and said, 'That's what's the matter. No cabbage farmer.'"

"And she went home to Walt."

Ginny shifted awkwardly on the bench. "I don't, like, *know* she went home to Walt. All I know is she said what she said and she left. And I never saw—" Ginny's voice broke.

Connie waited for her to regroup. "What was the problem with Aggie's father?"

"Aggie's mother. They don't get along. I mean, like, not at all. They won't, like, get under the same roof. I guess Aggie figured if she could only have one of them, it should be her mother."

"One more question and I'll get out of here. What time did Aggie leave your house with the dress?"

Ginny wiped her face with her fists. "Ten-thirty. I know because Duncan kept, like, sticking his nose in. Finally I told him it was past his bedtime, get lost. That really got him crazy, that I said in front of Aggie it was past his bedtime. He started yelling how he hasn't gone to bed at ten-thirty in, like, ninety years. Like we're supposed to think he usually stays up smoking and drinking all night, right? Anyway, it was ten-thirty. I looked at the clock when Duncan said it. And about a minute after that, Aggie said that thing about the cabbage farmer and left."

Connie sat digesting this information until she felt the ground shudder under her. She looked over her shoulder and saw Faye Turkle charging the picnic table.

Apparently her time was up.

* * *

"Friday, at Martelli's," said Walt.

That was the last time he'd seen Aggie. And getting those three words out had made Pete feel like Spanish Inquisitor of the Year. But once Walt got started he didn't turn back. It seemed he didn't much care for Aggie's father or Aggie's mother, and there had been a minute during the rehearsal dinner when he hadn't had much use for Ginny Turkle, either.

"She was supposed to come home. Aggie was supposed to come back here after some party at Ginny's. Then Ginny twisted the whole thing around. Opened her big yap and said Aggie could stay overnight at her house, drive to church with her."

"So you're saying Aggie never came back here after the dinner."

"No."

"What about the dress?"

"What dress?"

"The wedding dress," Pete reminded him patiently. "If she decided at the rehearsal dinner to stay at Ginny's, get dressed at Ginny's, wouldn't she have to come here to pick up her wedding dress?"

"Yeah," said Walt. "That's right. She said she was going to come home to get the dress and then go to Ginny's."

"Did she?"

Walt looked blank. "I don't know. Andy shanghaied me. I didn't get back here till almost ten."

"But is the dress here?" asked Pete patiently.

"I don't know. I didn't look. She kept it hanging on the curtain rod in the spare room."

Pete pushed back his chair. "Mind if I take a look?"

Walt rose and led Pete up the stairs into a room that had that uninhabited but ready-to-serve-if-needed look. It was clean, but stark—a bed, a bureau, a chair, a small night table. The curtain rod was empty of anything but stiff white curtains. Pete noticed a blue suitcase next to the bureau on the floor. "Overnight guest?"

Walt followed Pete's pointing finger and stared at the bag a long time before he spoke. "That's Aggie's."

Pete tried not to wince.

"The dress should have been on that curtain rod. There was a bag for it in the closet." Walt moved doggedly across the room and opened the closet door. Over Walt's shoulder Pete saw nothing but empty hangers. No dress. No bag.

Walt fumbled through the hangers anyway. "Not here."

"Okay. Back to Friday night. You came home and did what?"

"Got undressed. Went to bed."

"Did you go right to sleep?"

Walt nodded. "I get up at daybreak."

"You slept through till daybreak?"

Walt nodded again.

"Then what?"

"I woke up."

"And no Aggie?"

"Aggie was at Ginny's."

"Ginny says not."

Walt blinked.

"You saw no evidence that she'd been here?"

Walt's face was a blank.

"Think, Walt. Was her pillow mussed up? The sheets?"

Walt shook his head. "They asked me that. They kept asking me that. So that's why. No. I don't know. I'm telling you, I didn't even look. I thought she was at Ginny's."

"Okay," said Pete tiredly. "You slept till daybreak and woke up. Then what?"

"I went downstairs. I found the note."

45

"Where was it?"

"Stuck in the screen door. I read it. I went crazy. I guess I smashed up some windows. I don't know what happened after that."

"It was close to noon when we got here. You'd been sitting on the porch since daybreak?"

"I told you. I don't know. I guess so."

No wonder nobody thought Walt would talk. But was it that he wouldn't talk, or that he honestly couldn't remember? He had certainly seemed to Pete to be in some sort of shock the day before. Now, though, slowly, painfully, the words were coming out. Pete tried again. "You didn't seem surprised to get that note. Weren't things with you and Aggie—"

It was just Pete's luck that from someplace below them a car door slammed. Walt went to the window and looked out, but whatever he saw didn't seem to rush him down the stairs.

A woman's voice called, probably through the screen door. "Hello?"

Walt didn't answer.

"Walt? Are you here? Are you all right?"

The screen door banged and Walt gave up. He bolted out of the room and down the stairs.

Pete followed at a more sedate pace.

"There you are. You nearly gave me a heart—"

As Pete stepped into view at the top of the stairs the words were cut short.

"Why, hello, Pete," said Patrice.

CHAPTER
7

At dinners and all small or informal parties, the roof of a friend serves as an introduction, and strangers who find themselves seated together always talk.

Pete wasn't sure how he'd ended up at Mable's Donut Shop with Patrice Fielding. Patrice had said something about desperately needing caffeine. Walt had countered with something about picking tomatoes. So of course Pete had felt it was only right to offer to take Patrice for coffee. Besides, he was starving.

The first thing Pete noticed, strictly in the clinical sense, was that up close and without the distraction of blue cellophane, Patrice Fielding was a knockout.

The second thing he noticed was that she'd been away from Nashtoba for some time. She ordered a cafe latte with a dash of cinnamon and got a look from Mable that would have curdled it if she'd gotten it. Next Patrice tried decaf cappuccino. Mable brought her instant Sanka and a pitcher of milk so cold it was sweating. Mable brought Pete, without asking, black coffee in a thick white mug and two honey-dipped donuts.

Patrice looked tactfully aside as Pete made short work

of the donuts. He hadn't eaten since the previous night. Between bites Pete managed to notice Patrice's profile was even more striking than the full frontal.

"Poor Walt," she said finally. "No matter what everyone says, he doesn't deserve this."

"Deserve which?"

"Oh, you know. Aggie. Her leaving him like that."

"But it didn't surprise you, Aggie leaving?"

"No."

"Why not?"

Patrice gazed at Pete in a way that seemed to eliminate any edge his fifteen years' seniority should have given him, as if it was such a dumb question it required no answer, or that the answer was so obvious even a moron like Pete would catch on soon enough. He decided to try another direction. "Andy says you and Walt used to be an item." Andy hadn't said that, exactly. What he'd said was, Walt had pounded out someone who had bothered Patrice. Pete had extrapolated from there. Apparently, he'd ended up on the mark. The signs of any superiority Patrice had had disappeared, and a look of annoyance took their place.

"I would hardly have called us an item."

"No?"

"There was a brief period in high school where we saw something of each other. And when I say brief, I do mean brief. It lasted only as long as it took me to realize where it was going. Or I suppose I should say where he was going, which was in direct contradiction to where I was going. It surprised me, really, to find that Aggie was attracted to him. But when I went off to college he turned all that voltage of his on Aggie. Considering her situation, I suppose I shouldn't be so surprised that it took effect."

"What situation?"

"Oh, you know. Her parents were . . . estranged, I

believe is the word, since there never was a divorce. Aggie lived with her father most of her life. He's been completely devoted, but you know how it is. Children from broken homes sometimes rush to put down their own roots."

So they were offering Pop Psych 101 in college now. Pete took a long pull at his coffee. Patrice, he noticed, hadn't touched her Sanka, not that he could blame her much.

She caught him watching her and smiled. "Since we seem to be on the subject of ancient history, I was surprised to see you with your ex-wife yesterday. Things aren't back on?"

"Locked on," said Pete and returned to Aggie as fast as he could. "You didn't sound surprised yesterday that Aggie had decided to leave Walt."

"And I'll sound the same today. No, I'm not surprised. Aggie was not the fool she often got taken for. It was only a matter of time before she saw her future written on the wall and fled from it in terror. She was unhappy. I could see that as soon as I got back. I hadn't seen as much of her as I would have liked, living in New York the way I do, but when I came home for the wedding I noticed at once there was a big change in her. On Friday it became quite clear that her marriage was not the joyously anticipated event it should have been. That night at Ginny's it was obvious her second thoughts were torturing her. My feeling was, better now than later, although there is a school of thought that it is actually easier and cheaper to get a divorce later than to cancel a wedding at the last minute like that. And I suppose Aggie must have given some thought to the sheer humiliation. After all, what do you do? There would have been no time for a mailed retraction. I doubt she could even have reached everyone by telephone. So what do you do? Station someone at the church door, turning people away as they arrive? And all those gifts. They would have had to return them." Patrice's face turned thoughtful. "Of course I suppose he'll have to return them anyway. After all, the marriage never did take place."

"So you got the feeling Aggie was having second thoughts on Friday?"

"How could she not? And I felt the least I could do was to give her the opportunity to confide, but she didn't pick up on it. I left shortly after that."

"Before Aggie?"

"Yes, before Aggie."

"So you don't happen to know if Aggie stayed or not."

"She didn't stay. Ginny told me the next morning. She went home to Walt and—" Patrice looked away.

Pete took the opportunity to study the profile for a second time. Patrice had said she'd sound the same today as she did yesterday, but she didn't. Why not? True, Aggie's actions hadn't surprised her either time, but there was a difference in her attitude today. And suddenly Pete saw what it was.

"Yesterday at the farm you sounded angry at Aggie for what she'd done to Walt. Today you sound like it made perfect sense."

"Perfect sense? Just because I see the rightness of the end decision doesn't mean I can't be angry at the method she chose to effect it. To go away and leave the poor man nothing but a note? To leave him alone to face the hordes the next day? I told you, whatever I might have thought of Walt Westerman, he deserved better treatment than that."

"Maybe she was afraid to face him. Maybe she thought some of that voltage you talked about would end up around her neck."

"Oh, no," said Patrice quickly, but it sounded to Pete like something Mrs. Dillinger might have said to her local FBI agent. She studied Pete. "How well do you actually know Walt, by the way?"

"Not much," Pete admitted. "One more question. About that doll of Aggie's. The one without the arms."

"What doll?"

And how well did Patrice really know Aggie? wondered Pete.

When Pete got back he found Connie on the screen porch. It looked like her thermostat was finally beginning to adjust, but she still didn't look like herself. Pete wondered what it would take, short of a knock-down-drag-out, to get her to make an appointment for a checkup with Hardy Rogers.

"Well?" she asked.

Pete leaned against the rail across from her and tried to pretend he felt a breeze on the back of his neck. "No dress. But Walt talked. A little." He told her what he'd learned from Walt and from Patrice. Connie, in turn, told him about this visit of hers to Ginny Turkle.

"So it's official," she concluded. "We're missing a wedding dress."

"*We're* not missing anything. And nothing's official, either."

Connie ignored him, of course. "I suppose there's one more person to check out. Aggie's mother. Ginny says she's staying at the Whiteaker. That was a third option, that Aggie change at the hotel, stay with her mother."

"Connie—"

"I'd go myself, but you're much better with people's mothers. The minute I see one I keep thinking she's going to tell me to stand up straight and take that gum out of my mouth."

"Connie."

"Look, you didn't see him sitting there. Well, okay, yes, you did. But you didn't have to hang around with him as long as I did. He's just a kid. He's got his whole life ahead of him."

"And a good chunk of it behind him. Some of which he spent committing a variety of crimes and misdemeanors."

"You know, you didn't used to be such a stick-in-the-mud. You've jumped into a million murder cases and Willy's thanked you for it. And he'll thank you for this."

"No he won't, because I'm not doing it."

Suddenly Connie went that waxy color again and Pete's anxiety drove his patience, or at least his cool, right out of him. "Connie, what's going on here? What's the matter with you?"

"You think I've got an incurable disease? Well, I'm sorry to disappoint you. I'm hot." She got up and went into the bathroom.

Pete waited a few minutes, but she didn't come out. He could hear the faucet all the way out there on the porch. Well, all right, it *was* hot. Even Pete, who knew he should be tackling a few of those lawns, or at least a dump run, found himself thinking about the Whiteaker instead.

It was, after all, on the water.

He pulled into the hotel parking lot and looked, as he always did, at the harbor. It was as hot and still and blank as the sky itself. One luffing sail sat stranded in the mouth of the harbor, one motorized skiff pulled into the dock and a man and three cranky kids got out. Pete left the truck and climbed the wide steps of the hotel veranda.

One o'clock on Sunday in mid-July and the Whiteaker Hotel was just about as full as it got. The tables on the porch were loaded with vacationing brunchers, or weekenders stopping for a quick lunch on the way out. As Pete approached the desk he wondered for the first time if Alicia Scott had already checked out.

No, she hadn't. And when she opened the door to Pete he soon found out why not.

"One minute," said Alicia Scott as she returned to the telephone. "No, I told your associate this at ten o'clock this morning. I want *six* vases of lilies, three on each side of the casket. No, I did not tell him *three* vases, I told him *six*. Yes, the silver. To go with the silver handles. And the ivory . . . Yes. Yes. Yes. All right. No, there will be no viewing hours. The casket will be open in the front of the church. Center stage. Yes, that's right." The phone went down. A hand went up, not to the eyes, as Pete first feared, but to the hair. Alicia Scott wound a renegade lock into the straw wave that crested her face and turned to Pete. "Bartholomew, isn't that right? I'm sorry to keep you waiting. I have much to do in two short days and I do not need to spend half of one entire morning arguing over a viewing. I feel when the viewing precedes the service, the service itself becomes somewhat anticlimactic. I'm sure you see my point."

Luckily for Pete, she didn't wait to find out if he saw it or not. She draped herself into one of the wicker chairs in front of the window and beckoned Pete to the second. Already sorry he'd come, he sat.

"What was it you wished to speak with me about?"

"I . . ." Pete paused, stymied. He'd been about to offer his condolences, but somehow the businesslike woman in the chair opposite had caused his tongue to dry up. "I'm very sorry," he finally croaked. "I mean about Aggie."

"Yes, yes, yes. You're very kind. Very kind indeed. These are difficult times for all of us, I'm sure. Now you said you wished to speak with me about something?"

Pete began with the hardest question first, but it

seemed to Pete it was harder for him to ask it than it was for Alicia to answer. She stated without fuss that she'd last seen her daughter after they left the restaurant Friday evening.

"I was to help her dress in the morning. She seemed to balk at the idea of staying in a hotel on her wedding eve, so it was decided she would stay with her maid of honor. When I arrived at the Turkle residence in the morning, however, I was informed by the maid of honor that Aggie had returned to the farm the previous night."

"So you went to the farm?"

Alicia stood and looked out the window. "Since I was not informed of my daughter's decision to return there, I concluded my presence was not desired there. I returned to the hotel and presented myself at the church, alone, at the specified time."

Pete smiled. "Or a little after the specified time."

Alicia turned. "The mother of the bride is expected to be late."

"Oh. I was afraid you'd had some car trouble."

"What made you afraid of that?"

"Your shoes. The mud on them."

She arched one eyebrow. Pete never could figure out how people did that. "My car is not the type that is subject to breakdown. My shoes were muddy because the main hotel parking lot was full and I was forced to use the adjacent, unpaved lot."

"So Aggie never came here with her wedding dress."

"No. I told you. What is this all about?"

"The wedding dress. It seems to be missing."

"Missing?"

"Missing. I thought you might have some information about it."

"I know nothing whatsoever about the whereabouts of the dress. Is there anything else? I am, as you can see, quite busy."

"That's it," said Pete. "Thank you." He moved toward the door, but before he got through it she had already picked up the phone.

"Yes. Good morning. I'd like to arrange for a catered buffet luncheon for Tuesday at noon. Perhaps one hundred. Yes, thank you, I'll wait."

Two things occurred to Pete as he left the Whiteaker Hotel. One was that Alicia Scott seemed to move from planning a wedding to planning a funeral with barely a hitch.

The other was that the Whiteaker Hotel supplemental parking lot was dry as dust.

CHAPTER

8

Brides have been known to choose colors other than white. Cloth of silver is quite conventional, and so is very deep cream. Also permissible is parlor pink . . . But cloth of gold or any other definite color suggests the habiliment of a widow rather than that of a virgin maid.

Connie lay on the porch slider, abandoning all attempt to fight herself to her feet. Dump runs, mowing lawns, giving swimming lessons, trips off-island, nobody in their right mind would expect them to do things like that in this heat. And if she'd elected to tell the truth earlier, she'd have admitted that the reason she hadn't gone to the Whiteaker to talk to Alicia Scott was because she felt like hell. But so did a lot of other people, she rationalized. Walt, for one. Undoubtedly Alicia Scott, Ginny Turkle . . . Ginny Turkle.

Something, somewhere, wasn't quite right. Pete's report of Patrice's view of Aggie's and Walt's relationship didn't jibe with Ginny's view. Which one was right? As much as Connie wanted to believe in Ginny's version, the fairy tale version, every time she turned around she was confronted with Aggie's note. Aggie had decided to get out. But when? If Ginny Turkle was right, it happened late, after Aggie left Ginny's Friday night. But she

56

must have had doubts in the weeks and months before that. Or had she? How hard would it be to find out?

Connie heaved herself to her feet and went into the kitchen. She fumbled through the phone book, found and dialed the Turkle's number. It meant one more storming of the Bastille that was Faye Turkle, but in the end she got put through to Ginny and was delivered a neat list. Dress shop, photographer, reception site, florist, jeweler, stationer. After a few minutes studying the list Connie felt better. She got up. She'd start at the top of the list. Chez Renee, the bridal shop.

Chez Renee was small. The bridal gowns on display were large. The minute Connie walked in she felt as if she were suffocating in satin, pearls, and lace. There were four women in the shop, which, as far as Connie was concerned, were three too many, but she could see that two of them worked there—a knife-thin, middle-aged saleswoman walked slowly along a series of hooks, pulling out dresses for two other women who were obviously mother and daughter, the younger a pouty version of the older. Each time the saleswoman displayed a dress the daughter looked at the dress and the mother looked at the daughter. So far, the daughter seemed to have rejected every offer with an impatient shake of the head.

The fourth woman sat behind a reception desk piled high with *Brides* magazines. She wore a neat suit of the particular green that seemed to be in vogue at present but made this particular woman look like a giant pea pod. She was probably middle-aged but looked older. She rose when Connie walked in and handed her a white card with the name of the shop and the quotation, "Where the fairy tale comes true."

Fairy tales again.

"Renee?" asked Connie.

"Jeanine." Connie bet it was plain old Jean on the birth certificate. "May I help you?" Jeanine added, somewhat dubiously, Connie thought. She must not have looked too bridal. But the minute she stated her business Jeanine launched eagerly into a postmortem on Aggie Scott.

"Yes, she bought her gown here. Let me see." She flipped through a thick appointment book. "The first visit was April 26th. There were four in all, the last being Friday. I've been able to think of nothing else since I heard the news. It's all so senseless. If only someone had warned her."

"Warned her? About what?"

"About him. I mean, really. Everyone knew."

"Knew what?"

"Well, his past. He was always a problem. A truant, for one thing. He skipped so much school he stayed back twice. And you must have heard about the drinking. Or what happened when he went to work in May's jelly shop. The very first week she was short four jars. Walt swore up and down he never touched them, but really, why should anyone believe him?"

Connie was about to give a few reasons, most of them provided by the Constitution, but from behind them came a piercing bellow. "I'm *not* going to walk down the aisle dressed like Barbie. I told you what I want. Lace sleeves. No back. Straight skirt. With a slit."

The daughter sailed out of the shop. The mother hurried after her.

"So walk down the aisle dressed like a hooker," said Jeanine. "But you won't do it in one of our dresses. Honestly. Now I was just talking to May earlier about this. About Walt Westerman, that is. This isn't the first mysterious death he's been connected with. I suppose you remember what happened to his parents?"

"I thought they died in a car accident."

"Yes, but both of them at once? At eleven o'clock on a Saturday night? Doesn't that strike you as odd?"

"Not if they were coming home from the movies."

"Well, they weren't coming home from any movies. I'll tell you what May says they were doing. She says they were bailing out Walt at the police station. He'd been caught drinking again."

Which meant Walt should have been in the car, but Jeanine didn't pause long enough for Connie to interject this thought.

"So you see the pattern, I think. Just as well those poor parents aren't alive to see this. And just think of *her* poor father, what he must be going through. She was the apple of his eye. That's what he called her. Such a striking girl, too. Those blue, blue eyes and dark, dark hair. Unusual, wasn't it? And to think that before her mother arrived to save the day she was planning to get married in a fifty-dollar blue dress."

"She came here with her mother?"

"Yes, she came with her mother and her mother came with her credit card, and thank the good Lord for both. Honestly. Although I won't say we didn't have our work cut out for us as it was. The mother kept gravitating to the basque waists. The basque was entirely too much for such a small girl. Eventually I managed to sway her in the direction of a simple princess line in shantung silk with an alençon lace yoke. Worth every cent of the three thousand."

Connie was still struggling with the basques and shantungs and alençons when Jeanine hit her with the numbers. Three thousand . . . *dollars?* Where did you keep something like that, wondered Connie, in a vault? Suddenly she was struck with a thought. "Is the dress still here?"

"Here? Lord, no. I grant you, this entire affair was so last-minute, we were certainly thrown into a tizzy, but we did the last fitting Thursday and they collected the dress on Friday, never fear. You absolutely must have that last minute fitting, you know these brides and their nerves. They either waste away to nothing or gain ten pounds. I don't know which is worse."

And now they were down to the subject, at last. "Aggie was nervous?"

"All brides are nervous. It's their wedding day. Their one big chance. But I must say we did them proud. When I think of that lovely girl walking down the aisle in a fifty-dollar blue dress it makes me perfectly nauseous."

At the word nauseous Connie's stomach did a sympathy flip. "And did Aggie seem nervous? I mean any more nervous than the rest?"

Jeanine thought. "She did seem to be quite subdued. But for pity's sake. Look what she was taking on. For life. It would be enough to sober anyone. But you should have seen her in that dress. She looked like a dream. Her mother floated out of here on cloud nine."

Just then another young woman, with mother in tow, entered the shop. She paused in front of one of the hooks and gasped. "Oh, Mom, look. It's just what I've been dreaming about since I was six."

When Connie was six all she'd dreamed about was horses. She supposed, all in all, it explained a lot.

Andy Oatley was upstairs, supposedly catching up on his sleep, but all he could think about was Walt and his final words to Andy that morning. "If you want to help, go home and check on the folks. Keep them away from here. They don't need this, they've been through enough."

So Andy had gone home and told his folks that Walt wanted to be by himself. Andy's father had just nodded. Andy's mother had aged another quick year and gone off to make his father his poached egg on toast. And Andy?

Andy had lain there, trying not to think about Aggie, trying not to think about Walt. His relationship with Walt was a strange one. Close and not close. Andy supposed the common room and the common genes accounted for the close, but it was a couple of centuries of opposite life experiences that accounted for the not close. Walt was not like Andy. And as much as Andy had looked up to Walt, Andy wasn't much like Walt. Sometimes he felt like he didn't even know Walt. He felt like he knew Aggie better, but Aggie was easy. What was that expression about wearing your heart someplace right out where everybody could see? Well, that was Aggie.

Andy rolled over on his stomach and punched his pillow twenty or thirty times to try to keep himself from crying outright. He'd better stop thinking about Aggie or he'd have to punch a hole right through the wall next. Now that was like Walt. Andy opened his left eye till he could see the plaster patch over the hole Walt had made. And patched. Andy's dad had seen to that. He'd seen to a few other things, too. But who could blame Walt for throwing a few fits? Who could say what it must have been like for a sixteen-year-old kid to open his living room door one night to the news that his parents were both dead. How would Andy have coped with an aunt and uncle scooping him up out of the city and plunking him down in the middle of some godforsaken island someplace, having a fourteen-year-old cousin in his face everywhere he went? Okay, there'd been fist fights and drinking and school troubles, but nothing worse, never anything worse.

Until this.

But Pete was going to talk to him. Pete would get Walt to see sense. He'd have to. Once Walt told the cops what he knew, they'd get off his back. There was no way Walt killed Aggie. Not Aggie. Not anyone.

And then Andy remembered about the gun. A stolen

gun. Walt could be in big enough trouble just for that. Andy wondered what the penalty was for possession of a stolen handgun. Not that Andy couldn't guess who stole it, or where it had come from.

Andy heard his mother's voice on the porch. "Eat yet?" Who was she talking to?

"Well—"

Pete. She was talking to Pete. He'd talked to Walt and he'd come to tell Andy what had happened. And by the wavering going on in his voice, Andy figured he was probably starving to death and trying to be polite.

Andy jumped up. He was starving, too. He was always starving, but those eggs of Connie's hadn't sat right. She couldn't cook to save her life. But she was nice. Well, maybe *nice* wasn't the exact word. *Nice* was somebody like Aggie, somebody who wouldn't say a cross word to you even if you spit in her face. Connie had said enough cross words to Andy to grow hair on his chest. Okay, so he'd deserved some of them. All right, he'd deserved most of them. He didn't know what it was, but every time he had to do something in front of somebody his arms and legs stopped listening to him and went their own way instead.

As Andy hit the stairs he heard his father's voice drift up the stairwell. "Andy's asleep. I wanted him to bunk down over to Walt's for a spell, but Walt, he wouldn't hear of it. I'll wake the boy if you need him for something."

"No," said Pete. "Don't wake him up. It'll wait."

"How's he working out for you, by the way?"

Andy paused on the last step.

"Great."

Yeah, right. Nice fake, Pete.

"Never can figure it," said Henry, but he sounded pleased. "Can't bust his way out of a paper bag, that Andy. Walt, now, that boy has something in him. Mostly it's the devil. But when it isn't, he can do a day's work. Do just about anything he puts his hand to. Imagine a city boy like that taking that old farm and making it pay out. Seemed for a while things were going to turn out all right for him."

Andy heard a series of noises—lumps being reamed out of his father's throat—a familiar sound, at least since yesterday. "Me, I thought little Aggie coming along was as good as news got, but Estelle, she saw nothing but trouble ahead. Proves she was right. This time, at least."

"You were at the church with them on Friday," said Pete. "You saw them at dinner. Did you have a chance to talk to Aggie?"

"Always make a chance to talk to Aggie. Couldn't find a nicer little girl than Aggie. Only thing wrong with her was loving certain people too much."

And what did that mean? wondered Andy. Did his father think Aggie loved Walt too much?

"Did Aggie say anything to you on Friday about her plans for the night?" asked Pete.

"Not to me personal, like. But I caught wind of it. What I say is, they're together before, they'll be together after, why not let 'em be together during? Seems to me they could have used each other's company. But Alicia, she raised such a rumpus it ended up Aggie spent the night with her girlfriend. That's what I heard, at any rate."

"Heard where?"

"Heard here," said a voice to Andy's immediate right, and his mother came out of the kitchen with a plate of sandwiches and two long, sweating glasses of tea and lemon over ice. She gave Andy one of those disapproving looks he didn't mind because he deserved, eavesdropping on the stairs like that. She pointed to the second glass. "Figured you'd smell it. Come along and keep Pete company while he eats."

Andy followed his mother onto the porch. "Now, Henry," she said, "your lunch was over an hour ago. You'd best get moving if you plan to change that oil before night."

Andy's father eased out of his rocker, nodded to his son, and went inside, his eyes still shadowed the way they'd been since yesterday. Pete must have noticed. He shot Andy a warning look. So they'd talk later about Walt.

The two of them sat down to eat. The house was one of those ancient Capes with a stone foundation that had sunk in the northeast corner, and Andy had to cant himself to port to offset the starboard pitch. While they lit into the sandwiches Andy's mother took up where his father left off, but Andy wasn't fooled by her tone. He could hear the struggle with the sorrow when she breathed. So maybe Walt was right. Better to keep them away. They were getting old, they couldn't take this. The thought made Andy feel oddly bereft. And Walt didn't want him around, either. Not that Andy could blame him. Probably all his life Walt would look at Andy and think there he is again, that pesky little kid.

"Yes, Aggie stayed at the Turkle house," his mother went on. "That's what Faye Turkle said. But she was gone come morning, lock, stock, and barrel. And while we're on the subject, let me just say this."

Andy rolled his eyes at Pete.

"I don't want you taking wrong what I said yesterday out at Walt's place. I said that not knowing poor Aggie was dead. Aside of Walt there's no one more grieved about that young woman dying, lest it's my husband. But I stand by my gut, and my gut told me it would come to this, or something near enough so as not to matter much. Young Walt's had his troubles, I'll be the first one to admit to you that fact. But if he'd had one decent chance at the right sort of woman he'd have made her a fine husband. I was against him pairing up with Aggie Scott and I'll tell anyone who cares to ask me why that was. Aggie Scott's family life. No mother. Girl left to raise herself by hook or by crook."

"Come on, Ma," said Andy. "She had a father."

"No small girl can turn out strong who's left to raise herself," she repeated. "But that's only part of my objection. The other part is just that. Aggie Scott's father. He spoiled that child rotten. Treated her like a queen, gave her everything before she even wanted it. What could our Walt give her compared to all that? A farmer's life. Scraping and saving and a heap of hard work. I told Walt no good would ever come of a situation like that. Sooner or later the whole house of cards would come crashing down and land right on his very own poor head. Any little nig-piggling thing, she'd go running home and he'd get the blame. And she did. And he did. Sooner rather than later. And look where it got him."

"Look where it got her," said Andy. "She's the one who's dead."

"And through no fault of Walt's," said his mother. "But while we're on the subject, young man, did I or did I not tell you that selfsame thing about Maxine Peck? I know what her mother's thinking, and I don't blame her one bit. That girl still in high school and you twenty-three and out working for your keep."

Andy could feel his face turn red. If there was anything he hated in life, it was the way his face turned red.

"Maxine's mother feels Andy's very trustworthy," said Pete.

Which Andy was. It was Maxine her mother shouldn't trust. Andy thought of a certain situation that had cropped up last week right on Maxine's mother's couch. It had ended in another fight that had caused Andy to go dateless to his cousin's wedding. Maybe his mother was right. Not that he was too old for Maxine, but that

Maxine was too old for him. Not that he could ever admit that.

"We've gotta go," said Andy, fast.

Pete threw a thank-you-for-the-lunch over his shoulder and they walked down the porch steps.

When they were out of earshot Andy said, "You talked to Walt?"

"I talked to him. I don't think it's so much that he's holding back anything. I think it's possible he went into some kind of shock. He honestly doesn't seem to remember much."

Andy tried to look like Pete had cheered him up. But all he could think of was maybe Walt couldn't remember because he'd done something he couldn't stand remembering.

Pete clapped a hand on his shoulder. "I'll tell you what. We'll keep asking around, see if we can't come up with something that helps. And you, too. Keep your ears open." A sidelong look. "In particular, we've got that gun to worry about. The chief's pretty sure Walt's not coming clean about that and I know how he thinks. That if Walt's lying about the gun, he must be lying about the rest."

Andy ducked his head. He was a beet again. He could feel it. He swore one of these days he was going to cut his head off, right at the neck.

CHAPTER
9

Having pictures taken before the ceremony is a dull custom . . . But to attempt posing at the moment when the procession ought to be starting is as trying to the nerves as it is exhausting, and more than one wedding procession has consisted of very "dragged-out" young women in consequence.

Andy Oatley had been wrong when he said Walt Westerman had no friends. He had one, Connie discovered, in the person of the photographer, Lit Smith. Lit was called Lit, or Little, because at one time he had been the smaller of the two Smiths. The larger Smith, his father, was called Big Smith. The fact that Lit Smith now towered over Big Smith, and most of the rest of Nashtoba, for that matter, hadn't done a thing toward loosening the name's grip.

But if Connie had named him she would have named him Ichabod. He opened the door all knees, shoulders, elbows, and Adam's apple. His hair was swept straight back from a sloping forehead and tied with a leather thong at the nape of his neck, from which point it continued to flow downward in a long blond plume. When Connie brought up the subject that had drawn her to his door, Lit leaned against the doorjamb, crossed his arms, and studied her.

"You saw Walt? He's all right?"

"I don't know as I'd say all right."

"Yeah. Guess not. I didn't want to go out. Knowing Walt, he'd just about hate that. Still, you kind of want to make sure."

"Walt hired you to take the wedding pictures?"

"I wouldn't say hired. Back in March when Walt told me about the wedding I offered to snap a couple shots. A wedding present. But that was for the first plan."

"The first plan?"

"A few people back at the farm. Walt said 'snap a few shots.' Then Aggie and her mother came to see me. All of a sudden we're talking formal shots on the lawn. Six takes of cutting the cake. Eight more of the bouquet getting tossed. So I called Walt. I asked him if he knew what had happened to his plan. He said, 'Do what Aggie wants.'" Lit shrugged. "He was crazy about her. He said he'd pay for it if I could wait, but I said no way, you're talking to your old pal Lit. Besides, the mother said she'd spring for it. I wouldn't have taken it, though. So you figure he's okay? Heard he was throwing things around, smashing up the place."

"That was when he found out she wanted to leave him. Did you hear about that?"

"Yeah, I heard."

"Were you surprised?"

Lit looked up at the sky, down at the ground, and, finally, in the general vicinity of her eyes. "Not much."

"Why not?"

"Old Walt, seems like he gets it every time. Right in the old nuts." He cast a doubtful glance at Connie. "If you catch my drift."

Connie caught it. At least she caught it to the extent that she could vividly recall the expression on Pete's face that time she'd backed into him with a broom handle. "When did Aggie and her mother come to see you?"

Lit thought. "Must have been May. Early May. I'll tell you exactly if you want me to." He disappeared, and when he came back he said, "Yup, May 1st."

"And do you remember how Aggie seemed when she was here?"

"What do you mean?"

"Did she act like the typical excited bride, or did she act like somebody who was contemplating a cut-and-run? Did she seem . . . happy?" Connie finished lamely, but apparently the simplistic adjective was all it took. Lit didn't pause for further thought.

"Happy? No chance. Matter of fact, if she were a guy, I'd say somebody had a shotgun to her head."

A shotgun wedding. Connie almost laughed. The only trouble was, it wasn't funny. But the analogy did serve to tell her what she'd come to find out. By the time Aggie saw Lit, she'd seen the light, so to speak. The prospect of marriage to Walt had begun to look grim. Still, she'd tried to go through with it for a while. She'd kept up the farce for another two and a half months, as a matter of fact. Only at the eleventh hour had she tried to back out. But what about Walt? In all those two and a half months, hadn't he sensed something wasn't right? Connie decided to ask Lit.

"How was Walt through all this?"

"Walt? He just wanted to marry Aggie. He didn't care about the rest."

"The rest?"

Lit held an imaginary camera to Connie's face, panto-mimed depressing the plunger and said, "Take six."

When Pete pulled into his driveway the police chief's red and white Scout was already in it. As Pete approached the driver's side window something about the chief's body language as he climbed out of his car told

Pete this wasn't the thank-you visit Connie had predicted.

"What the hell is this?" said Willy.

"Let's see. July 16th."

On the whole, the chief's body language didn't improve much. "I got a call from this maid of honor's mother. She said Factotum was harassing her daughter. Were you?"

"No," said Pete. "We were talking to her. Connie talked to her. It's a free country."

"It's not as free as you think. You can't go around harassing people. What's Factotum doing in the middle of this?"

Good question, thought Pete. "Andy was worried about Walt, so I said I'd go talk to him."

Willy still looked unhappy, and on the whole Pete couldn't blame him much. Pete decided to try to cheer him up by telling him about Aggie's doll, the one without the arms that had somehow found its way into the well. When he got through Willy pulled out a notebook and wrote in it. Pete peered over his shoulder and saw the name Hendrick.

"Who's Hendrick?" asked Pete.

Willy snapped the notebook shut. "The farm's previous tenants. I've just come back from there. They claim the bucket, the chain, the cup."

"But not the pennies?"

"No," said Willy. "Or the gun."

"And you believe them?"

"More than I do Walt. And you still haven't explained what you're doing harassing people."

"I told you. I went out to see Walt at Andy's request. And Connie had a few things she figured I should ask while I was out there."

Pete took it as a compliment to Connie when after a short pause the chief said, "Like what?"

"The wedding dress."

"The wedding dress."

"One of the reasons you're looking at Walt in the first place is that Ginny Turkle said Aggie left her house for his house Friday night. And she took the dress with her when she left, that's why Connie went out to the Turkles to check. But the dress never made it to Walt's."

"Who says?"

"I told you, I went over there. I talked to Walt. He took me upstairs and he showed me the place Aggie hung it. No dress."

Willy shook his head smugly. "This is why I'm a cop and you're not. You don't let a suspect show you an empty hook and let it go at that, you go over the place with a flea-comb. But, as a matter of fact—" Willy reached down and picked up what appeared to be a brand new car phone.

"My, my, my," said Pete. "Aren't we getting high-tech."

Willy ignored him. Pete could only hear snatches of his half of the conversation, but he caught the word "inventory" and "Westerman place." When the chief hung up he looked a little less smug. "You're right," he said. "No dress."

As Connie strode through the lobby of the Whiteaker Hotel she noticed two white-coated waiters wrapping the mahogany stair railing in green garlands. "Did I miss Thanksgiving?"

"No," said the younger, more serious-looking of the two. "It's a wedding."

Connie sighed. If there was anything she hated, it was a joke that fell flat. She started toward the hotel office just as the hotel owner, Jack Whiteaker, came out of it, carrying two huge, white bows. He saw Connie and flashed a mouth full of white teeth. He hung the bows from the newel posts and swiped a lock of hair off his suspiciously dry forehead. "All right, boys. Now the red carpet. Set it up on the landing, but don't unroll it. The minute Alf sees the horse and buggy, he'll give you the high sign."

"A horse and buggy are going to ride down these stairs?" asked Connie.

Jack Whiteaker grinned. "Only a matter of time. Last Saturday they water-skied here. Nice to see you, Connie. Something I can do for you?"

"It looks like a bad time. I was hoping for a word. I guess you pack these weddings in pretty tight."

"This time of year I do. Everyone who's ever spent a week's vacation here wants to get married on Nashtoba. But actually, you couldn't have timed your visit better. We've pretty well wrapped things up and they won't arrive for another hour. Here, come into the office."

He led Connie behind a mahogany counter that still gleamed despite a good ninety years of living, and into a cozy room that Connie suspected contained the only air-conditioner on Nashtoba. She collapsed gratefully onto the love seat.

"I'll be back with my PJ's and toothbrush," she said.

"My pleasure." Jack grinned again, or, rather, he kept on grinning—he hadn't actually ever stopped. But once Connie mentioned the subject she hoped to address, every single one of Jack's abundant white teeth disappeared from sight.

"From day one this Scott wedding has been my biggest nightmare. No, I take that back. Not the biggest. The biggest was the time a best man made an off-color toast about the bride and the groom slugged him. I'm not sure who slugged the groom. Perhaps an usher. It was definitely the bride who slugged the groom's father. When the second row of tables went over, I called Will McOwat. When they started laying hands on Will, he arrested the whole lot." Jack shook his head. "Pressure. It's all way too much pressure. And liquor. But you wanted to know about Aggie Scott's wedding."

"Other than the obvious end result, why was it a nightmare?"

"Please. A mid-season wedding with less than three month's notice? She waltzed in with her mother in late April and laid down the list. Four suites of rooms, sit-down dinner, nine-tiered cake, dancing, the works." He whipped back that thick shock of hair again. Connie noticed it looked grayer since she'd last seen him.

"Why didn't you say no?"

The white teeth made a brief, sheepish appearance. "I had every intention of doing so. But that was before I calmed down enough to hear them talk. It was the mother, actually, whose attitude I objected to. When I attempted to explain the various difficulties, the young woman seemed to understand fast enough. She mentioned something about going back to pizza and beer at a farm someplace. I assume it was a bed-and-breakfast establishment, something of that sort. I don't know where. There's nothing like that on Nashtoba. At any rate, the daughter seemed to want to put on a good face for my sake. She seemed like a nice, thoughtful young woman and I hated to disappoint her. It's a terrible thing, her getting killed like that."

"Yes," said Connie. "It is."

"That's why I relented, because I couldn't bear to disappoint the daughter, but I think *she* felt more sorry for her mother than for herself. All through our little discussion she seemed to be trying to cheer the mother up. At least she enthused about the virtues of pizza and beer quite a bit. But the mother only got more and more grim-faced. So finally I said that I supposed I could put together an attractive buffet in the dining room and confine the regular diners to the veranda. I told them in no uncertain terms it would be a squeeze, and the daughter acknowledged that. She sounded as if she truly hated to put me to all this trouble, but the mother jumped on the offer and that was that. Then the mother brought up the dancing. I told them dancing was out of the question, due to the space constraints. The daughter said it was all right because the groom didn't dance, but the mother rode right over her. She said there would be plenty of other guests there who did dance, but I held my ground. I reiterated that there was no possible way to fit in dancing space with the numbers they were suggesting. The mother became distraught. She had dreamed for years of dancing at her daughter's wedding, she said. Finally the daughter asked her, with the first hint of discord I'd heard since she'd arrived, whom she intended to dance with, since the groom couldn't, and her father wouldn't, or vice versa, or something to that effect. That seemed to nip the dancing idea in the bud."

"So an agreement was reached. Buffet in the small room, no dancing. How many tiers on the cake?"

Jack Whiteaker grinned. "I'm afraid I knuckled under completely on that."

Connie thought. "And after all that, there was no wedding. You must have lost out on a few bucks."

Jack's grin left in a trace. "There was no wedding. Ordinarily the deposit is nonrefundable, but I didn't have the heart to keep it. What with the extenuating circumstances—"

The extenuating circumstances being, of course, that the bride was dead.

CHAPTER
10
---

*. . . boutonnieres sent by the groom, should be waiting in
the vestibule. These should be in charge of a boy from the
florists, who has nothing else on his mind but to see that
they are there, that they are fresh, and that the ushers get
them.*

Betty's Bud Boutique was next on Connie's list. Connie
almost retreated at the sign in the window: "Betty's Buds
are Best!" But it had to be done. Actually, it didn't, but
Connie was going to, dammit. She plowed through the
door and up to the desk.

Unlike Jeanine, Betty was in no mood to talk. All
Connie could get out of her was that in the middle of
May, Alicia Scott and her daughter had come in and
looked through books. Betty either had not heard or did
not care to repeat any discussion that had taken place.
They had left without placing an order. The mother had
returned at a later date and had ordered bouquet,
centerpieces, boutonnieres, etc., featuring, for the most
part, pink and white roses. At this second visit the
daughter had not been present.

By the time Connie left Betty's Buds she was so hot
she was dizzy. She got back into her car, but she hadn't
gone far when the dizziness seemed to affect first her

vision, then her stomach. She pulled over in front of Beston's Store. She trudged up the steps as if she were at the Maginot Line, about to face the enemy. She wouldn't have stopped if it wasn't an emergency. She was dehydrated, she told herself. All she needed was a cold drink. And the nearest, wettest, coldest thing was the Coke machine on Beston's porch. The problem was, there was no way around the three perennial porch-sitters on the way to the Coke.

"Well, well, well," said Bert Barker. "If it isn't Miss Merry Sunshine. What's the matter, not hot enough for you yet?"

The huge pile of gleaming flesh next to Bert Barker chuckled. "Now, Connie," said Ed Healey. "You just bring that sody pop right over here and set down. It's no weather to be driving around in a car with no top."

Evan Spender, the third bench-sitter, shot Connie an eye-smile that a less desperate person might have missed. She slammed her money into the machine, extracted a long, cool, bottle and considered her choices. Evan was more work—since he never talked much it would be left up to Connie—but Bert was too annoying and Ed was too fat. If she sat next to Ed, they'd stick. Connie sat down next to Evan. As it turned out, she needn't have worried about making conversation—Ed Healey simply raised his voice a notch or two and kept going with the usual subject.

"Hottest day since 1917. Bet you didn't know that, Connie. I thought yesterday was bad, till I heard today was even worse. But yesterday was no day for a wedding, no siree."

"Jesus God Almighty," said Bert. "Did you die overnight and forget to stop talking? There was no wedding yesterday."

Ed picked up a section of the *Sunday Herald* and fanned himself. "I know that, Bert. But the guests had to get all dressed up, didn't they not? The wedding party had to stand around in a hot church for close to an hour, didn't they not?"

"Serve 'em right," said Bert. "If you ask me, if they'd eloped they'd have saved everybody a lot of grief. Not to mention the expense. Buying clothes, buying presents—"

"Aah," said Ed. "Those elopements never take. Look at Aggie's parents."

Connie perked up her ears. "Aggie's parents eloped?"

"Yep. Didn't last long, though. Six years, wasn't it, Ev?"

"Six or seven, thereabouts."

"Have to hand it to Ben," said Ed. "He did a nice job raising Aggie all alone like that."

"How did it happen that the father got her?" asked Connie. "That wasn't done much back then."

Bert opened his mouth. "Damn women. If you call Alicia Scott a woman. Fool went and—"

Ed shot an elbow into his ribs.

Bert shut his mouth.

As far as Connie could remember, it was a first.

When Connie arrived home, the police chief was sitting in his car in the driveway and Pete was leaning on the open window. Things seemed a bit strained as she approached, and recalling her last words to the chief, she thought she could understand why. "Hi," she said. She tried to say it enthusiastically, to make the one word sound like an apology, but it came out like something from a tae kwon do class instead. She tried again. "How's the case?"

"Not good," said Willy. "Pete's just reminded me we need a wedding dress."

Connie looked at Pete. "Not at her mother's?"

Pete shook his head.

"And it's not at the dressmaker's, I checked. What about the rest of it?"

"The rest of what?"

The two men looked at her blankly.

"The stuff that should go with it. There are things you need besides the dress."

"There was a suitcase in the spare room at the farm," said Pete.

"Aggie's escape bag," said Willy. "We checked."

"What was in it?" asked Connie.

Willy reeled off a list of items—nightgown, slippers, shorts, T-shirt, the usual toiletries, nylon stockings . . .

"I'd like to look at that bag," Connie said.

Willy considered her at some length. Finally he leaned over and opened the passenger side door. "Your coach awaits."

They found Walt kneeling in the damp earth among the tomato plants, fumbling with bandaged hands to fill a wooden crate.

The chief explained that they wanted to check Aggie's suitcase one more time and Walt acted like he'd hardly heard them, but the chief seemed to accept a half-raised hand as a sign to go ahead.

It was not pleasant re-entering the farmhouse. Someone had cleaned up the glass, but the gaping wounds in the windows made Connie want to close her eyes as she walked past. The chief led the way upstairs and into the spare room. He hefted the blue suitcase, laid it flat on the bed, snapped back the locks, and bowed to Connie. She stepped up and pushed back the lid. The police had made little effort to keep the things in the case neat. Jumbled on top of each other were shampoo, hair dryer, toothbrush, toothpaste, body lotion, bra, panties, white cotton nightgown, blue T-shirt, denim shorts, rubber thong sandals. When Connie saw the white ballet slippers and two unopened packages of white nylons she stopped. "This is no escape bag. This is the bag she packed for Friday night. See?" She picked up the ballet slippers. "The shoes to wear with her wedding dress."

"Those slippers?"

"They aren't slippers." She picked up the package of nylons. "You don't wear nylons with slippers."

Willy looked unconvinced. He fingered the denim shorts, the T-shirt. "What about these?"

"She's not going to eat breakfast in her wedding dress. She packed these clothes to wear Saturday morning. Or later Friday night. Or both. This isn't any escape bag, this is the bag she planned to take to Ginny's."

"Then what's it doing here?"

"She forgot it."

"Or she came back with it. Just before she got killed. By Walt."

"In that case, where's the dress?"

Willy rubbed a large hand over his long face. "Good question," he said.

Connie was disappointed when Duncan answered the door at the Turkles. She'd kind of hoped Faye herself would arrive to see Connie standing there with the police chief, but as it was, Duncan looked pretty impressed, the way any stop-sign-stealing fifteen-year-old should.

"We'd like a word with your sister," said Willy.

"Mom!" Duncan hollered over his shoulder. Obviously, he'd been trained to clear all visitors.

Faye lumbered into the hallway, caught sight of Connie and the chief, and said, "What? Again? The two of you?"

"A matter of a blue suitcase," said Willy. "I would appreciate a word with Ginny."

Faye turned on Duncan. "Get your sister."

Faye didn't ask them in. Neither did she budge when

Duncan returned with Ginny. They crowded awkwardly around the open doorway—Ginny, Duncan, and Faye on one side, Connie and the chief on the other.

"We're attempting to track the movements of a blue suitcase," said Willy. "Aggie Scott's blue suitcase. Did you see it at any point on Friday?"

"Sure I saw it," said Ginny. "I carried it out to the car for her. The dress was an armful all by itself."

"You saw the suitcase go into the car?"

"I put it in there. Aggie hung the dress in the back and I put the suitcase on the seat in the front."

"This was when she left here on Friday? At approximately—?"

Ginny flashed a look at Connie. "At *exactly* ten-thirty."

"Thank you," said Willy. "My apologies for disturbing you."

"May we assume this is the last we'll be seeing of you?" said Faye.

"You may assume we will do what we have to do to track down this young woman's killer," said Willy. He turned and strode toward the car.

Connie caught up to him halfway down the walk. "I think you've been watching too much *Dragnet*," she said.

CHAPTER
11

On returning home from a party, [a young girl] must not invite or allow a man to "come in for awhile." If he insists, she should answer casually but firmly, "Sorry! It's against the rules. Good night."

I don't care," said Connie. She kicked fitfully at the loose sheet and managed to bring her heel down sharply on Pete's kneecap. Pete groaned and looked at the clock. They were in the middle of an argument that had begun the minute Connie got back from her excursion with the chief and had continued until now, eleven o'clock Sunday night, in bed, with the windows wide open and the lights out and the heat smiting them each time they moved. "I don't care," Connie repeated. "The fact remains that it still doesn't prove anything. Just because Aggie's overnight bag was in Walt's house, that doesn't mean Aggie was there last."

Pete massaged his kneecap. "Sure it does. Ginny Turkle told you Aggie picked up the dress and the bag when she left Ginny's. She hung the dress in the back and put the bag on the seat in the front. This was what, Friday night at ten-thirty."

"So Aggie and her bag and her dress arrive at the farm

at ten-thirty-something. The bag makes it upstairs, but somehow, for some unknown reason, the dress does not. This is what you're trying to tell me."

"Sure. She takes the bag out first, because it's beside her on the seat. She goes upstairs—"

"But Walt never sees her."

"Walt *says* he never sees her."

Connie gave up fighting with the sheet and shot out of the bed. Pete could just see her in the moonlight as she crossed the window, but lost her as she turned and flopped into the rocking chair. The only reason he knew she'd flopped into the rocking chair was because he could hear her rocking.

And talking.

"I don't get you sometimes, Pete. Why can't you start from the place any normal person would start? Why can't you believe what somebody tells you? He says he never saw Aggie after they left the restaurant. Instead of spending half the night trying to think up reasons why Walt would lie, why don't you try to think up reasons why he might not have seen her?"

Pete didn't see why he had to spend half the night doing any of this, but what he did see was that there would be no sleep until they did. He sat up, grabbed Connie's pillow, and balled it in with his own until he'd formed an uncomfortable bolster. "It won't take half a night to think up a reason why Walt would lie. He would lie if he killed her."

"Okay, fine. We'll do it your way. Walt lied. And he lied because he killed her. All right? Now, can we try it my way? Or is your way the only one we're allowed to consider?"

"I'm perfectly willing to consider your version as long as you acknowledge the validity of mine. Okay. In your version Walt never sees her. Why not?"

"How about because he wasn't there?"

Pete shook his head. "Walt left Lupo's and got back here before ten. He told me so himself."

"All right. I suppose if we believe Walt in one thing, we have to believe him in another. So think. He was already here when Aggie arrived with the bag and the dress. Why didn't he see her?"

"Because he was asleep," said Pete enviously.

He was surprised when he heard hands clapping in the dark. "Asleep! Exactly! Walt was sound asleep when Aggie got there. Okay. So she sets down the bag in the spare room. Then what?"

"Then Aggie writes the note, Walt wakes up and finds her writing the note, they argue, and he kills her."

Silence.

"All right," said Pete. "I'm sorry. That wasn't fair. We're still on your version. We have Walt asleep, Aggie putting the bag down in the spare room. Ordinarily she'd go back to the car to get the dress."

"I suppose you've looked in her car."

"I looked in the car Saturday morning. I'd have seen a dress. Besides, the cops have been all through the car. If the dress had been there, Willy would have said."

Silence.

"This was Aggie's second dress," said Connie finally. "The first one was blue and cost fifty dollars. The woman at the bridal shop made it sound like the crime of the century to get married in a fifty-dollar dress. And I don't think she was too crazy about the blue. She—"

"Don't switch dresses in the middle of the stream," said Pete. "We've still got one dress in Aggie's car. What happened to it?"

"I'll tell you what should have happened to it. Aggie should have gone down to the car, gotten the dress, brought it upstairs, hung it on the curtain rod, and gone to bed."

"But she didn't."

"Okay. Why didn't she?"

Pete yawned. "Because Walt woke up and found her writing that note. I'm sorry, but it's the only explanation that fits. If you come up with another one, I'll be as happy as you are, but I'd be happier if you'd come up with it tomorrow."

"All right, all right." Connie got up, crossed the window again, slid back into bed, and searched around for her pillow. When she found it she yanked it from behind Pete so fast his head cracked into the headboard. Pete doubted other people ran into this element of danger in bed.

He sighed and closed his eyes.

"Pete."

"Tomorrow. Please."

"That's the trouble," said Connie. "I keep waiting till tomorrow. But nothing happens. And now it's round two and still nothing. Which makes it five weeks. And two days."

Pete opened his eyes.

After some seconds Connie said, "Did you hear me?"

"I'm not sure."

"I said I'm late. Five weeks and two days, as a matter of fact. Oh, I've missed before, it happens with these pills once in a while. But just once, never twice. And this feels different. *I* feel different. You know, sick. Tired. *Fat.*"

All of a sudden Pete didn't feel so hot himself. "Did you do one of those tests?"

"Right. Can you see me walk into Beale's Pharmacy, pick up a Clearblue Easy, and walk out? It would be all over the island in two minutes."

Pete reached over and switched on the light. When he looked at Connie she looked . . . well, *scared* was probably the best way to put it. "Be that as it may," he said as gently as he could. "Don't you think it might behoove us to find out?"

"Yeah, I know." She didn't say anything else.

Pete sat up and ran his hands over his face, trying to come up with something rational, something calming to say to her. To *him*. "These things happen," he said.

"Yeah, but not to us. I don't know what went wrong. So I forgot a couple of pills. The minute I realized, I doubled up, but—" She stopped.

"Why didn't you tell me? We could have . . . *I* could have—"

"I know. I don't know. I figured what difference could a few measly pills make? Christ, there's about a million of them in the pack. You figure you could miss four of them without—"

This time Pete was sure he hadn't heard her right. "Four? You forgot four pills?"

"Yeah. I guess after the first one I kind of lost track."

Pete gave himself a minute to neutralize his voice. "Connie," he said finally, carefully. "In the morning. We go to Beale's. We get one of those . . . what's it called?"

"Clearblue Easy. Haven't you seen the ads? I swear to God, it's been on television twelve times a day for a month. Blue, you're pregnant. Clear, you're not. And they claim it's so damned easy." After a minute she said, "Hell, why are we sweating about this before we even know what's what?" She reached across him and switched out the light. "I'll go to the pharmacy in the morning. There's nothing we can do now but sleep."

Right, thought Pete.

Sleep.

CHAPTER
12

There are occasions when a young woman is persuaded by her parents into making a "suitable marriage."

It was easy, all right.

It was also blue.

And as Pete looked at Connie's white face he realized with chagrin that he had no idea how she would feel about this. Oh, he knew how she felt philosophically, but Pete was now discovering that a general philosophy didn't help much when it came down to a specific case. Their specific case. Neither of them had ever put children at the head of their life-goals list. Did that mean they wouldn't be good parents? Did it even mean they didn't want to be parents? Maybe they would have gotten around to it eventually. Maybe they would have gotten around to it before this if their marriage hadn't jumped the track. But what would Connie say about this now? What should Pete say? It suddenly occurred to him there was one option he should probably make clear.

"So we get married. A couple of blood tests, a license, we'd have it over with by the end of the week."

Of the various responses he might have expected, the one he got was last on the list.

Connie said nothing. She walked out the bedroom door. Pete heard her feet on the stairs. He heard the front door open and close. He listened for her car, for the muffler that he'd been meaning to replace, and heard nothing. He went to the window and looked out. There she was, crossing the marsh, working her way along the shallow creekbed toward the beach.

So we get married. And this from the man who not two days ago had so romantically dubbed their first wedding a "mistake." But they could get married, Connie thought. Anybody could. There was no road test for a marriage license the way there was for a driver's license. But come to that, hadn't she and Pete already taken a sort of a road test, a test run, so to speak? And more to the point, there were no tests to find out if you were qualified to be parents. Anybody could try it out, and due to what Connie could only think of as an idiotic system, the people who worried about it the least were the ones who tried it out most.

For some reason Connie found herself thinking about the Scotts. Aggie Scott had hardly had a mother at all. The marriage had clearly not been good, but everyone seemed to agree that the child had turned out all right. Until she'd turned up dead, of course. And Walt. Walt had not had an easy childhood. He'd lost both his parents and taken a serious nosedive, but now he'd settled down and was . . . okay, either Walt had eventually turned out all right or Walt was a murderer.

Connie laughed wildly. A half-dozen ducks leaped out of the marsh grass to her right and beat the air in a frenzy to escape her presence. Nice. She pressed on until her bare feet left the cool mud of the marsh and touched the hot sand. She crossed the beach to the water, dead calm and tepid under the hazy heat. She walked in ankle-deep and looked down at her quivering reflection. Oh, she saw a lot of things in herself, things that didn't bode well for either a husband or a child. She suspected there were as many selfish reasons for having children as there were for not having them. At least she knew there was more to it than these on-again-off-again bouts of maternal instinct. Didn't she have enough trouble sorting out her own life? Didn't Pete? For that matter, didn't Aggie and Walt? But maybe, just before it had all gone to hell, they'd figured they'd finally gotten life sorted out. It was a concept to which Connie could relate.

Suddenly Connie realized she could walk the beach till she was blue in the face, but she wasn't going to come any closer today to sorting out her thoughts. She'd buried her head in the sand too long to be able to pop to the surface in one clean shot. Better to go back to Aggie's and Walt's problems while she subliminally adjusted to this latest "mistake."

Connie about-faced and returned to the house, but she didn't go in. Despite numerous lectures by the police chief, she and Pete still left their house wide open and their keys in their cars. Connie got into the Triumph and left.

Rita Peck arrived at her desk at Factotum Monday morning at eight-thirty on the dot. She spent the first few seconds checking the tiny mirror she kept in the center desk drawer to make sure her collar lay right and her hair had arrived behind the desk in the appropriately preened state. She checked her nails, perfect shell-pink ovals, for last-minute chips or cracks. She realigned the notepad that had been mysteriously moved from the right- to the left-hand side of her desk overnight, checked the canister of pencils to make sure they were sharp, flipped through the files marked "Work in Progress," and transferred one crisp folder to the "Work Completed—Send Bill" rack. After tapping the files into military precision she checked the answering machine for messages that might have collected during the night. Miraculously, none had. Rita squared up her chair and settled down to work. She expected a normal sort of Monday-in-July day—collecting and sorting calls from the year-rounders who needed the house painted or the cellar cleaned or the mooring dug up, the calls from the seasonal customers who wanted Factotum to do a clambake, or give them sailing lessons, or take the kids to the beach.

But it wasn't a normal workday. The first thing that came by her desk was an unusually silent Connie, with a bag from Beale's Pharmacy in her hand and a grim-reaper look to her face. The second thing to come by was Connie again, this time on her way out, still silent, with the grim-reaper even more firmly entrenched.

Then it was Pete. At least he paused on his way by.

"Good morning," said Rita.

"What?" said Pete.

"I said good morning. Frivolous of me, I know. But I do occasionally like to begin my day with some small pleasantry."

"Oh," said Pete. "Good morning. Where's Andy?"

Rita looked at her watch. "Where he usually is at eight-fifty-two Monday morning. Late. Now I suggest you and Connie start with the Harrisons. You'll need at least a day or two to get everything moved into the guest house, don't you think? When Andy deigns to appear I'll send him off to the dump and then get him started on those lawns. I think we can spread out the cars and the road trips over the next few days, and I've decided we'd better move to group swimming lessons. Bunch everyone up somewhere in the middle of the week."

"What's the deadline on Harrison, Friday? You'd better send Andy out. The lawns will have to wait."

"Oh?" said Rita. "And what will you be doing?"

"Aggie Scott."

Rita's good mood dropped straight into the basement. First of all there was the reminder of the weekend tragedy. That, alone, was enough to put Rita off breakfast and lunch. But second was the unwelcome news that Pete had seen fit to stick his nose into yet another murder. Rita was beginning to think there was something seriously wrong with his common sense. But she'd given up arguing over it. She riffled the files in the "Works in Progress" rack and said, "Well, I suppose Connie will make sure Andy doesn't break anything really valuable, like his head."

"Better leave Connie alone for a bit."

"I see," said Rita. "Fine."

A pained expression crossed Pete's face. Rita studied him for a minute and softened her voice. "Pete? Everything's all right?"

He looked around at ceiling and floor as if he'd never seen them before. "Look," he said finally. "I'll work in the dump and I'll try to get out to the Harrisons' to help Andy with the big stuff later this week. I'm sorry. It's this Aggie Scott thing. It's getting to everybody."

He left.

Rita stared after him. She stared after him for some time, as a matter of fact, and when she finally stopped staring she'd come to two conclusions. One was that if Pete saw fit to take two of Factotum's four employees out of the lineup they were going to need some additional help. She picked up the phone and verbally shook her seventeen-year-old daughter Maxine out of bed. The second conclusion she came to was . . . Well, she supposed she could sum it up best with one sentence.

Aggie Scott, my foot.

* * *

Pete's Monday morning always started with Sarah Abrew. Ordinarily it was Pete's favorite job—reading the paper to the old woman who could no longer see the fine print. But today he approached Sarah's tiny half-Cape with trepidation. Sarah might not be able to read the paper, but she could read plenty of other things. Voices. Moods. Pete decided the best tack was to arrive in a rush, read the news, and get out.

But for some reason, an hour later, he was still sitting on her couch.

Sarah sat in her usual chair, a huge, thronelike thing that left her feet barely touching the floor, her spiky white hair just cresting its back. They'd started by doing what everyone else on the island of Nashtoba was doing—talking about Aggie Scott—and it wasn't long before Sarah's watered-down blue eyes were throwing their usual sparks.

"Every time I saw that little girl my guts wrenched. Walking around town clinging to her father's hand like he was the king of creation, afraid if she let go, he'd disappear, too. For two cents I'd have gone up to that mother and spit in her face. Ran off and never once looked back."

"Is that what happened?"

"That's what happened. That little girl was five years old when her mother walked out, and that was the last she heard from her. Not a visit, not a call, not a note. For seventeen years."

"Until last month."

Sarah made a sound somewhere between an elephant's sneeze and a hog's grunt. "Until last month. As if you could squeeze a lifetime of mothering into one month."

Or fathering. Suddenly the potential for drastic change in the next eighteen years of Pete's life loomed before him like Mount Everest.

Sarah must have said something that Pete missed. "Hello? Take yourself with you next time you go out."

"Sorry. I was thinking about something."

"Now what's she done?"

"What?"

"Connie. Or is it your turn to louse up? I'm losing track."

Pete supposed this one would have to get chalked up to Connie, except that it didn't seem fair to give her all the blame just because she'd gotten stuck with all the responsibility. No. You make certain commitments, you share certain risks. He knew that. Connie was the one who didn't seem to. Five weeks and two days and this was the first time she saw fit to mention it? But at least that he could do something about. He hoped.

The warmth of gnarled fingers under his chin brought his eyes up from the rug. "I don't know what it is this time," said Sarah, "but I'd be willing to bet you good money it's not as bad as you think."

Pete was sorely tempted to come clean and collect. Instead, he kissed her cheek and left.

Andy pulled into the farm at eight-thirty and found Patrice Fielding getting ready to pull out. She got out of her car, a red convertible Mazda like the one Andy had been admiring in the Price Imports lot, and climbed into Andy's truck. Andy tried not to look surprised.

"He's somewhere out there," she said, pointing to the corn. "I offered to come back later and take him to lunch, but he continues to insist he needs no help. What do you think, Andy? *Is* he all right?"

"No," said Andy. "But I think he wants to be by himself." He could feel Patrice staring at him. He stayed facing front.

"It's nice that he has you. I wish I had a brother."

"We're cousins."

"But you grew up together, didn't you? Some of the time, at least. You're like brothers, aren't you? You even look alike."

Andy snorted. Walt, tall and dark and eyes so black they never let out a single thought? And Andy, a blocky little Scandinavian whose thoughts people seemed to read without trying. Like right now, for instance.

"It wouldn't be apparent to the casual observer, I suppose. But I see it clearly. Not in the specifics, but in the general, overall quality of the product." She smiled. "There are differences, of course. Walt has cockiness without the confidence. You have the reverse."

Confidence? Andy? He was so surprised he forgot to blush.

"And Walt will undoubtedly get worse. Aggie had to have been a terrible blow. Now he'll probably charge off and do something foolish to prove his manhood."

"I don't think so," said Andy. "I don't think he's got the steam. I think right now it's going to take all he's got to get through the day."

"Of course, you're right." She smiled again. "It's been nice to have a chance to talk, Andy. We should do it again sometime."

"Well, sure."

Patrice held out her hand for him to shake, just like a man would. Andy took it. She didn't shake hands anything like a man, he noticed.

She got out of the truck. So did Andy. He'd gotten as far as the grass between driveway and cornfield when a second car pulled up. Ginny Turkle's VW. Andy saw two red heads inside, bobbing around through the windshield. After a few minutes the voices got loud enough for Andy to make them out.

"And what's he supposed to do?" That was Ginny.

"I don't care!" shouted Duncan.

"He's counting on you."

Duncan leapt out of the car, hotfooted it across the field, down the road, and out of sight.

Andy stood where he was and waited for Ginny to come up.

"I'd trade him in for a dog, but the kennel wouldn't take him," she said. "He's supposed to be working for Walt. Now he's, like, totally freaked. Like if he sets foot on the place *he's* going to croak."

"Where's he going?"

"Home."

"Walking? All that way? He'll fry up."

"Well, good."

Ginny walked toward the field. Andy fell in beside her. They found Walt in the corn, peeling back an ear, puncturing a kernel.

"Time to pick," he said as they came up. "Where's Duncan?"

"Can't come. I'm filling in for him."

"Me, too," said Andy.

Walt shot him a look. "No, you're not. You've already got a job."

"Well, I don't," said Ginny. "Not till five o'clock." Summers, Ginny was a waitress at the Arapo Yacht Club. She grabbed a bushel basket and retreated to the end of the row of corn.

"Folks doing all right?" asked Walt.

Andy nodded without speaking, but apparently today his face was a regular old open book.

"Look," said Walt. "Don't you go leaving Pete in the lurch. Me, I'm better off by myself."

Which meant, as far as Andy could figure out, that he was still that pesky little kid.

Either that, or Ginny Turkle didn't count.

CHAPTER

13

To begin with, before deciding the date of the wedding, the bride alone, or more probably with her mother, must find out definitely on which day the clergyman who is to perform the ceremony is disengaged, and make sure the church is bespoken for no other service.

Somewhere in the course of the mostly sleepless previous night it had occurred to Pete that there was one other participant in the Friday festivities that should be worth a chat, and preferably before Pete became saturated in *eau de dump.*

As it turned out, he needn't have worried about the dump odors. He found the Reverend Rydell crouched over the spigot in the backyard at the parsonage, trying to remove what looked, and smelled, like a healthy dose of horse manure from the sole of a black boot.

When the Reverend saw he had a visitor he straightened. "Ah, Pete. I've been attempting to pay a call on our friend Walt. I found him among the fertilizer. Or perhaps I should say the fertilizer found me. There. I believe that's the worst of it. Now, come, sit. I'm delighted to see you."

The Reverend scrubbed his hands vigorously under the tap, withdrew a large brown plaid handkerchief from the pocket of his pants, and wiped his hands and sweating face. He led Pete to some iron lawn furniture under a dogwood tree and flopped into the nearest chair. Pete selected the least resistant-looking specimen and eased into it. To his surprise the chair was comfortable. But Pete wasn't. He thought about it and decided it might have had something to do with the length of time since he'd last been in a church.

The same thought seemed to have crossed the Reverend's mind. "I must say I'm surprised to see you. It's been some time. Excluding, of course, the recent unfortunate—"

"Yeah," said Pete. "Well."

The Reverend smiled. "No matter. It seems to be a trend. Or perhaps I should say it was a trend; we're experiencing a bit of a resurgence of late. All you baby boomers seem to be returning your children to the flock. Perhaps that's all you need, Pete, a few small-fry of your own to lure you back."

Pete opened his mouth to tell the Reverend not to hold his breath, but shut it without speaking. What would they do about something like that? He remembered being a kid, spending every Sunday morning in church, thinking here it goes, a whole quarter of the weekend shot. Is that what parenting meant, inflicting the agonies of your youth on the youth of your kids?

"Yeah, well," said Pete awkwardly. "I came to talk to you about Friday night. I'm trying to track Aggie's movements. I'm told you talked to her in the parking lot."

"I talked to Aggie many times in many places." The Reverend wiped his face again and Pete noticed his pale blue shirt was decorated under the arms with saddles of sweat.

"Would you mind telling me what you talked about on Friday night?"

"About forgiveness. When I first spoke with Aggie on the subject she seemed to harbor a great deal of resentment."

And who could blame her? thought Pete, but he made an effort to sound polite. "I understand her mother walked out on her when she was five and never came back."

The Reverend, still smiling, shook his head. "Aggie's words precisely. But I'm afraid I must correct you in much the same way as I corrected her. Alicia Scott did not walk out on her daughter, she walked out on her husband."

"That's a pretty fine distinction for a motherless five-year-old to make."

"As I said to Aggie, what was done in the past was done in the past. Perhaps her parents acted rashly. What could Aggie do now about this ancient history? Nothing. Nothing except forgive. The matter was now in her hands. And this was how I counseled her."

"And how did you counsel Aggie's mother?"

The Reverend made use of his handkerchief for an extended interval. When he resurfaced, the smile was stiff. "Unfortunately, Aggie's mother did not seek my counsel."

So the burden was all Aggie's. Somehow, it didn't seem fair to Pete. But back to the point. "Did Aggie say anything on Friday that would give us a clue where she might have gone that night?"

The Reverend looked puzzled. "Gone?"

"There are several versions of where Aggie ended up that night, who might have seen her last. She was supposed to have stayed at Ginny Turkle's, but Ginny says she left for Walt's. Walt says she never arrived. The police chief doesn't seem to believe him, especially in light of the note she left."

"And what does this have to do with you?"

Good question, thought Pete. "Let's just say I know a few people who do believe Walt."

"Ah, Walt. A disturbing young fellow. I asked to speak to them both before the ceremony. It is customary. He came, but it was obviously under duress. He made it clear that the only reason they were using my 'facilities,' as he put it, was because the guest list had gone to hell and the church had a bigger parking lot."

Pete grinned, saw the Reverend's face, and swallowed it. "Did Aggie say anything to you about her plans for the evening? The reason it's important is that she was killed within a few hours of your chat that night."

The Reverend hesitated. It seemed to Pete he was a bit taken aback by his proximity to the fatal event. "No," he said finally. "Aggie said nothing about her plans. We spoke, as I said, of forgiveness. I felt I had left the job half-done." By now, Pete noticed, the sweat circles under the Reverend's arms had advanced to his belt. He looked at his watch. "Excuse me, I'm afraid I have another engagement for which I cannot be late. Have you seen Walt? Yes? Is he managing to cope? My one regret is that my attempts to communicate with him have been so vigorously repulsed."

That was his one regret? Pete could add a few others. That a young life had been snuffed out. That another looked good for passing in jail. That somewhere on the island of Nashtoba an unmarried ex-wife of his was walking around five weeks and three days pregnant.

And counting.

"Amethyst," said the jeweler with distaste. "For an engagement ring, no less. I attempted to discourage him, but I'm afraid he insisted."

Amethyst. It was different and Connie liked it. But Earl Sorensen didn't. "My efforts to convince the young man to look at this purchase as a lifetime investment were fruitless. I then attempted to illuminate him as to the inappropriateness of amethyst as an engagement ring, but he was adamant. There was some sort of a reason for it, of course. I'm afraid the details escape me. And I must say, when they returned for the wedding bands, she conveyed to me that she was pleased with his choice. But she was quite young. Perhaps in time she would have developed a more refined taste."

With superhuman effort Connie refrained from airing her thoughts. "When did this take place?" she asked instead.

Earl Sorensen looked pointedly at an expensive watch, but since Connie didn't move, he backed through an office door and returned carrying two slips of paper. "The engagement ring was ordered February first, delivered March thirteenth. The wedding rings were ordered March fourteenth, picked up on the twenty-fifth."

"Two wedding rings?"

"Two. Both uninspired. Very cut-rate."

Connie thought of her own wedding band, swimming around in an otherwise empty jewelry box on the top of her dresser. She wondered if Pete still had his. Knowing Pete, he'd probably chucked it in the ocean. She supposed Earl Sorensen would call their bands uninspiring and cut-rate, but when Pete had put it on her finger she'd felt like they'd cornered the market on the most valuable commodity there was.

But Connie wasn't standing here with gritted teeth just so she could reminisce about her own bizarre marital fate. She asked the question she'd come to ask.

"When they returned for the wedding bands, did they seem happy?"

Earl Sorensen was no Lit Smith. He couldn't seem to comprehend the question. Or maybe it was just that he couldn't comprehend the connection between happiness and wedding rings. "I found them highly annoying. They seemed more concerned with the inscription than with the quality of the product itself."

"But how did they act? Excited? Nervous? Grim? Boisterous? Were they both the same or did one act differently?"

"They were both completely silly. They beamed at each other. They occasionally beamed at me. I could hardly keep their attention focused on the jewelry. They were one of the more difficult couples. The minute I seemed to make headway with one of them, the other one would interject some foolishness about a tractor, or some such."

"Then what happened?"

"I believe it was the young woman who first mentioned the need for a new tractor. The young man capitulated at once. They selected two rings that were utterly bottom-of-the-line, and that was the end of the entire matter."

"And the inscription?"

Earl Sorensen's lip twitched. *"I give you my love and my life.* I suppose I should have known better than to expect Shakespeare."

And what would he have preferred? wondered Connie. *Get thee to a nunnery?* But Connie wasn't too crazy about the inscription Aggie and Walt had chosen either. The love part was all right, but the life? Did that mean if you forfeit the love, you forfeit the life?

It was one thing to decide to give your life to somebody. It was another to have it taken away by a pair of hands around your neck.

After the dump Pete stopped home just long enough to clean up and to see if Connie was there. Connie wasn't. Rita was.

"Entirely against my better judgment I've sent Andy and Maxine out to the Harrisons together. The only way I could get either of them to move was to bodily move the fight. And there ends any hope of anybody doing any work, but at least I don't have to watch. You've had three calls. That is to say, Factotum has had many calls, which makes no difference since we've apparently come to a complete and total grinding halt, but you, personally, have collected three calls. One was from your sister Polly. She's thinking of coming to visit later this month."

"What? She just left."

"She left two months ago. The second call was from the police chief. He said don't call him, he'd call you."

"Did he say he'd been talking to Polly?" asked Pete suspiciously. The chief and Polly had a thing going. Or were on the verge of having a thing going. Or weren't on the verge. Polly'd had a bad time with a man once, and Willy knew this. He was trying not to scare her off, but at this point it was hard to say if it was working or not.

"The chief didn't mention Polly," said Rita. "The third call was just now, from Ginny Turkle. Actually, she was calling for Andy, but when I told her you were just pulling up she said to send you out to Walt's place. She sounded odd. She said to tell you not to tell Walt she called and she hung up."

When Pete reached the crest of the hill above the farm, the first thing he saw was a plume of smoke. He accelerated down the hill and saw that the plume was coming from the barn. He tore out of the truck, but he hadn't gone far when he realized the plume wasn't coming from the barn but from behind it. As he rounded the corner he stopped in his tracks.

Walt Westerman stood in front of a smoldering pile of smoke, soot, and flame, feeding a pile of rags into it with a pitchfork. At least Pete thought they were rags until he saw a pair of white ballet slippers.

Pete walked up to him. "What are you doing?"

The face that turned to him was grim and streaked with soot. "Leave me alone."

"Walt. It hasn't rained in weeks. This whole place is like a tinderbox. One spark on the barn roof and it's up in smoke."

Walt turned to look at the barn, but he didn't move from the fire.

Pete gave up on reason and resorted to action. He ran back to the barn and found an outside spigot. He uncurled the hose, cranked the faucet on full, and towed the hose back to Walt's bonfire. When he got within range he trained the hose on the flames. Thick clouds of black smoke and steam wheeled into the sky above their heads.

Walt dropped the pitchfork. "I don't care," he said. "It's no use." He wandered off toward the fields.

Ginny Turkle came out of the house and ran across the lawn toward Pete.

"Thank God you came. I didn't know what to do. I was helping him with the corn. All of a sudden he, like, asked me would I do something for him. He wanted me to get Aggie's stuff out of the house. He wanted everything out, the stuff in her closets, the drawers, her desk, even the stuff in that suitcase. I brought down the suitcase and the clothes and went back to empty out the desk. When I came back he was, like, burning her clothes. Burning everything. He ripped the box out of my hands and . . . and—" She stumbled to a halt.

"Go back inside," said Pete. "Call the Harrisons. Edward Harrison, out on Stone Point. They should be in the book. Ask to speak to Andy and tell him to get out here. Tell him Walt's—"

"Tell him Walt's gone off his *nut.*"

Ginny ran toward the house. Pete gutted the last of the flames, picked up the box Walt hadn't yet managed to feed into them, and started toward the barn, but as he did so Andy pulled up. Pete went to meet him. He chucked the box into the back of his own truck and walked with Andy toward the field where Walt stood, explaining as he went.

Pete had to hand it to his youngest and usually most ineffective employee. He approached Walt talking and walking and never let up. "I tell you, Walt, you'd better have something cold in that refrigerator. I've been up in a hot attic in this one-thousand-degree heat and I'm about ready to pass out." He led Walt toward the house.

Pete didn't follow them. He stalled around at the truck until Ginny Turkle came out. "Everything okay in there?"

"Yeah." Ginny sounded surprised. She must have had previous Andy-experience similar to Pete's. "Anyway, thanks for coming. I was, like, sort of scared." She looked anxious to get out of there now. She hopped into her car and peeled off.

Pete followed at a more respectable pace. When he crested the hill he saw nothing but Ginny's trail of dust and a crowd of two that Walt's plume of smoke had attracted. A short, tanned, middle-aged man and a tall, pale, middle-aged woman stood craning their necks over the rise. The man raised a hand and Pete slowed to a stop.

"Got some trouble down there? Barn on fire or something?"

"Everything's okay. They were burning some rubbish."

"Burning rubbish? In dry weather like this?"

"I know. I talked to him. He's thought better of it."

"Walt?" asked the woman.

"It's under control," said Pete.

The woman shot a sideways look at her husband. "I hear you've been asking around."

"Now, Loretta," said the man.

Pete's antennae perked up. Behind the man and woman a dirt drive disappeared into a thatch of scrub pine and oak. In the distance Pete could just make out the chimney and a small patch of gabled roof with a window winking in the sunlight. Not much of a view, but they'd managed to see the smoke all right. And that single window overlooked the road. "I'm trying to collect some information about the events last Friday night," said Pete. "Was there something—?"

"Go on," said Loretta. "It's not like he's the police. Though why you couldn't tell the police what you saw I still don't know, Cal Fontana."

"And have them call me crazy? No thanks."

"They came here right off," said Loretta. "But Cal forgot all about it till later, when we heard about the time she died that night. Go on, Cal, you tell him."

Cal wrapped his lower lip over his upper one and clamped his jaw down tight, but it didn't make any difference, since Loretta opened hers.

"Three in the morning, it was. Prostate troubles he's got. Up and down, up and down, I swear to you, twelve times a night. But three A.M. was the time you saw her drive in, isn't that right, Cal?"

"Three-thirty," said Cal.

"Saw who drive in?"

"Why, Aggie. Aggie Scott, in that little white Ford of hers. Young Walt, he come in about 9:30."

"Nearer ten o'clock," said Cal.

"Nine-forty-five," said Loretta. "I was just going to bed myself. Cal, he was already dead to the world. That prostate of his keeps him hopping up and down so much he never does get caught up. But he was up at three and saw her come in then."

"Three-thirty," said Cal.

"Three, three-thirty, it don't matter a lick," said Loretta.

Pete had to agree with her.

Three or three-thirty, Cal had seen Aggie Scott come home at least three hours after she was dead.

CHAPTER
14

The invitation to the ceremony is customarily engraved on the first page of a sheet of white notepaper. A very smart one is that with a raised margin formed by a "plate mark." At the top of the sheet the coat of arms—if the family has one—or sometimes the crest and motto only.

The police chief wasn't at the station, but Jean Martell seemed to think it would be nice if Pete sat around most of the rest of the day on the off chance he showed up.

"Tell him to try me at home," said Pete and left.

He soon wished he hadn't. When he walked into Factotum he walked into yet another in an ongoing series of the Peck family debates.

"Allow me to clarify one small point," Rita was saying to her daughter. "Andy gets called away on an emergency involving his cousin and you decide that if Andy was 'taking a break,' as you choose to label this family emergency, you must be due for a break yourself?"

Maxine shrugged a pair of smooth shoulders under the kind of top that Connie used as underwear.

"Did you lock up?"

"What do you mean, lock up? Nobody locks up. Who said anything about locking *up?*"

"Did it ever occur to you," said Rita dangerously, "to

wonder why I gave you those keys in the first place? Did it ever occur to you why the Harrisons gave me those keys? The Harrisons aren't from here. The Harrisons believe in locking up."

Maxine pulled at the bangs that had once been the same gleaming black as her mother's, but were now streaked with three distinctive blonde stripes. "So let them. Besides, you didn't give me the keys, you gave Andy the keys, so go yell at him, why don't you? You're the one who *screeched* at me for eighteen hours this morning that Andy was in charge and I was supposed to do whatever he said."

Rita looked in Pete's direction with an expression that meant he was about to be called on to mediate, and suddenly Pete did something he'd never done before. He panicked. He'd done it a million times, this surrogate-father act. Why, now, should the prospect freeze him in his tracks? Because this could soon be for real. For life. With his own flesh and blood. But what was the big deal? If he told Maxine to run back and lock up she wouldn't be scarred for life. Conversely, however, the Harrisons would never know their house had been left open for a half an hour or so. Unless, of course, the first burglary in the history of Nashtoba happened to be taking place as they spoke. . . .

If the police chief hadn't walked through the door right then who knows what Pete would have said. He whisked the chief into the kitchen and launched into his story about Loretta and Cal. At least he tried to launch into Loretta and Cal, but the chief wouldn't let him get past the plume of smoke that had brought them out to the road in the first place.

"What plume of smoke?"

"Walt was burning some stuff."

"What stuff?"

"Aggie's stuff. Clothes, books. These people at the top of the hill saw the—"

Willy headed for the door.

"I haven't finished," said Pete. "I haven't even got to the part you're supposed to worry about. The people at the top of the hill saw Aggie Scott Friday night."

"The Hawthorne woman. I know. I talked to her Saturday."

"Not Hawthorne, Fontana. Cal Fontana."

"I talked to him, too."

"Yeah, well you better talk to him again. He's remembered some stuff since you saw him. Like Aggie driving home at three-thirty in the morning."

The chief shook his head. "Aggie was dead at three-thirty in the morning. It's been confirmed by autopsy."

"Maybe you should see if they'd care to revise their estimate. Three or three-thirty. That's what Cal said."

Pete had to go over it twice before Willy went to the phone to request a double check on the time of death. Apparently the answer he got didn't please him. "Then triple-check," he snapped. He slammed down the phone and left.

When Connie got home she found Pete upstairs, sitting cross-legged on the bedroom floor. There was an empty cardboard carton beside him and the rug was covered with an assortment of papers and books. He looked five years older than he had that morning.

When she walked in he looked up. "How are you?"

Connie shrugged. She supposed she hadn't needed any Clearblue Easy to tell her what her body had been screaming at her for weeks. She bent over and picked up a spiral-bound notebook. "What's this?"

"Stuff of Aggie's." He filled her in. Bonfires. Fontanas. Aggie driving around in the middle of the night.

At first Connie saw it the same way Pete presented it—a major newsbreak. It accounted for Walt not seeing Aggie at ten-thirty, when everyone assumed she'd arrived home at the farm. But it didn't account for the missing dress and it didn't account for the fact that Walt still should have seen her when she got home at three in the morning, or, if he was a heavy sleeper, when he woke up on Saturday. It still left the farm as Aggie's last known stop. It still left Walt's head in the noose.

She looked at the spiral notebook in her hand. It was labeled "invitations." She flipped it open and found a list of names. Some of them were familiar. Most of them weren't. One name, Gene Tilton's, had been written in and later crossed out.

Pete picked up a bunch of envelopes wrapped together with a rubber band. They were unsealed and he'd opened one up. "Look at this."

It was a plain blue piece of notepaper, the same kind on which Aggie had written her farewell note. It was folded in half. Connie unfolded it and immediately recognized Aggie Scott's childishly round hand. *Walt and Aggie would like you to help celebrate their marriage on April twenty-fifth at four o'clock at their house. RSVP please.* Of course, "RSVP please" meant "please respond, please," but Connie wasn't about to quibble. She thought the invitation was short, sweet, and to the point. And, obviously, it had been written before the Whiteaker Hotel had entered the picture. She looked at the pile of matching envelopes in Pete's hand. And, also obviously, these invitations had never been sent.

Pete was talking again, this time about his conversation with the Reverend, but it seemed to Connie the most important question he could have asked had been overlooked. Had Aggie seemed happy when she met with the Reverend? Aggie had beamed at Walt all through their visit to the jeweler's in March. At the photographer's in May she'd acted as if there were a shotgun to her head. Something must have gone wrong between March and May. What?

Suddenly Connie thought of something. How could she have been so stupid? Lit had even used the conventional words.

A shotgun to her head.

"Pete," said Connie. "Was Aggie pregnant?" She explained about Lit's shotgun metaphor.

"I doubt it. I think Willy would have mentioned it." But he reached for the phone, called the station, and left another message for the chief to get in touch. When he turned around he coughed and right away Connie knew this was it.

"Speaking of shotguns—"

"I know."

"No, Connie, I don't think you do. And do me a favor. Stop treating me like I'm a one-nighter you picked up in a single's club someplace."

"What's that supposed to mean?"

"It means first you wait five weeks to clue me in on this little problem and then you walk out the door without a backward glance. I'm half of this, remember? Talk to me. Tell me what you're thinking, what you want."

Suddenly Connie felt as if a huge water balloon inside her chest had burst. "All right. Okay. You want to know what I'm thinking? I'm thinking I didn't want it to be like this. I'm thinking this is lousy timing. I feel like we've only just stopped teetering on some ledge. I'm thinking I won't be any good at it. And I'm thinking I'm thirty-eight. *Thirty-eight.* How many more chances have I got?" She stopped, out of breath, heart slamming against her chest.

"Okay," said Pete. "All right."

"All *right*? You think it's all right? We've just barely remembered how to make a bed together and now this."

"I know." Pete crossed the five feet that had somehow appeared between them and the next thing she knew she'd grounded her face in his neck. When he spoke his voice seemed to come at her straight through his chest. "It'll be all right. Really."

Connie pulled back and looked at him. *I'm half of this.* A kid could do plenty worse than a half like Pete. For the first time some of the terrible weight seemed to lift.

"Well?"

"All right," said Connie. "But if your worst nightmare comes true, say the kid ends up in a chorus line in Vegas, will you remember it's half your fault?"

"I'll remember," said Pete.

Andy Oatley sat at his cousin's kitchen table feeling pretty much like a jerk. A fourteen-year-old jerk. For a minute there he'd thought maybe the day had started to pick up. It sure hadn't started off so hot. He'd arrived at Factotum to find out that, in a moment of complete and total brain-freeze, Maxine's mother had decided that he and Maxine should go out to the Harrisons' and move all their stuff into the new guest house. *Together.* They'd lasted fifteen whole minutes before the first fight broke out, and Andy had been on the verge of taking a walk when the call had come about Walt. That had freaked him out fast enough. But eventually they'd settled down at the kitchen table and things had been going all right. Walt had seemed to forget he'd spent most of his life treating Andy like he was three instead of twenty-three. He'd seemed to actually not mind him being around, as a matter of fact. Then Andy had asked him about the gun. Walt had jumped up, told Andy if he knew what was good for him he'd keep out of it, and walked out.

Well, maybe Andy didn't know what was good for him, but just maybe he knew better than Walt what was good for Walt.

Andy left the kitchen, got into the truck, and headed for the causeway as fast as he legally could.

Walt has no friends, Andy had told Pete, but he used to have friends, if you could call them that. And as much as Walt had tried to keep them out of Andy's reach, Andy had managed to catch up with them enough to pick up some juice. The so-called friend Andy was after now was Frankie Reese.

Frankie had a room in Bradford above a used car lot. It was handy for Frankie, having the car lot downstairs, since that's what he did for a living—sold cars. Most of them were hot.

And so were the guns.

Frankie Reese was out on the car lot chalking a price on a windshield when Andy showed up. He recognized Andy right off. He dropped the chalk and waved him out back and up the stairs to his place. The hot-car business on Cape Hook must not have been too good. Frankie lived on top of a sheet of ripped linoleum in the middle of a bunch of plastic furniture. He tossed Andy a beer out of a small refrigerator and said, "Heard about Walt's girlfriend. What's going on?"

"They're trying to nail Walt. Some friends and I are trying to help him out."

"What have they got?"

"The gun. It'll cause him trouble if it gets traced back."

Frankie scratched his head. His head was shaved down to a gray shadow, but still, a few flakes of dandruff drifted onto his shirt. "What are you asking? Can they trace it to me? No chance."

With intense effort Andy kept the column of air from exploding out of his chest. So he'd been right. The gun was Walt's. He'd bought it off Frankie Reese. It was exactly what he hadn't wanted to hear. So now what?

"When did he buy it, do you remember?"

"What do you think this is, the Registry of Motor Vehicles?"

"Approximate. This year, last year?"

"Over a year ago. At least."

"Did he say what he wanted it for?"

"How do I know? Why don't you ask your cousin?"

"He's pretty shook up, he's not talking much. We're just trying to get a few places before the cops."

"I get it. You want to know if he said, 'I need a gun, I gotta whack my girlfriend.' No, Walt didn't say anything like that. He said something that made no sense. That's why I remembered it, it made no sense. Something about liking to sit near the exits in the movies. Hadn't seen him in six, seven years, he shows up looking for a gun and talking about movies. So what'd he do, blow her head off with that Colt?"

"No," said Andy.

The room was hotter than the Harrisons' attic and something in it smelled like rot. He left without saying good-bye. He couldn't have, even if he wanted to. Somebody had just tied his throat in a knot.

CHAPTER
15
---

*What people in deep mourning may do without criticism
can perhaps be denoted in one sentence: They may do
nothing that indicates taking part in social gaiety. In
other words, they may not go to balls or dances or large
dinners, nor join conspicuously large groups; but they may
of course continue to play golf . . .*

They were back in the First Parish church. It was just as
hot and the guest list was much the same, but that was
where all similarity ended. Instead of roses, there were
lilies. Instead of dresses made of blue cellophane, there
were dresses made of subdued grays and blacks.

And instead of a red carpet in the front of the church,
there was an open casket.

Pete couldn't look. No matter how gleaming the black
hair, how smooth the white cheek, how rosy red the lips,
he couldn't think of Aggie Scott as beautiful. He could
only think of her as dead.

Walt Westerman sat in the front pew on the left. Alicia
Scott sat in the front pew on the right. Neither one
looked to either side, but while Alicia's eyes were glued
to her daughter's casket, Walt, like Pete, seemed to find
the sight too painful to take. He stared at a spot between
his shoes. Most of the other people in the church stared
at the back of Walt's head and Pete could almost hear the

words humming in their heads. *Did he kill her? Did he? Did he? Did he?*

The door in the back of the church banged open. Pete heard the sounds of rustling cloth, of indrawn breath. He didn't turn until a shape entered his peripheral vision, and he saw that a man was walking down the center aisle in the middle of Aggie Scott's funeral service, lurching unsteadily on his feet.

Ben Scott.

In the front of the church the Reverend Rydell broke stride for the space of a heartbeat and then kept on droning. Ben Scott reached the casket and paused, head bowed, back bent. When he turned, he turned left.

Walt Westerman mustn't have looked up until he saw the feet. By the time he saw the hands they were already reaching for his neck. The words that ripped out of Ben Scott's throat came from somewhere dark and dead. *"You,"* he rasped. "This is what it felt like. Your hands around her neck."

Walt Westerman was tall and fit and young, but Ben Scott was big and broad and bent with rage. The two men were locked together by the time Pete barreled out of his seat and up to the front. Andy, Evan Spender, and a thin man Pete didn't recognize materialized along with him. The thin man and Evan grabbed Ben Scott. Pete and Andy grabbed Walt. The thin man took an elbow that must have knocked his ribs into his spine. He staggered backward. Walt suddenly broke loose and let fly with his fists as if he didn't care where they landed. One landed close enough to Pete's jaw to make him see red, and the next thing he knew he had Walt pinned against the pew. He leaned there and breathed while Evan hustled Ben Scott out of the church. Finally the Reverend Rydell stepped up. Walt must have looked limp enough by then—the Reverend tapped Pete's arm, helped Walt out of the seat, and drew him into the vestry.

Pete looked around. The thin man seemed to have disappeared. Andy followed the Reverend and Walt into the vestry and Pete was alone in the front of the church with Aggie Scott. As it had on the day of the wedding, the congregation buzzed. Obviously, thought Pete, Ben Scott had no doubt that it was Walt Westerman who had killed his daughter. And having witnessed one of Walt's knee-jerk responses in the flesh for the first time, Pete was more than ever inclined to admit the possibility. Pete began to return to his seat, but suddenly he realized he'd had enough of church. He exited left.

Pete came out into the churchyard just as the thin man emerged from behind a thick tangle of honeysuckle and rambler roses, handkerchief to his mouth. He didn't look like he took blows to the solar plexus too often. He was dressed in a well-tailored linen suit, soft blue shirt, and shiny, black loafers. With tassels. His chin was shaved to the bone and his hair, although thinning, was combed straight back with confidence. He looked to be closer to Pete's age than Aggie's. Pete reached into his pocket, pulled out some Lifesavers, and offered them up.

"Thank you."

Pete offered his hand next. "Pete Bartholomew."

"Gene Tilton."

Gene Tilton, Gene Tilton. Where had Pete come across that name before? The hand that took his was clammy, but judging by the strength of the grip, the man was rallying fast enough. "You were a friend of Aggie's?"

"I knew her. I'm a friend of her father's. I'm staying at Ben's house."

"Oh," said Pete. "Is he—" He hesitated. He'd been about to say "Is he okay?" but obviously he was not.

"The gentleman in the gray sport coat saw that I was

indisposed and he very kindly offered to take Ben home. But I should go now. He shouldn't be left alone."

"No," said Pete. He wanted to add something, some message for Ben, but he didn't know what. Here Pete was, twisting like a pretzel, contemplating the momentousness of bringing a child into the world. What would it cost a man to watch his child go out of it?

Gene Tilton said good-bye and walked across the parking lot to his car, a Jaguar sedan. Nice stuff.

After a minute Andy Oatley came out of the side door of the church, leading his cousin Walt by the elbow. Pete shot Andy an inquiring look and got a thumbs-up-thumbs-down mix. Andy packed Walt into his truck and pulled out. Pete was trying to figure how to collect Connie and get out of there without going back into the church, when there she was, beside him, putting an arm around him. It seemed she'd been doing that a lot of late.

"All right?" she asked.

Pete nodded. "You?"

"I wasn't the one who got in a brawl in the middle of a funeral. Was he out of his mind or just drunk?"

"Ben? Out of his mind, I think. Tell me something. Gene Tilton. Why does the name ring a bell?"

"Aggie's wedding invitation list. He was the one who was written in and then crossed out."

"Ah," said Pete.

The phone was ringing when they walked in the house. Pete snatched it up.

"No change on that time of death," said Willy. "They'd stretch it the other way if she hadn't been seen alive at ten-thirty, but they won't budge past midnight."

"So that means—"

"That means the Fontanas may have seen Aggie Scott's car, but there was no way Aggie was driving it."

"You think they made a mistake?"

"Not necessarily. We picked up some unidentified prints off the wheel, the upholstery. Not Walt's. Not Aggie's. I'm checking with Strong's garage on servicing, but it's not likely. We know Aggie drove the car to Turkle's that night and these prints were superimposed over Aggie's."

"Was she pregnant?"

"Who, Aggie? No. Why?"

"There were reports she wasn't the glowing bride she should have been. So what's next?"

Silence. When the chief spoke again something had changed. It wasn't so much as if the chief had given up on Walt as a suspect, it was that he seemed less happy with the way the pieces were, or weren't, fitting. The ashes from Walt's bonfire had proved unrevealing. There was still no trace of the wedding dress.

"I tell you what I'd do if I were you," said Pete. "I'd work on this car thing. I'd talk to those people on the hill again. Somebody must have seen who was driving."

"I've talked to them and got zilch. That's the problem with this place. Once I sound like I'm challenging somebody's story they hang onto it like the last raft in a flood. They don't want to admit they can't see as well as they used to, or they had no clue what time it was, or they forgot, or made a mistake, or plain old lied outright. This is when that second man comes in handy. New face, new story."

The only trouble was, the second man was in the hospital, having his appendix out. "Any news on Ted?"

"He's fine. Or he will be. In two weeks."

"Oh," said Pete.

"So if you happen to be driving by—"

"Driving by where?"

"Fontanas. Hawthornes. That area."

"What are you trying to say?"

"Nothing. At least not officially. But it would be interesting, don't you think?"

"Right," said Pete.

It might not be the thanks Connie had assured him was coming, but at least it was the official invitation.

Unofficially, of course.

Pete went upstairs and found Connie facedown on the bed.

"All right?"

"You mean am I still pregnant?"

He sat down beside her and brushed damp hairs off her hot neck.

"I can't believe this," she said. "Can you believe this?"

"Not yet."

She rolled over and sat up. "But we're really going to do it? Marriage, kids, station wagon, the whole bit?"

"Marriage, definitely. Kid, in the singular, at least for now, yes. But I draw the line at the station wagon."

Connie grinned weakly. "I hear minivans are hot. I guess I'd better make an appointment with Hardy Rogers. And one for our blood tests."

"And we'd better call the folks."

Connie lay down and groaned. "This is so embarrassing, marrying the same man twice. I feel like Liz Taylor. And just about as fat." She shot back up. "Pete. I want to ask you something and you're going to want to fudge the answer. Don't. I need it to be heartrending, gut-wrenching honest. Will you promise?"

"All right."

"If you hadn't knocked me up, do you think we'd ever have gotten married?"

"Sure we would. I don't have to wrench and rend over that. Maybe not right now, but so what? You think after we've been married fifty years it will matter that it might have been forty-nine? I doubt it."

He could see her searching his face. It didn't scare him. He'd meant it. As a matter of fact, he was starting to get excited about it.

"I hope it turns out like you," she said.

Now that scared him, all right.

CHAPTER
16

Most people very much dislike being asked their names. To say "What is your name?" is always abrupt and unflattering. If you want to know with whom you have been talking, you can generally find a third person later and ask, "Who was the lady with the gray feather in her hat?"

Pete left the house feeling peculiar. It was finally beginning to sink in. He was going to get married and have a kid and be like the rest of the world for once. It felt, well, *normal*. Before that, of course, he was going to take the police chief's hint and spend the rest of the afternoon wandering in and out of Walt Westerman's neighbors' houses. He supposed it didn't pay to get too normal all at once. And besides, he'd stuck his big nose into this. It would take some nerve to pull it out the minute the chief decided he could make some official use of it. Unofficially, of course.

He stopped first at the Hawthorne house. The Hawthornes were an interesting generational mix—the elder Hawthornes continued to house an unmarried son, a divorced daughter, and the divorced daughter's ten-year-old twins. Pete had heard that twins were known to put an extra strain on a marriage. What if he and Connie had twins? Instead of taking turns getting up at night, they'd all be up all night every night. Connie was never at her best when she didn't get her eight hours. Pete never did respond well to being wakened from a dead sleep.

The divorced Hawthorne didn't help Pete's anxiety any. She opened the door screaming over her shoulder. "Daggett! Crockett! You better be out of that sprinkler by the time I get back!" When she saw Pete she rearranged her features into something more agreeable. "Well, hello, Pete. Fancy meeting you here. Haven't seen you in months. Feed store, wasn't it?"

"No," said Pete with certainty. He was pretty sure he'd never been in a feed store in his life. The trouble was, he couldn't remember the divorced Hawthorne's name, either. "I wondered if I could talk to any of you who were home Friday night."

"Home Friday night? You struck the jackpot, right here. Usually I'm out, Friday night being date night."

Pete looked at her uncertainly. Was that a joke? Did divorced mothers of twins actually date?

"This Friday I was home because D and C had the grippe. You know, the old throwing and going. Let me tell you, it wasn't pretty. When one was throwing, the other was going. We went through three pairs of pajamas. Each."

Pete found himself taking a step back. As he did so, he looked up to the second story and saw what he took to be two dormered bedroom windows and a smaller pane between them that he assumed was the bathroom.

"Those bedrooms. Is one of them yours?"

Whatever-her-name-was arched her neck. "My, my, my. Aren't we getting personal. No, they keep me and the boys in the downstairs den and spare room. It keeps the noise down overhead. That's my brother Gav's room on the left and Mom and Pop on the right. But don't think you'll get anything out of them about Friday night. Mom and Pop are dead to the world by eight-thirty.

Gav's a regular night owl, but he was out all Friday night." She leaned out the door, allowing a wing of dirty blonde hair to swing forward suggestively. "Girlfriend's house. The boys were drowning the TV out."

"I'm interested in any cars you might have seen go by, either at that time or at any time later that night."

Suddenly the woman's expression went from false coyness to sincere distress. "I saw Aggie. That must have been close to ten-thirty. Heading toward the farm. I told the chief that."

"We're double-checking. You recognized her car?"

"I recognized the car and I recognized Aggie. I was on this porch getting some air. I could see her black hair."

"In the dark? At ten-thirty?"

Doreen. That was her name. Doreen. She crossed her arms and planted her feet. "I'm telling you. I saw Aggie."

Pete didn't push it further. "And after that? Did you see any other traffic?"

Doreen shook her head.

"What time did you go to bed?"

"I was up all night, I told you. There weren't any cars going by here after that."

"You didn't see Aggie go out later? Or come back in?"

"Nope. She went home and stayed there. Everybody knows that. She was dead and jammed in that well by midnight that very night."

Pete insisted on talking to the rest of the family, but it only confirmed what Doreen had told him—the brother was out all night, the parents were asleep.

And Daggett and Crockett were throwing and going.

Connie felt much better. She supposed it was the rest. Either that or it was the psychological benefit that comes with resolve. She called Hardy Rogers' office and made an appointment for the morning. She briefly considered calling her mother, but somehow she wasn't in the mood.

She thought about calling the assistant town clerk, who was a justice of the peace, but she needed to talk to Pete first. How were they going to do this? *When* were they going to do this? Soon, she hoped. How had Pete put it? "A couple of blood tests, a license, we can have it over with by the end of the week." As marriage proposals went, it had to be down near the bottom of the list. She remembered his first one. She'd wakened one morning early to find him propped on an elbow, watching her. "I think I'd like to marry you," he'd said. Connie's answer had been less than memorable, but considering it was out of a dead sleep it could have been worse. "You'd better think again," she'd said. But much to Connie's surprise, they had gotten married. She'd never imagined herself as the type. Her mother had, though. She'd even imagined the details—white train sweeping down the aisle of the church, followed by three hundred people, most of whom Connie had never met, crammed into the Wharton Hotel in South Jersey, eating Surf 'n Turf. Connie had tentatively suggested they hand over the cash instead and she and Pete would fly to some exotic location where they'd quietly tie the knot. After a brief episode of cardiac arrest on Connie's mother's part, they'd compromised on the plain hem of an understated cream-colored silk floating over her father's prize crab-grass, followed by cocktails and hors d'oeuvres for one hundred and fifty-eight. It had only been three times the work and twice the cost of the Wharton's Surf 'n Turf.

Connie wondered now how Walt had proposed to Aggie. However he'd done it, once he'd done it, they'd moved fast. He'd picked up the engagement ring on March thirteenth. The very next day he and Aggie were back in Sorensen's picking out wedding rings. And when had they planned to get married? Connie picked up the blue invitation. *Walt and Aggie would like you to help celebrate their marriage on April twenty-fifth at four o'clock at their house.*

April twenty-fifth. Not a month and a half after Walt had proposed to her. Connie liked their style. She walked across the hall to the other room, the room that still had not been given an identity and continued to hold everything Pete and Connie didn't know what to do with. She supposed this was where they'd have to put the kid. Then what would they do with the junk? She flipped through the center drawer in an old mission oak desk and unearthed the second invitation, the one Aggie and Walt had actually sent them in June. Engraved on the usual creamy paper Connie read that their presence was requested at the marriage of Agnes Rose Scott and Walter Smith Westerman on July fifteenth, two and a half months later than the first proposed date.

It was like living in a fun-house mirror, Connie decided. There were two versions of everything, one of them upside down and inside out. Two different invitations. Two different weddings. Two different dates. Two different versions of the relationship between Aggie and Walt. That, she supposed, was the biggest discrepancy. Which was closer to the truth, Ginny Turkle's *Sleeping Beauty,* or Patrice Fielding's *Nightmare on Elm Street?* How could two close friends think so differently about it? Connie wondered if the two women had ever talked about it, and if they had, what had been the end result. She wasn't sure it was worth another trip to the Turkle house to satisfy her curiosity. But as she looked at the invitation in her hand, she remembered she did have one more stop to make.

She got dressed and went out.

Pete found the occupants of the house next to the Hawthornes on their porch. They were a young couple, relative newcomers to Nashtoba, who never did recipro-

cate when Pete introduced himself, so he never did find
out who they were. They looked like each other—both
tan with straw-colored hair, hers even shorter than his.
They insisted that between the hours of ten and midnight on Friday *no* cars had gone by, either toward the
farm or away from it.

"We were right here on this porch," said the young
woman, pointing to a small wicker couch. "We didn't
once budge. It was too stinking hot in the house. We
didn't see any cars."

"Nope," said the young man. "No cars. Not Friday
night. We'd have remembered the minute we heard she
croaked."

Pete thanked them and left. As he got into the truck he
saw her grab the waistband of her husband's pants and
pull him onto the wicker couch. As he drove away he
couldn't see them at all.

All in all, Pete decided, their Friday night couch
testimony probably didn't count for much.

The stationer's was over on Cape Hook, in Naushon.
As her exhaust pipe rattled over the causeway and the
traffic immediately picked up it occurred to Connie that
she and Pete should get off the island more, exercise their
coping skills. All these cars on the road rattled her. She
could count six in her rearview mirror, at least. When
she pulled off the highway onto Old Naushon Road her
heart rate slowed, but so did her car. Actually, it came to
a grinding halt, as the car in front of her waited to turn
left. Connie tried to curb her impatience. Three cars
went by, the car in front of her turned, and she pro-
ceeded, reading signs, until she found it—J. Pinckney &
Co., Stationers.

J. Pinckney's daughter manned the desk. She was a
trim, no-nonsense woman with a short, blunt, no-
nonsense haircut. She consulted an order book and came

up with the date. May seventh. And she remembered the two Scotts.

"My father took one look at them and told me to handle it. They looked like trouble—or at least the mother did. The daughter looked like she'd rather be at the beach. But as it turned out they weren't any work at all. I handed them the sample book. The mother riffled the pages and showed one of the more expensive samples to the daughter. The daughter asked if we had it in blue. The mother said of course we didn't. We didn't, either, so I didn't have to add much. Same with the print, the envelopes, the response cards, the works. The mother would show something to the daughter, the daughter would nod, that was it. They even had the wording all written out. She handed it over, wrote out the deposit check, and left."

"But how did they seem?" asked Connie. "How did the daughter seem?"

"She seemed like she liked blue," said Pinckney, Junior. "After that, I couldn't tell you. She never opened her mouth."

"But was she smiling? Did she look comfortable? Uncomfortable? What?"

"Like I said," said Pinckney. "She looked like she'd rather be at the beach."

Connie thanked her and left.

At the Turkles', she couldn't believe her luck. Ginny Turkle in, Faye Turkle out. This time Ginny took her up to her bedroom. It was a hot choice and not as private as it first looked. Every so often Ginny's eyes shifted focus from Connie's face to the doorway behind her and she'd scream, "Duncan, this is the last time I'm telling you! Butt out!" But in between the sibling wars Ginny was forthcoming enough to make it seem worth the trip. All Connie had to do was to mention Patrice's gloom-and-doom forecast on the Scott-Westerman marriage and Ginny was launched.

"What do you expect from Patrice?" said Ginny. "It was all sour grapes, that's what it was. Or didn't you know they used to go out?"

"Yes, but when Pete talked to her she gave him the impression she was the one who bailed out."

"Patrice? Like, *right*. The minute Walt met up with Aggie he dumped Patrice flat. But he wasn't a sleaze about it. First he went to Patrice and said he didn't want to go out with her anymore. Then he asked Aggie out. But Patrice was, like, ripped. Next thing you know Patrice is telling everybody what a juvenile Walt was, how he wasn't, like, growing the way she was, how she was leaving him in the dust. But this is what's weird. After that was when Patrice became friendly with Aggie. Started, like, calling her up, going shopping and stuff."

"I'm surprised Aggie went for it."

"Then you don't know Aggie." Ginny's eyes filled. "Aggie was, like, the world's nicest human. She couldn't stand it when people didn't get along. She couldn't stand not to be nice to people. It was like she even wanted Walt to stay friends with Patrice."

A fallback position in case Aggie backed out? "What do you know about this Gene Tilton?" asked Connie.

A sly smile touched the corners of Ginny's mouth. "I know he practically lived at Aggie's father's house."

"We wondered what the story was. We found his name crossed off the wedding list."

Ginny hooted. "That would have been Walt. Still jealous, I guess."

"Of Gene? Why? Did he and Aggie go out?"

"I don't know if you'd call it *out*. Aggie was still living at home. The first time Aggie's father invited Gene for the weekend, Gene asked Aggie to dinner in Bradford. Aggie didn't know her father wasn't coming along and she said yes. She didn't, like, mean it to be a date. She was going out with Walt. But Walt went crazy when he found out and they had this big fight. Still, Gene Tilton kept showing up at her house on weekends and finally Walt went, like, so completely berserk they actually busted up. But all that trouble ended when Aggie moved out of the house and in with Walt."

"This bustup. When was that?"

"Oh, that was all over a year ago. They'd been living together since last summer."

"And despite all that fighting you still weren't surprised by that note?"

"Look," said Ginny. "She's, like, sitting in my house practically crying into her Chardonnay because she misses the guy so much. She bolts right in the middle of everything, because she can't, like, stand to be away from him for a night. One night. How could she go from feeling like that to writing him that note?"

"So how do you account for it? How do you account for that note?"

Ginny Turkle's eyes clouded. "That's the trouble. You don't."

CHAPTER
17

The bride and groom stand before him and the service is read. Afterwards those present congratulate them, and that is all . . . At such a marriage the bride rarely wears a white wedding dress and veil, but it is entirely proper for her to do so if she chooses . . . If the marriage is performed by a magistrate, however, a wedding dress is entirely out of keeping.

Hardy Rogers consulted a small chart and looked up with steel blue eyes twinkling. "Estimated due date, March fifteenth."

Beware the Ides of March. It figured, thought Pete. But at the moment he wasn't as worried about next March as he was about the next few minutes. Hardy was now drawing Connie's blood, and as soon as he finished, Pete would be next. He hated needles. It had been a long time since anyone had stuck him with one, and somehow, in the interim, the fear had grown worse. Hardy placed a small, round bandage on the inside of Connie's elbow. Pete tried not to look at the huge vial of Connie's blood lying next to him on the counter.

"You said everything looks all right?" Connie asked. She didn't seem to realize she'd already asked it twice. "I took all those birth control pills afterward. And I've been so sick. At least I was. It seems to have stopped all of a sudden."

Hardy looked up. "It has, has it?" He looked again at the chart, eyebrows clapped together, but said nothing until he turned to Pete. "Here, you. Roll up that sleeve."

Pete rolled up his sleeve. It was only a long, thin piece of metal. It was going to pierce his skin, it wasn't going to pierce his heart. He didn't much like it, but he didn't have to watch it. He looked out the window.

The next thing he knew he was flat on his back, looking up at the overhead light and listening to a conversation that sounded like it was taking place somewhere east of Mars.

"It's these strong, silent types who always go down first. The tougher they are, the faster they drop." That was Hardy.

"Sounds like Walt Westerman. Did he faint?" That was Connie. And what the hell did she care about Walt Westerman? Pete was the one who was lying on the rug.

"No, Walt didn't faint, but that little girl was hanging on to him so hard he wouldn't have gone anywhere if he did."

"Aggie? She was nervous?"

"Nervous? No, just silly. Hugging and kissing and holding his hand. 'Course that was the first time. Second time around she'd quieted down a mite."

Second time. The words brought Pete fully around. He struggled to sit up. "What do you mean second time?"

"Stay down there a minute, I'm not catching you twice." And Hardy went straight back to Aggie and Walt. Nice. "The marriage license is only good for sixty days and Aggie's and Walt's ran out. Had to do the whole thing over again come June."

"And you say Aggie seemed unhappy the second time?" Connie again.

"I never said that, now, did I? I said she wasn't as silly. But she was still looking at him like he was God's gift.

All right, young fellow, on your feet before I have to charge you rent."

Pete got up. Hardy stuck a bandage on his punctured arm. He was left to cope with his punctured dignity himself.

Connie drove them to the town hall, despite Pete's insistence that he was all right. At least for a minute there he'd been all right. Connie drove like she was the only one on the road, which on Nashtoba wasn't so much of a problem because she usually was. But she also drove like she was the only one in the car, which in this particular case she definitely was not.

"Will you slow down? My life's starting to flash before my eyes."

"If you press fast-forward you won't get so depressed."

Pete gave up. "So what's the plan?" he asked. "How do you want to do this?"

"Quietly," said Connie. "If such a thing is possible around this place. And the sooner the better."

"Tomorrow, town hall?"

Connie nodded. "We'll need witnesses."

"Willy should be able to cut loose for fifteen minutes someplace."

"Good. And I'll ask Polly."

Pete looked sideways, surprised. "I don't know if she can get off on such short notice. She's got that job on the paper."

"I know, but I'd like to ask. I think she'd like it. If she can't do it we'll nab Rita off the desk."

Nashtoba's town hall was one of those Queen Anne wonders, full of dormered angles and turrets and odd-sized windows, as if the windows had been stuck in wherever the owner could find enough flat wall space or happened to be in the mood to look out. All of Nash-toba's important business was done in the town hall—

tax collecting, public works, building permits, voter registration, the voting itself. The marriage licenses were issued from the town clerk's cramped office under the eaves on the second floor, along with the beach and dump stickers and fishing and shellfishing licenses. When Pete and Connie walked in, the town clerk, Myra Totobush, looked up.

"Well, well, if it isn't the Bartholomews. And don't I just wonder what they might want? Now let me see. You got your dump sticker in June. And your fishing/shellfishing license last March. And you don't need a beach sticker, you've got a beach right in front of your house. Could it be, could it possibly be, that you're finally going to—"

"All right, Myra," said Pete. "What do we do?"

"You mean you don't remember? Here, fill this out. When's the big day?"

"Tomorrow."

Myra laughed. "Not in this state. You apply today, you've got a three-day wait."

Connie lay on the bed and watched Pete dial his sister's number, get the busy signal, hang up. "I've been thinking," she said. "Did you catch Hardy's remark about Aggie? He said in June, the second time they came for the blood test, Aggie was still looking at Walt like he was God's gift. If you ask me, that sounds like love."

"She never said she didn't love him. She said she didn't want to marry him. Or words to that effect. Not always the same thing."

Connie shot Pete a look. *True,* she thought. "But you do see my point? That as far as Hardy was concerned, the wedding plans seemed on course?"

"Sure," said Pete. He redialed. A second later he was speaking into the phone. "Hi, Pol."

Connie sat up.

"Yeah, I got your message. No, no. Hold it. *Hold* it. No, we're not. We're getting married. Saturday."

Connie heard a shriek followed by waves of tinny laughter. Pete handed her the phone. "She's going nuts. She wants to talk to you."

Connie took the phone. "Will you be my witness? We want you to be here if you can swing it."

"Can I swing it? Can I swing it? I've only been holding my breath for eighty-six years waiting for this. *Yes,* I can do it. What do I wear?"

"Whatever you want. I don't care."

"You don't *care?* What are you wearing?"

"I don't know. We're just going in to the town hall first thing Saturday morning and—"

"Go out this minute and buy something earth-shattering. And as soon as you get it, call me back. You don't want us to clash, do you? Who's the other witness?"

"Willy."

Connie wasn't sure, but she thought she heard some sort of disruption in Polly's breathing. But when she spoke she sounded casual. "Good. It will be nice to see him. I'll see if I can come up early and help out."

"Help out with what? We're just going to the town hall Saturday at ten o'clock."

"Yes, but then what?"

"Then nothing. That's it."

"That's *it?* Aren't you going someplace afterward?"

"We haven't thought about it. We only just decided all this."

"Well, you'd better get going. I know. We'll have a big wedding brunch before you leave. I know the perfect place. The Whiteaker Hotel on that big old porch."

Connie thought of Aggie and shuddered.

"So what do we do?" asked Polly. "Willy holds the rings, I hold your flowers?"

"Flowers?"

"You have to have flowers. And talk to Pete about the breakfast. And the trip. You can't just get married and go back to work."

"I'll talk to Pete. See you Friday."

Connie hung up.

"You didn't tell her about the Ides," said Pete.

"Neither did you."

"It's your witness."

"It's your sister."

They looked at each other.

"It's still not real, is it?"

"Something tells me sooner or later it's going to get real enough. I'll tell her when she gets here. And what haven't we thought about?"

"Rings, for one thing."

Pete went to the bureau, opened his underwear drawer, fished around in a white sock, and pulled out a gold band Connie had first seen over a decade earlier.

Connie opened her jewelry box and pulled hers out.

"Ah," said Pete. "Hedging our bets?"

They tried them on. It figured Pete's would fit perfectly. Connie's was a shade tight.

Pete put his ring away and began dialing. "I'd better call the folks. If they hear this from Polly first I'll be in the doghouse for life."

Suddenly Connie panicked. She didn't want to hear what Pete's parents had to say about all this. They'd have to consider her, at best, stupid. And at worst? Connie didn't even want to think about it. She decided it was as good a time as any to look for that wedding dress.

Buy something earth-shattering. Like what? What did Emily Post recommend for a wedding in the town clerk's office? Nothing from Chez Renee, that was for sure. Connie drove past the bridal shop without looking and pulled up in front of Hansey's clothing store. Connie hated shopping. She dragged herself up the steps and into the ladies' dress department and flipped through the size ten rack. She blew past the whites and blacks. There was no need to get overly dramatic about this. She paused over a beige suit until she realized it reminded her of Alicia Scott. She skipped over a smocked thing that looked like it came out of Heidi's backpack and likewise dismissed something with puffed sleeves that reeked of Snow White. Finally Connie pulled two dresses off the rack and took them to the fitting room, a plainish yellow and a two-tone blue. When she zipped into the yellow dress the first thing she noticed was that she was wearing someone else's breasts. They percolated out of the scooped neckline and billowed into the tiny dressing room like a pair of uninvited guests. She unzipped the yellow and pulled on the two-tone blue, but in that one she looked equally strange, like a new recruit for the state cops.

As Connie stared at her ridiculous reflection in Hansey's mirror she was assailed with a fresh round of self-doubt. Who was she to decide she could be a good parent? What kind of nerve did she have to marry Pete for a second time? People like Aggie Scott chickened out on getting married the first time around. And Aggie had had a dress. Two, as a matter of fact.

Two.

Connie straightened halfway into her shorts.

How was it possible she'd forgotten about Aggie's *other* wedding dress?

CHAPTER

18

If a young man and his parents are very great friends, it is more than likely that he will already have told them of the seriousness of his intentions.

Pete hung up the phone with an ache in his right temple. Something had gone wrong, but he didn't know what. He played back the mental tape. *Connie and I are getting married.* So far so good. Happy laughter from both parents on their separate extensions. Or was it happy? Yes, dammit, it had been happy. Then what? *Well I'm not surprised.* That from his mother. *And you've got all the mistakes over with, right?* His father's little joke. Pete had chuckled politely. Actually, he'd expected to get teased a lot worse. *When's the happy event?* His mother again. Pete had told them about Saturday, about collecting Polly and Willy and dropping in at the town hall, and . . . And there it was. That was the minute it had begun to fall apart, the minute it had dawned on his parents that they weren't expected to fly up from Florida to join the fuss.

Now what? He supposed he should call back, explain

how this time it was going to be low-key, tell them about the Ides. What with the downturn in the conversation, he'd never gotten around to that. Stupid thing to keep calling it, Ides. His son? His daughter? Just the words gave him an adrenaline rush, but whether it was of fear or anticipation he couldn't yet judge. He wondered which they'd have, a son or a daughter. He suspected he'd do better with a daughter, wouldn't be so prone to force her into his old ruts. He tried to picture himself with a daughter, but for some reason the only clear image that formed was one of Ben Scott, hands reaching for Walt Westerman's throat.

Pete shuddered. New subject, please. But he tried, and failed, to move on to something else. For some reason he couldn't seem to get his mind off Ben Scott. He'd seemed so sure Walt had killed his daughter. Why? Did he know something Pete didn't? What the hell, thought Pete. Maybe he should try to find out.

Ben Scott lived in a darkly stained two-story colonial that seemed too big for one person. The driveway was hedged with reeking privet that loomed over Pete and nearly suffocated him. There were two cars in the driveway—Gene Tilton's Jaguar sedan and an old Buick Skylark. It was Gene Tilton who opened the door, but Ben Scott's voice roared from the background the minute the door was cracked.

"Who is it? Who? What? What do they want?"

Gene Tilton turned without speaking and motioned Pete to follow him. He was led to a poorly lighted dining room, where Ben Scott sat at the table, facing a blank wall, his massive upper torso hunched over his hands. He looked up. "Who are you? What do you want?"

Good question, thought Pete, already regretting his peculiar decision to come here. He answered the first question, ignored the second, and cleared his throat. "May I say how sorry—"

"No, you may not. None of you know the meaning of the word sorry. You don't know the first thing about my daughter. You don't know what she was, or what I've lost." The heavy shoulders pivoted until they faced Gene Tilton, who had stepped to the side, out of Ben Scott's line of vision. "And neither do you, Gene. But you could have, couldn't you? You could have known her, loved her. And if you had, she'd be alive now. That man would never have had her. He'd never have killed her."

"You can't always choose who you love," said Gene Tilton softly. "And you certainly can't choose who loves you. You know I was fond of your daughter."

"And she was fond of you. And she would have been fonder if you'd not hid your light under a bushel every time you came here. Big Harvard education, fancy car, $600,000 a year, and you can't even turn the head of a foolish little girl straight out of the schoolroom." The blackened visage swung Pete's way again. "And you? What do you want? How many times do I have to ask you?"

What the hell, thought Pete. "I came to ask a few questions about Walt Westerman."

Ben Scott's knuckles whitened.

"You say he killed your daughter," Pete added hastily. "I wondered what makes you so sure when the police aren't."

"I'll tell you what makes me sure. Walt Westerman was a no-good bum. And my daughter was beautiful and kind and good and she loved her father. Then she met him and I lost her. He killed her."

Pete shot a look at Gene Tilton, but his eyes were fixed on Ben Scott. "If you have some definite evidence—"

Ben Scott took an unsteady step toward Pete. Pete

took a good strong step backward. Gene Tilton moved behind Ben, arms loose at his sides, ready to move, but next to Ben Scott Gene Tilton looked like a coat hanger. Pete was relieved to see that Ben Scott stayed where he'd stopped.

"How much more evidence do you want? My Apple knew what was right. She saw she'd made a mistake, she tried to leave him, and he killed her."

"But you don't know—"

"I know like I could feel him choking it out of her. He——" Ben Scott raised his hands to his face and stumbled backward. Somehow Gene Tilton managed to steer him in the direction of the chair. Again, the shoulders fell forward over the hands, and this time they began to shake. Gene Tilton signaled to Pete. He led him out of the dining room, through a set of wide French doors and into a terraced garden.

The garden surprised Pete. The overgrown hedge in front, the despairing man inside, didn't go with the light and air and beauty that now surrounded him. But as Pete looked around he saw that much of what bloomed and prospered were the low-maintenance things like hydrangeas and day lilies, and that in the high-maintenance flower beds the weeds had encroached.

Gene Tilton extracted a slender cigar from the breast pocket of his shirt and offered it to Pete. Pete shook his head. Tilton clipped it, lit it, sucked on it, and stood admiring it for some seconds before he spoke. "You're a braver man than I," he said finally. "Whatever possessed you to come here asking questions about Westerman?"

Pete grimaced. "Stupidity. I have a young friend, a cousin of Walt's, who's about as determined that Walt didn't do it as Ben Scott is that he did. I know where my friend got his conviction. I wondered where Ben got his."

"That's easy enough. Guilt."

"Guilt?"

"Walt Westerman didn't cost Ben his daughter. Ben tossed her away all by himself. Aggie was in love with Walt. It certainly seemed that Walt was in love with her, but Ben wouldn't hear of it. And Aggie wouldn't give him up. Finally Aggie got sick of her father's efforts to derail them and she moved in with Walt. After that Ben refused to speak to her."

"Or to come to the wedding?"

"He's a stubborn old cuss. As I'm sure you just saw for yourself."

"And where do you fit into all this?"

"Minimally. Ben and my father were old friends. My father died not long ago, and I suppose for Ben I took my father's place. Or maybe the more truthful answer would be that Ben took his. Whichever way it worked, when Ben invited me down that first time, I came for my father's sake. I suppose I came after that because I felt sorry for him. And by the time I realized what he was up to, it would have been awkward to stop."

"I gather what he was up to was fixing you up with Aggie."

Gene nodded. "The minute the specter of Walt Westerman reared its ugly head he counterattacked. But it didn't make a dent. Aggie wanted nobody but Walt."

"And you? What did you want?"

The cigar occupied Gene Tilton for some seconds. It seemed to have gone out. He relit, redrew, re-examined. "I'm quite sure what I wanted never entered Ben Scott's head. But if it had, I'm equally sure it would never have occurred to him that any man could find the Apple of his eye, as he called her, lacking in any respect. As a matter of fact, I was telling the truth when I said I was fond of Aggie, but she was very young and she was very much in love with someone else. I don't know about you, but I've never found that combination particularly enticing."

Pete decided it would be wise to plead the fifth on that. "So despite his little games, you and Ben have stayed close."

"Close?"

"You came to his daughter's funeral. And you're still here now."

Gene Tilton dropped the cigar onto the grass and ground it to shreds under his heel as if it were an old cigarette. "You saw him at the funeral. You saw him now. He's in no shape to be left by himself. Unfortunately, there seems to be no one else."

"What about the wife? Do you know anything about what happened with her?"

"Nothing. Only that she left when Aggie was small. I got that from my father. Ben himself never mentions her. So the police don't think Westerman did it?"

"They used to. They may get back to it in the end. Right now they've got some questions. Like what happened to her wedding dress, who was driving her car around at three in the morning, things like that."

Gene raised an eyebrow, but he didn't linger on the subject. His next comment was about the heat. Pete agreed that it was still hot and with that the conversation seemed to run out.

"I go back through the house?" asked Pete finally.

"You don't have to. There's the gate."

But Pete was stubborn in his own right. He'd come in on the wrong foot. He wanted to try to go out on the right one. He went back through the French doors, into the dining room, and found Ben Scott where they'd left him, slumped over his hands.

"I'm sorry for the intrusion, Mr. Scott. Would you let me say just this much? I may not have known Aggie well, but I knew her well enough to know that any man would consider a daughter like that a gift. I didn't come to

142

cause you more grief. I came to try to help find out who killed her."

"Which is what we all want," said Gene Tilton from the door.

But Ben Scott didn't speak.

Connie hadn't meant to eavesdrop. She saw the car, one of those tiny, sporty convertibles that only seemed to be sold in primary colors, parked in Walt Westerman's drive. She saw the top of a man's dark head angled downward in the middle of the corn. As she approached she could hear voices.

"Remember?" the woman's voice said. "If you say you don't I'm afraid I'll have to kill you. Two feet in the air, the door opening, the look on her face—"

Laughter. It didn't seem possible, not from that dormant volcano, Walt. Connie pushed through the lush corn stalks and the laughter cut short.

Yes, it was Walt. And Patrice Fielding stood with her hand on his arm, every designer stitch, every hair on her head in place. And this after riding around in a convertible. Whenever Connie got out of her convertible she looked like a building supply store for the local bird population.

"Oh," said Patrice, "it's you. No matter, I'm just leaving. Good-bye, Walt."

"Yeah, bye," said Walt.

Patrice disappeared through the corn.

Walt looked up at the sun and said, "Lunch."

A jerk of the head seemed to indicate that Connie was to follow him. They walked in silence into the farmhouse and through to the kitchen. Walt pulled a package of sliced Swiss cheese out of the refrigerator and waved it at Connie.

"No, thanks."

143

He opened a cupboard and found bread. He cemented a half-inch of cheese slices between the bread with yellow mustard and bit into it. He fished in the refrigerator, pulled out two Cokes and slid one across the table to Connie.

"Thanks."

She hadn't expected this grudging welcome, but it turned out the explanation was simple. Once the first wad of cheese and bread went down his gullet he said, "So you don't think I did it. Why not?"

Good question, thought Connie. Then she remembered what the chief had said. "Maybe I don't want to."

Walt bit, chewed, swallowed, watched her. "Aggie was like that."

"Like what?"

"Wouldn't see the bad in people."

"What people?"

"All of them. Me. Her father. Her mother. Rydell. They walked all over her. And she let them."

"How so?"

"She let her father cram that walking washout down her throat. Gene Tilton."

"No, she didn't," said Connie, but suddenly she wondered, or did she? She'd intended to leave Walt Westerman. Maybe she'd intended to leave with Gene Tilton. Connie moved quickly to the next person on the list. "Her mother seemed all for you two getting married."

"She was all for Aggie getting married. It didn't matter who to."

"Maybe she didn't know you."

"Didn't know me and didn't try to. Didn't know Aggie, either. But Aggie wanted to please her. Aggie wanted to please everybody. Even the Reverend."

"Was the Reverend against you?"

"He was against leaving us alone," said Walt violently.

144

"He was against people leaving people be. He wanted everybody up in heaven smiling at everybody. He told Aggie to forgive her, Aggie forgave her."

"Oh," said Connie.

Walt pushed back his chair. "What do I care? I'm not going to be up there with all those hypocrites. What did you come here for, anyway?"

Whatever Connie's original reason, it now escaped her. She hunted around for a substitute excuse and finally found one. "That doll they found in the well. Andy says it was Aggie's. He says she kept a doll with no arms on her dresser."

"Yeah," said Walt.

"Isn't that a bit . . . odd?"

"Yeah," said Walt. But after a minute he seemed to relent. Either that, or he actually wanted to talk. "Aggie's mother gave it to her when she was little. It broke and her father threw it out. She found the body in the trash and took it back."

"And she kept it all these years? Moved it with her to the farm?"

Walt looked at Connie like she was a dunce. "It was from her mother. It was all she had left of her."

"Oh. And how did it get in the well?"

"Aggie, I guess. I saw it missing from the dresser and asked Aggie. She said it was broken and it was silly to save it and she'd thrown it out."

"When was this?"

Walt seemed to give it some thought. "I don't know. A month, two months back."

After her mother had re-entered her life in the flesh. And suddenly Connie remembered why she'd come here in the first place.

"I was wondering about Aggie's wedding dress."

"It's not here. I showed them already."

"Not that one, the first one. The blue one."

"Oh." After a minute Walt said, "What do you want with that?"

"I wondered if she changed her mind. Decided to change dresses. Since the other dress is missing—" Connie let the sentence hang. She wouldn't have known how to finish it anyway.

But Walt acted as if it actually made sense. He also acted acutely embarrassed. "I burned it," he said. "I burned everything. Or tried to. After you came here to look at her suitcase. I looked at it, too, later. I kept looking and looking. I kept thinking if I looked hard I'd figure it out."

"Figure what out?"

Walt didn't answer. He went to the sink and chucked the sandwich knife into it, sweeping the crumbs from the counter with the side of his hand.

"Were you trying to figure out why she left you?" asked Connie. "You wouldn't have found the answer in that bag. She didn't pack that bag to leave you, she packed that bag to marry you."

Walt didn't seem to hear. He gripped the edge of the sink as if he wanted to push it through the floor. "So I didn't want to look anymore. Not at that, not at anything. I burned the old dress, I burned the stuff in the bag, I would have burned it all if they'd left me alone. You think I care if the barn goes? You think I care if this whole place burns to the ground?"

"You'd have cared later."

He didn't seem to hear that, either. "It's all I asked for," he said. "Just that one thing. Just *why.*"

But whom did he ask? God? Aggie? Apparently neither had answered.

And when Connie left he appeared to be trying his luck with the drain in the sink.

CHAPTER
19

*[The best man] must see that the groom is dressed and
ready early, and plaster him up if he cuts himself shaving.
If he is wise in his day he even provides a small bottle of
adrenalin. . . .*

Andy Oatley returned to Factotum at lunch. He'd
thought long and hard, or pretty hard, anyway, about
what to do next. It had come down to one course. But
first he wanted to run it by Pete. He hung around, trying
to stay out of Rita's reach, until Pete's truck pulled up.
He dove out the door and jumped into the passenger seat
before Pete could bail out. It was a trick he'd learned
recently from Patrice.

"What's up?" asked Pete.

"I've got one of those things. Hypothetical. You
know."

Andy watched Pete's eyes focus down. "Meaning?"

"Meaning I tell you about this hypothetical thing and
you tell me what you'd do."

"If it weren't so hypothetical."

"Yeah." Andy inhaled. "If air feels hot in your lungs
does that mean it's hotter out than 98.6?"

"Hypothetically? This is it?"

"No," said Andy, wishing it was. "It's this. Say you found out somebody you knew did something illegal. Purchased a stolen handgun, something like that. What would you do?"

Pete didn't say anything. All he did was keep looking at Andy. Andy hated it when he did that.

"I'm no snitch," said Andy. "Let me just tell you that."

"Does this person know you know about this illegal act?"

"No."

"Then I'd tell him," said Pete. "And I'd do my best to convince him to tell the police."

"Like how would you do that?"

"By explaining what we talked about before. That the police probably know he's lying about this already, and if they think he's lying about this, they'll assume he's lying about the rest."

"And if he says 'bug off'?"

"I'd give him a chance to think about it. Bring it up again later, if he still says bug off, we'll give somebody else a shot."

"Like Willy."

"Like me, first. It'll look better if he fesses up himself. Let me know how you make out."

Andy took a good, long look at Pete. It suddenly occurred to him he was overdue with something. "Thanks," he said. "I mean, for all this." He started to get out of the truck and stopped. "And what you said to my dad. About me working out great. Maybe I'm not, but I will."

This time Andy got the long look.

"I know you will," said Pete.

* * *

Pete found Willy in an unlikely place—his office. He was sitting behind the plain, massive desk that Pete was sure must have worn dark with time, not work.

"Find anything?"

"Nothing. Nothing on the car, nothing on the dress, nothing on anything. Bob Strong says he hadn't serviced the car in months, but we checked his prints anyway. Not a prayer. So what do you want?"

Pete shuffled his feet, cleared his throat. "What are you doing Saturday morning?"

"Well, I won't be sleeping late. Goddamned Ted. Not that he's much use, but at least he can file papers." Willy's eyes narrowed. "Why?"

"I need a witness. I'm getting married."

Pete supposed a dispassionate third party might have been amused at the changes that came over Willy's face. First it went blank, as if he were waiting for the punch line. When none came, the eyes widened until the stubble on top of his head bucked. "Holy shit," he said. "You and Connie?"

"Who do you think?" said Pete, annoyed.

Willy grinned. "I never thought she'd get that desperate."

"Yeah, well, I never thought she'd get that pregnant."

Willy's grin vanished. But then he seemed to realize Pete was doing it.

He came around the desk and clapped him on the back. "Come on," he said. "I'm buying you a drink."

When Pete got back Connie was on the phone in the kitchen. She rolled her eyes at him. *"No*, Mom. Yes, I know that. Yes, I remember. No. *What* pearls? *Who?"*

Pete grabbed a piece of paper and a pencil and wrote *Ask them to come if you want.* He shoved the paper at her.

149

Connie read the note. "Are you nuts? No, Mom, not you. I was talking to Pete. Look, do you want to come up for this thing? Saturday morning. Yeah. Yeah. Sure. All right, Friday night. No. Yes. See you Friday. Good-bye. Okay, I'll tell him." Connie hung up.

"All right," she said. "What the hell are you doing?"

"She wanted to come, didn't she?"

"Of course she wanted to come. And now you'll have to ask your folks and they won't be able to get a flight and we'll have to postpone the whole thing and I'll be the size of a weather balloon by the time they get here."

"They'll get a flight."

"And where are we going to put all these people? We can't put your father on the foldout couch with his bad back. We'd better give them our room and put my folks on the foldout. Polly can sleep on the couch in the office."

"And where do we go?"

Connie's face lit up and then immediately fell. "We can't afford it, can we?"

"You mean a real honeymoon? I don't see how, not with the Ides coming. Which reminds me, how did your mother take the news?"

"We had no time for those little details. We had to talk about important things, like Great-aunt Lucretia's pearls, which if I know my mother, she's packing as we speak for me to wear on Saturday. And that reminds *me*. About Aggie. She never did pack a bag to run away with, did she? Doesn't that seem strange to you?"

"Not if she got killed before she got around to it."

"But that means she'd have sat down to write that note before she packed her bag. And she left the note in the screen door. If she got that far she should have had her bag packed and with her."

"Your explanation?"

"I don't have one," said Connie glumly, more glumly, it seemed to Pete, than Aggie's unpacked bag seemed to warrant.

Pete reached across the table and brushed the knot between her eyebrows. "Look, there's no way we're spending our honeymoon night with our parents and my sister. I'll get us a room at the Whiteaker. So the Ides can go to U. Mass. instead of Harvard."

Harvard. Gene Tilton. Ben Scott. There it was again, the same old subject. They couldn't seem to let go of it. Pete told Connie about his visit and when he finished she gazed at him thoughtfully.

"Shaky," she said.

"What's shaky?"

"Gene Tilton, mainly. I find it hard to believe a grown man would play along with some juvenile scheme to throw him together with Aggie unless he wanted to be thrown."

"Meaning?"

Connie laughed. "Meaning absolutely nothing except that I'd bet Gene Tilton, like most men, doesn't like looking like a loser. You know, 'so what if you don't want me? I never wanted you in the first place.' A variation on the old you-can't-fire-me-I-quit."

"Or the old you-can't-leave-me-I'm-divorcing-you."

They looked at each other.

"Yes," said Connie softly. "Something like that."

"Saturday?" said Jack Whiteaker. "You mean *this* Saturday?"

"I'm not asking for water view." Pete didn't care if he'd be viewing the Dumpster. He spent every day of his life viewing the water. He just wanted a bed and room service and a hot shower and clean towels and a maid to clean it all up afterward.

"Yes, but your honeymoon, Pete. I'd have liked to do you up proud. If you'd given me a little more notice . . . Oh, well. You'll get the best I've got, you can count on that. And there'll be a bottle of our best champagne, chilled and waiting, on the house."

Whenever Pete drank champagne he broke out in a sweat. And Connie never drank anything but beer. "Thanks, Jack," he said. "That would be nice."

Pete retrieved his credit card and was about to leave when he remembered Alicia Scott. If she hadn't gotten the mud from the Whiteaker parking lot, where had she gotten it?

He asked Jack and was told she was still in residence. Pete climbed the stairs to her room and knocked on the door. No answer. He was turning away when he heard what sounded like air in an antiquated radiator.

In July.

In eighty-degree heat.

Pete knocked again. "Hello? It's Peter Bartholomew." This time it sounded like wind in a drainpipe.

Or a woman moaning.

"Are you all right?"

A cough, followed by what was clearly a moan. "Please—" Another cough. Another word that sounded like *huck.*

Or *help.*

Pete tried the door. It was locked, but the door was old and so was the lock and hadn't Pete seen enough old movies? He backed up and kicked, and for once it worked just like the movies. The wood splintered, the door swung open.

And Alicia Scott lay on the rug, curled in the fetal position.

Even under her makeup she looked the color of dust. Pieces of a broken chair rested against the wall.

Pete went to the phone and dialed. Then he knelt over her.

"Fell." she said.

Rita Peck was just realigning her desk for her lunchtime departure when Connie came by and stopped in front of her. "By the way," she said, "Pete and I are getting married on Saturday."

Rita's mouth fell open. She felt it fall and quickly snapped it shut. She jumped to her feet and lunged over the desk to hug Connie. "Oh, I'm so relieved."

"Relieved?"

"Well, you know. Thrilled. And how do you feel? You must be—"

"Pregnant," said Connie.

Rita made sure, this time, not to let her jaw slip so much as a quarter of an inch. "Well," she said.

Connie laughed.

Rita studied her, decided she seemed happy enough, and rearranged her face. "Well," she said again, "I think that's the most exciting news I've heard since I was. Pregnant, that is." Suddenly Rita remembered where her daughter Maxine was this very moment. Piercing her navel. She felt the shadow eclipse her smile and exerted herself to get it back. "Now, don't buy a thing until we comb my attic. I've saved everything. Crib, high chair, playpen, clothes . . . that's if it's a girl, of course."

"Boys have different cribs?"

Rita shot Connie a nervous look. She *was* kidding. She was sure she was. "Oh, Connie, this *is* exciting. But let's not put the cart before the horse. Saturday. You're getting married Saturday. Where, First Parish Church?"

"No, second floor, town hall. Clerk's office."

"Oh," said Rita. "Of course. How—" She had planned to add *nice,* but she'd seen the clerk's office. She switched it to, "How interesting."

There followed a pause. "Would you like to come?" said Connie finally. "Ten o'clock Saturday? You don't have to. I mean our feelings won't be hurt if you don't want to, I know you already came once."

Rita clapped her hands. "Oh, I wouldn't miss it for anything. And Maxine. She'll be so excited. So tell me everything. What you're wearing, what happens afterward—"

Suddenly Connie looked perplexed. "I don't know about that part. There's some talk about a brunch."

"Oh, let's do a nice luncheon. I always wanted a nice wedding luncheon."

"Luncheon," said Connie.

Rita patted her hand. She pulled a fresh legal pad into the middle of the desk. She removed a newly sharpened pencil from the pencil holder. "Don't worry," she said. "We'll just start at the top. That way we won't forget anything."

It wasn't Pete's favorite place, Bradford Hospital. So why was he there? Because he'd found her. Because she'd lied to him. Twice. And because if he didn't hang around to find out what was wrong with her, who would? The emergency room wasn't exactly crowded with well-wishers.

Pete eventually managed to get the scoop out of the nurse. Two broken ribs and a punctured lung. They were admitting her. Yes, Pete could see her, but only until they'd gotten a room ready.

The nurse led Pete to Alicia's cubicle, pulled back the curtain, and left him. Without the starched support of her makeup and clothes, Alicia looked twice the age and half the size. She mouthed one word when she saw Pete. "Fell."

"Some fall. What'd you fall off, the bed?"

"Chair broke. On the bed. Smoke detector."

She elaborated once she caught enough breath. She'd put the chair on the bed to reach the smoke detector, which had somehow mysteriously gone off. The chair was old and it had broken. That's how she'd fallen. First onto the chair and then off the bed and onto the rug. Pete let her struggle on until she exhausted herself.

"Who did it?" he asked.

She closed her eyes. "Fell," she said.

CHAPTER
20

In the cities where a Social Register or other Visiting Book is published, people find it easiest to read it through, marking "XX" in front of the names of family members and intimate friends who must be asked to the house. . . .

Connie sat at the kitchen table and stared at Rita's list. If she started right now she'd be busy every minute of every day for eight weeks. When Pete walked in she said, "Fine mess you've got us into. By the way, Rita's coming Saturday. And probably Maxine. Where have you been, anyway?"

She listened, appalled, as Pete told her about Alicia Scott. When he finished she sat there in silence, thinking furiously. She looked up when she saw that Pete was counting something on his fingers.

"What are you doing?"

"Counting wedding guests. I make it twelve."

"Where the hell do you get twelve?"

"You. Me. Polly. Willy. Our parents. Rita and Maxine. And we can't very well invite Rita and Maxine and not include Andy."

Connie counted after him. "That's eleven."

"And Sarah. Don't you think?"

"Cripes, yes, we have to have Sarah. Okay. Twelve."

"And that's not counting Elsie McAllister."

"Who the *hell* is—"

"The assistant town clerk. The justice of the peace. Speaking of which, did you happen to notice their office? There's no way thirteen of us can fit in there."

Connie looked down at Rita's list. She had a sneaking suspicion that Rita had been secretly planning weddings for years, on the off chance that Maxine would ever take a wild turn toward the conventional. What the hell, thought Connie. According to number six on Rita's list, they were going to have to clean the house, anyway. And it made no sense to drag everyone down to the town hall if they had to come right back here for this luncheon or brunch or whatever it was. "Why don't you see if Elsie can come out here Saturday? We'll pool everybody in front of the stone wall. The ramblers are out, it'll save on number four."

"Number four?"

Connie pointed to Rita's list. "Florist."

Pete didn't for one minute believe Alicia's story about falling, but before he took the tale to the police chief he wanted to make sure. He found Jack Whiteaker grabbing a quick sandwich in the office. He filled him in on Alicia's state and Alicia's tale, but he hadn't gotten far into the smoke detector story when Jack Whiteaker began to shake his head vigorously.

"Not possible. That smoke detector never went off. We'd have gotten the signal here in the office."

"Mind if I take one more look at that room?"

Jack looked doubtful. "We've moved her things. For security purposes. Seeing as the door was broken."

Pete wasn't sure, but he thought he detected an accusatory note in there somewhere. "I'm not looking to paw through her underwear. I want to check out that chair, the smoke detector."

Jack agreed reluctantly. He accompanied Pete upstairs. A workman was already busy replacing the door frame. Pete and Jack stepped around him and into the room. It didn't take Jack Webb to be able to pierce the necessary holes in Alicia Scott's story. Even if the smoke detector had gone off, it wasn't located over the bed, but about four feet to the right of it. Putting the chair on the bed to reach it? Sorry. And what had set the detector off in the first place? If Alicia smoked there was no sign of it, not even an ashtray.

Jack Whiteaker went to pick up the splintered chair where it lay in the spot it had most likely been thrown—against the far wall, luckily below, and not through, the window. Pete stopped him. "I'd leave that. The door won't matter, that was my contribution. But somebody else busted that chair and Willy's probably going to want to look at it." And so did Pete. He bent over the chair. It was a straight, ladder-backed chair with a solid seat. Three rungs and two legs broken. It looked to Pete as if the chair would have broken Alicia long before Alicia would have broken the chair. Pete looked around and soon enough found what he was looking for—the scarred surface of the oak bureau where the chair had presumably made contact, either before or after it had been swung at Alicia.

Pete hung around until Willy arrived. He told him how the land lay when he first came upon it, and he told him of his chat with Alicia in the hospital.

"She's lying her head off," Pete warned him. "She might not press charges. But you'll talk to her?"

"I'll talk to her. If it hangs together and she doesn't press charges, we will."

* * *

Connie couldn't seem to move. She sat at the kitchen table with Rita's list in her hand, fighting off waves of panic. Today was Wednesday. Not tomorrow, not the next day, but the next day was Saturday. Wasn't there one thing on the list she could cross off as done or unnecessary? How about number three—invitations? No. They still had to invite Sarah. That's what she could do, invite Sarah.

As Connie pushed back her chair the phone rang, and as surely as if the umbilical cord had been somehow reattached Connie knew it was her mother. She picked it up. "Hello?"

"Oh, I'm so glad I caught you in," said her mother. "I know you won't mind, but I promised him I'd check. You don't mind if Uncle Henry comes up."

"If Uncle Henry comes up when?"

"Why, for the wedding, of course. You remember he missed the last one. He was in Hong Kong and he was so disappointed. I told him I was sure you wouldn't mind if we brought him."

"Actually, we're trying to keep this low-key."

"Oh, I know that, dear. But it's just Uncle Henry."

Connie decided to try a diversion. "I've got something else to tell you. You're going to be a grandmother."

Connie's mother burst into tears. Connie couldn't tell if they were tears of joy, or tears of something else. But when her mother got her breath it became clear soon enough.

"We'd just about given up hope. Oh, your father will be delighted. Maybe this time he'll get his boy. That's all he talked about when I was carrying you. Teaching his son to golf."

"Tell him thanks."

"Oh, Connie, you know what he meant. And he did teach you to golf. At least he tried to. But you never did take to it. And it *was* a disappointment."

"I have to run," said Connie.

"I'll tell Uncle Henry you'd love to have him. He's bought you a lovely pair of candlesticks."

Connie hung up. So they were up to fourteen. She'd never been superstitious, but she had to admit she was just as glad to have unloaded that unlucky number.

Unlucky. Suddenly Connie's thoughts went back to Aggie. She remembered what Pete had said about all those pennies in the well. She wondered who'd chucked them in there. Aggie, she'd guess. It sounded like Aggie to believe in wishing wells. She doubted Walt believed in much of anything.

But enough of this daydreaming. Where was she? Connie snatched up Rita's list again. *Rings.* Now there was something she could cross off in good conscience. They had the rings, as long as she didn't gain another ounce before Saturday, which she would surely do now that she wasn't sick anymore and could start eating again. But so what? She'd soap up her finger ahead of time. Connie grabbed a pen and crossed off *rings* with energy.

But there was still something about rings, wasn't there? Yes. Not theirs, but Aggie's. That was something else she should have discussed with Walt. Earl Sorensen had said there was some sort of a story behind Aggie's engagement ring and Walt was the only one who could know what that was. Buoyed by the courteous if not eager reception earlier that morning, Connie decided to go back to the farm and ask him.

Walt was transplanting cabbages when Connie pulled up. She walked through the damp earth and crouched in front of him. "Need some help?"

Walt peered at her long enough to determine her sanity, or at least that's how Connie interpreted the look.

"I've got a few more questions," she said. "I can ask while we work."

That seemed to clear up the question of her sanity quick enough. Connie could see Walt was the type who would always look a gift horse in the mouth. But he also seemed the type who didn't take kindly to questions.

"I'd like to know how it's supposed to help things, you and Pete asking all these questions."

Connie tried a laugh. "Me, too, but we can't seem to help it. If we find a question, we have this crazy urge to dig out the answer. And how can it hurt?"

Walt looked as doubtful as Pete had when she'd tried that line on him. But he handed her a trowel and a tray of plants and showed her how to peel back the peat pots, how to set them in the soil at the same depth they'd started out.

"Two feet between rows. Two feet between plants. Fall cabbage is bigger."

Connie didn't dare ask "bigger than what?" She faced Walt across their respective rows and set to work in silence. Now that she was actually ready, it was harder to speak than she'd thought.

"Well?" said Walt finally.

"All right. Aggie's engagement ring. The jeweler says there's some story to it."

"No story. Aggie read it in some book. Amethysts are love charms. We joked around about it. I said I'd better get her a zillion of 'em to—" He stopped.

"To what?"

"To make sure she'd stick around," he finished, as if it was a good joke, but Connie wasn't dumb enough to laugh that time.

"So I had them put three in her ring. See how great it worked? She chucked the ring in the well. That's what the cops said. Next."

Connie assumed he meant next question, but she wasn't sure she had one. She tamped the dirt down around a cabbage plant and reached for another pot. There seemed to be an endless row of them and the afternoon sun was hot. She waved her trowel at the fields around them. "You do this all yourself?"

"Now I do. Aggie used to help. And Duncan Turkle, but he can't now. Ginny says he's sick but that's not it."

"It isn't?"

"He liked her," said Walt simply.

It took Connie another minute to digest that one. "Speaking of that well," she said finally. "They found a lot of pennies in the mud."

"Yeah, Aggie did that. I'd see her out there every night after dinner, tossing in a penny. I told her she was wasting her money."

"What was she wishing for?"

"Never said. Bad luck to tell, that's what she told me. Figure it was something useless. World peace, probably."

The attempt at callousness didn't quite come off. But callouses can't form until the wound closes up. Walt moved down the row. Connie hastened a plant into the hole she'd just dug. "Tell me about the wedding. The first one. The one Aggie wrote those invitations for herself. What happened to that wedding?"

"Her mother. Or the Reverend. Take your pick. He's the one who talked her into calling her mother. Her mother's the one who came and fouled everything up. We had it all fixed. It was supposed to be right here, at the farmhouse, with Elsie McAllister. My aunt and uncle, Andy and Ginny to stand up with us, pizza and beer afterward. Then Aggie runs into the Reverend Rydell and rings him in on it. The next thing I know the sky's falling in all over the place. He gets her to write her mother. I didn't even know Aggie knew where her mother was, but I didn't argue. She was running low on family, I couldn't blame her for wanting her mother around."

Yes, thought Connie, and suddenly it seemed even clearer what had drawn Walt and Aggie to each other—both were orphans of sorts.

"Her father didn't come?"

"I didn't figure he would. She wrote him right off and asked him to come, but he didn't even answer her letter. He didn't like me much."

"But her mother came."

"Her mother came, all right. And wrecked everything."

"Couldn't you say something?"

"I said plenty. But all it did was get Aggie upset. She'd just got her mother back. She didn't want to rock the boat. I guess she didn't mind it, this new version of our wedding. I thought I knew her. I thought we were alike. Turns out we sure weren't. So when Lit called and told me what was going on I said 'do what Aggie wants.'"

"So you went along?"

"I kept trying to hang on to the fact that the minute the show was over, I'd have the part I wanted, the part that would count. So I went along. Even at the church on Friday. I admit I'd about had enough. I was in no mood for Aggie going off somewhere that night. But in the end I shut up."

And Aggie went off to Ginny Turkle's.

Odd that Connie would be thinking of Ginny Turkle the very minute she pulled up.

She traipsed through the garden and stared down at Walt with hands on hips. "I told you I'd be back."

Connie handed Ginny her trowel and stood up. "Be my guest."

Walt hardly seemed to notice the change of shift.

CHAPTER
21

. . . the proportion of guests who will take a long trip seldom exceeds that of the immediate family and such intimate friends as might be asked to the smallest of receptions.

Rita Peck launched herself from the desk and attacked Pete as he walked past. When she got through with the hugging and kissing she said, "I knew it, of course. Everyone knew it. It was only a matter of time. But this is probably just what you needed, a little boot to get you off your duff. Now don't you worry anymore this week about Factotum. Andy and Maxine and I will take care of everything. You have other things to do. Don't you think a swing from that big oak on the south side of the house would be nice? I've always thought that was the perfect spot for a swing. We never could find a tree just right at our house. Oh, I can see her already, swinging from that old oak with her braids sailing out. I always wanted to braid Maxine's hair, but she would never stand still long enough. Not once."

"Yeah," said Pete, "Well—"

"I've told Evan and he's delighted. Just delighted."

Evan. They'd forgotten about Evan, Rita's gentleman friend.

"Evan can come? Good. By the way, there's been a change of scene. The backyard."

"Thank *heaven*," said Rita. "I hated to think of you in that musty old office. Of course this means we'll need to add a few things to that list."

Pete retreated hastily to the kitchen before Rita could hand him her codicil. He was about to reach for the phone to call his parents when Andy and Maxine came through the door.

Andy charged him with a high-five that nearly sent his chair over. "Hey, Rita just told us. Congratulations. You should have told me before."

"Yeah, well, we had other things to talk about." He gave Andy a searching look. Andy gave his head a near-imperceptible shake. What did that mean, that he hadn't talked to Walt, or that Walt hadn't taken the hint?

Pete turned to Maxine. Her expression, Pete decided, could best be described as "you mean you old guys still do it?" She turned pink around the edges of her eyeliner, mumbled a good luck with more feeling than was exactly complimentary, and shot out the door, pulling Andy after her.

When Connie came in she took one look at him and said, "What's the matter?"

"Nothing. Just feeling ancient."

"Tell me about it. I'm so tired I could go to sleep on this floor." She sat down and untied her sneakers, which were crusted in mud. She walked barefoot to the door and deposited them on the porch.

"What have you been doing?"

Connie told him. Cabbages. Dolls. Engagement rings. Wishing wells. Sabotaged weddings. When she mentioned Elsie McAllister Pete snapped his fingers. That's what he was supposed to be doing. He reached for the phone.

"By the way," said Pete. "We're up to fourteen. We seem to have added Evan Spender."

"Fifteen," said Connie. "My uncle Henry."

Pete opened his mouth, but the phone rang under his fingers. He picked it up. "Hello?"

Willy didn't say hello back. "When you talked to Alicia Scott did she happen to mention where she was going?"

"Going?"

"As in gone."

"Gone?"

"Checked out. Against orders."

"Damn. Now what?"

"Now I find her." He hung up.

"What?" said Connie.

Pete told her.

When the phone rang again Connie said, "Don't answer it. It's my mother."

Pete picked it up. Close, but no cigar. It was his ex- and future father-in-law. Pete greeted the coming-back-for-more-are-you? routine with good cheer, but suddenly the conversation seemed to have escaped him. Finally he put a hand over the mouthpiece and asked Connie, "What's all this about golf?"

"It seems I've been a terrible disappointment to him on the links. He's hoping our son will take to it better."

Pete eventually transferred the phone to Connie and went out to the porch. Golf. Is this what he was letting himself in for, a golfer? Pete had never golfed in his life. He gazed over the marsh to the sound. What he couldn't teach his kid about the water probably didn't exist and he could hold his end up in the rest—baseball, football, hockey, even soccer. But golf? He remembered Connie's crack about the Vegas chorus line. She'd been joking, but it was no joke. It could happen. Their kid could decide to do any number of things that Pete and Connie found distasteful, and all Pete and Connie could do would be to smile and take it.

Pete shuddered and turned toward the kitchen, but as he did so his gaze came to rest on Connie's muddy sneakers. There was something familiar about them. Not so much the sneakers, but the mud. Then Pete got it.

From inside he heard Connie's voice grow louder. *"No,* Mother. We are not inviting the Julius cousins and that's final." There was another indistinct mumble or two and the phone clattered onto its rest.

Pete picked up the sneakers and went inside.

"This murder would make perfect sense if Alicia were the corpse," said Connie. "We'd know right away it was Aggie who killed her. And if there was ever a more justifiable homicide—"

"Speaking of Alicia, I think I know where that mud on her shoes came from." He held up Connie's sneakers.

Connie peered at the shoes. "You think Alicia helped Walt plant a few cabbages before the wedding?"

"No, but I wouldn't mind having another talk with him."

"I'll go with you. We're big buddies now. Besides, I've only been out there twice today."

Pete looked at his watch. And if they stopped at the town hall on the way, they might just catch Elsie McAllister.

She was just packing up to go home, but when she spied them through the glass pane in the door she waved them into the office, beaming vigorously. Pete knew better than to take it personally. Elsie McAllister beamed at everybody. She had the kind of skin that looked like it had never seen sun or wind, and she favored the kind of clothes that billowed after her when she walked, like somebody's fairy godmother.

"I'm glad you stopped by," said Elsie. "Myra wasn't sure she told you. We need a copy of the divorce papers. Silly, I know. But you have to prove you got divorced before we can let you remarry. No rush, just sometime before Friday. Now let me see, it's ten o'clock, Saturday—"

"Would you object to a change of scenery?" said Pete. "The numbers are creeping up." He waved a hand around the tiny room. "We thought if you came out to the house everyone would breathe easier."

"Oh, certainly, I'd be happy to come out. We don't want anyone fainting, do we?"

Pete peered at Connie suspiciously. Had she gone blabbing it to everybody? But Connie wasn't looking. "Tell me something," she was saying to Elsie. "You were supposed to marry Aggie Scott and Walt Westerman. What happened, did the mother fire you?"

"The mother? Why, no." Elsie dropped into her chair and shook her head sadly. "Aggie came to me herself. Walter had arranged for me to marry them at their house, but that was before Aggie spoke to the Reverend Rydell. It seems the minute she mentioned she was getting married he assumed he would be performing the ceremony. She didn't have the heart to hurt his feelings, so she came to me to cancel the arrangement. She could much more easily have called, but she came here in person, to explain what had happened. She was a most thoughtful young woman. I'm sure she will be sorely missed by everyone."

Pete was sure she would be missed by everyone, too.

Even, maybe, her murderer.

When they reached the farm they found two cars in Walt's driveway. One was Ginny Turkle's. The other was

Patrice Fielding's. It seemed to Pete that for a self-proclaimed loner, Walt Westerman got a lot of company.

There was nobody in the field so they began to walk toward the house. Halfway there Connie grabbed Pete's sleeve and stopped him. "See? If Alicia had come to the farm, this is where she'd have parked. The question is, why would she cross that nice, damp dirt instead of walking up the drive to the house?"

Pete surveyed the layout. One thought occurred to him, but because it was too crazy he discarded it.

But Connie didn't seem to have the same scruples. "Obvious, isn't it? The short way to the well."

"Tell me you're not thinking Alicia Scott killed her own daughter."

"Why not? She's disappeared. *And* she eloped."

"What's that got to do with it?"

"She never had a wedding of her own. She'd been dreaming about Aggie's half her life. If Aggie decided to back out—"

"Come on. Alicia Scott kills her daughter because she won't get married?"

"Listen a minute, will you? We know that somewhere in the course of events, Aggie decides she can't go through with this wedding. Let's say she goes to the hotel Friday night to tell her mother. We know Alicia's been all gung ho about the wedding. And just think of the humiliation. Alicia doesn't sound like the type to let it all turn to dust without an argument. So assume they argue. Alicia gets so angry she goes for the throat."

"I think we'd better talk about this some time when you haven't just been talking to *your* mother."

"I'm serious, damn you. Alicia strangles her *accidentally*. The vagal shock, remember? It wouldn't have taken more than a second."

"So now what? She's got a dead daughter on the floor of her hotel room and she decides to blame it on Walt."

"Exactly."

"So she waltzes down the staircase of the Whiteaker Hotel, dragging Aggie by the hair—"

"Okay, I don't know just how she does it, but it has to be possible, doesn't it? She gets Aggie out of the hotel somehow, drives over here, drags the body through the field, getting her shoes muddy."

"The night before the wedding."

"Right."

"But she kills Aggie in her wedding clothes?"

"Okay. Hold it. Let me think. Maybe Alicia only brought one pair of dress shoes to the island. She might have worn the same pair Friday night and Saturday morning."

"I doubt it. At the very least she'd have cleaned them off before she put them back on in the morning. No, she got those shoes dirty just before the wedding and she was too upset to notice. And besides, you're forgetting about the note Aggie left Walt."

But Connie didn't seem to have heard him. She left the field and struck out over the grass for the well, still calling to him over her shoulder. "Aggie was tiny. I think Alicia could have managed her. She could have lifted her like this, dropped her over the side—"

Connie leaned over the well.

And snapped upright. "Pete!"

He didn't want to move. That was the funny thing. He stopped where he was and examined Connie's long, tense spine. She seemed heavier since he'd last looked and her hair had grown and gotten lighter over the summer. He hardly recognized her. There was no reason for him to go over there, to answer a call from some stranger, to look into the well and find another body lying there. . . .

But he was moving. Of course he was moving.

And looking.

A heap of filthy white froth lay crumpled in a ball at the bottom of the well.

"Three thousand dollars," said Connie. "That's what that thing is worth."

"Not anymore," said Pete.

CHAPTER

22

All gifts as they arrive should be put in a certain room, or part of a room, and never moved away until the description is carefully entered. It will be found a great help to put down the addresses of donors as well as their names so that the bride may not have to waste an unnecessary moment of the overcrowded time which must be spent at her desk.

Connie went to the farmhouse to call the chief as Pete stood guard at the well. Through the open windows she could hear the sound of pots banging around in the kitchen. She rapped smartly on the farmhouse door and listened again. The noise stopped and heads appeared in the hall—Ginny Turkle's disorganized red curls from the kitchen, Patrice Fielding's sleek coiffure from the living room. *The Witches of Eastwick,* thought Connie. Only the devil was missing.

"I need to use the phone," said Connie.

Ginny pointed to the hall phone. Patrice disappeared up the stairs and Connie heard low voices drifting down them. By the time she finished dialing, Patrice had reappeared with Walt, leading him down the stairs with that hand on his arm, the hand that always seemed to belong there. At the foot of the stairs Patrice disappeared into the living room, but Connie could feel Walt behind her, listening. She battled her way through Jean Martell to the chief and told him what they'd found this time. Before she'd finished she heard Walt's boots make for the outer door. One by one the witches reappeared and followed him. Oh, there's something in the air here, thought Connie. Something that could be, or maybe should be, cut with a knife. She replaced the receiver and crept down the hall to the kitchen. It appeared that Ginny had been making dinner—a huge salad had been tossed in a mixing bowl, a cold ham sliced and piled high on a platter, and corkscrew pasta boiled madly in a black pot on the stove. The table was set for three.

How cozy.

She backtracked to the living room. Cardboard cartons, newspaper, brown wrapping paper, packing tape, and scissors littered the floor. Perched on every available flat surface were the wedding gifts that Patrice had apparently been packing and returning for Walt. Connie looked around. A soup tureen, a cheese board, an embroidered tablecloth, ornate water goblets, nothing that looked like Walt, or even Aggie, for that matter. Connie wondered how much of the wedding list had been engineered by Aggie's mother. She stepped into the room and picked up a notepad that contained a neat list, again in Aggie's childish writing. *Mr. and Mrs. Richard Thurston, Spode casseroles.* A Fulton address. Connie skimmed the rest of the list and noticed a disproportionate number of Fulton addresses. At least Aggie had been organized. That should make the job easier, but it still wasn't going to be any day at the beach. For a second Connie flushed with rage at Aggie. How dare she leave poor Walt to cope with this alone? But then again, he wasn't coping alone, was he? And then also again, he deserved this and more if he'd killed her. Connie shuddered. Odd how the minute Walt's harem appeared her own sympathies for him faltered.

Okay, enough stalling. Connie turned on her heel and

hurried out the door. She managed to catch up with the women just as Ginny Turkle reached the well and looked down. "Oh," she gasped. "Oh, *Aggie.*" She whirled into Walt's arms and burst out crying. Walt looked more surprised than anything. He peeled her away, attempting to stand her up as if she were a lopsided mannequin.

"Patrice?" he said finally.

Patrice's features went through a series of contortions that finally settled on something like I-don't-have-time-for-this-I-have-an-important-meeting-at-eleven. She stepped up, grabbed the weeping woman by the elbow, and said sharply, "Stop this, Ginny, it isn't helping."

But Ginny didn't stop. Patrice jerked her toward the farmhouse. Walt watched them go. Connie watched Walt. Something—the sound of Ginny's sobs, the dress in the well, all these women in his face—something had gotten to him.

When the police chief arrived all eyes pivoted in his direction. He parked the Scout a short distance down the road and walked along it to the point nearest the well, looking at the ground as he went. From there he cut across the field in the most direct route from road to well, still looking down.

"If he's looking for prints, good luck to him," said Walt. "Whoever did this did it at night. I would have seen it in daylight. And the sprinklers go on at six every morning."

Convenient, thought Connie. As convenient for Walt as it was for anybody. He more than anyone would know that all tracks would be washed away at six in the morning. Who was to say Walt didn't chuck the dress in the well as soon as he knew the police were through searching? It would be the last place they'd look, since they'd already cleaned it out when they found Aggie's body.

And that was the first thing Pete said when the chief

reached them. "That dress wasn't in there Saturday morning."

"I realize that," said Willy. He sounded testy. He'd gotten a fresh haircut since Connie had seen him and it seemed to have minimized the contrast between receding hair and expanding forehead. Or maybe it was the growing number of worry lines that did it. He sprouted a few more as a dark-green compact car pulled into the driveway.

The Reverend Rydell got out.

Walt turned and ran.

The chief jerked his head toward the new arrival and said to no one in particular, "Get him out of here."

Connie's usual reaction to male authority was to plant her feet, but for some reason this time she found them moving toward the driveway to intercept the Reverend.

He took in the scene around him fast enough. "I see Walt appears to be fleeing. And the chief is here. Perhaps this isn't the best time."

"No," said Connie, "it isn't."

She could have sworn the Reverend looked relieved. He turned his gaze toward the two men in the field, who were approaching the well with a ladder they must have borrowed from the barn.

"What's going on?"

"They've discovered a key piece of evidence. Aggie's wedding dress."

"Her dress? In the well?"

Connie nodded.

As they watched, the ladder was eased over the lip of the well and the chief hoisted himself after it, plastic bag in hand. He emerged soon after with the muddy dress clearly visible through the plastic.

"You say this is key evidence?"

"They figured wherever the dress ended up Friday, that's where Aggie ended up," said Connie. "And wherever Aggie ended up, that's where she probably got killed."

The Reverend looked over his shoulder at the farmhouse. "I see. And I suppose now they arrest him."

"No," said Connie quickly. "Somebody could have planted it."

The Reverend looked at her curiously. "And the body?"

"Yes, and the body."

"I see." It had cooled off, but the Reverend was still sweating profusely. He withdrew a handkerchief from a back pocket and wiped his face. "There was a note, wasn't there? I don't suppose the chief is forgetting about the note? I seem to recall some of it. I saw it on the table when we gathered here at the house on Saturday. Not seeing eye to eye. A decision to part company."

Behind them, a screen door slammed. Connie turned. Walt Westerman rounded the corner of the house and entered the barn. A truck engine roared. Willy's head came up. By the time Walt had backed around and headed out the drive, Willy had intercepted him. An animated exchange appeared to take place through the truck window.

"I think I'd best go," said the Reverend. He wandered off to his car, eyes on the ground, still sweating.

Connie dropped into the kitchen chair and sighed. Pete gave her that Father Goose look he'd recently developed that meant either he was going to shove food in her face or tell her to lie down or . . .

"You look tired," he said. "Why don't you lie down while I make dinner?"

Suddenly Connie realized that was just what she wanted to do. Lie down. She was exhausted.

The phone rang. Connie didn't know why Pete kept answering the thing. This time it was his sister. Connie could hear her talking animatedly, although the words weren't clear. Pete worked in a few monosyllabic answers and motioned to Connie. Connie shook her head vehemently. "She'll call you later," said Pete and hung up the phone. He went to the refrigerator and removed a Ballantine. He tried to hand it to Connie, but she waved him away. He'd been there when Hardy said no alcohol, what was the matter with him? He popped the top and tossed back a healthy swallow. For a second she felt like killing him. She summoned all her waning control and asked politely, "What did Polly want?"

"I don't know. To yell, mostly. Willy called her to see how she was taking the big news about the Ides and now she's ripped I didn't tell her."

"What else did she say?"

"She's already booking the kid's trip to Walt Disney World. Oh, and she wants to know what you're wearing."

"I don't *know* what I'm wearing," snapped Connie.

"Hey, don't yell at me, I wasn't the one who asked."

"I noticed."

Pete turned from a study of the empty refrigerator. "Is there some sort of a problem here?"

"*Yes,* there's a problem. We're getting married in three days. We're having a baby in March. But apparently none of this concerns you. And why should it? You don't have to make a fool of yourself throwing up in somebody's dead pearls while the whole island—"

Pete set his beer can carefully on the counter. "Let's cut this here, shall we?"

"Fine." Connie stood up and stalked to the door. "I'm going to invite Sarah to our wedding. Assuming, of course, you still plan to be there."

Sarah Abrew leaned her head against the back of the old wood Adirondack chair and looked at the sky. Turning gold now. Another day gone by. It was cooler today, it would be cooler tomorrow, but Sarah was in no rush to get there. She was of an age where she no longer wished any day good riddance. There were enough of them already behind her, too few left in front of her, and too many pieces of the puzzle still missing. She supposed there'd come a day when she'd say, all right, I've done what I could, I've seen enough, I've had it.

But not yet.

If you please.

She heard the car long before she saw it. It sounded like Connie was having some trouble with her exhaust. She saw the small green saucer whip into her driveway, heard the hand brake screech, saw the long, gold streak that was Connie drift over the side and across the lawn. Sarah felt her heart leap with pleasure. And with a little of something else, too.

Connie folded up cross-legged on the grass at Sarah's feet. "Brace yourself," she said.

She needn't have bothered. Sarah had learned long ago to get braced whenever Connie hove into view. "Now what?"

"Pete and I are getting married. Saturday. Want to come?"

Sarah smiled. Now there was one big puzzle piece she'd been waiting for. But something didn't feel just right. She decided to wait for the rest before she spoke.

"Well?" said Connie. "Did you hear me? I said Pete and I are getting married."

"I heard you. Not that I needed to. I can still hear the echo from the last time you told me. What brought this on, the heat?"

"Of a sort. I'm pregnant."

And there it was. It figured those two wouldn't do it in the normal order. But even taking that into consideration, Connie's voice still didn't sound just the way it should. Damn this eyesight. She wished she could see her face. Sarah reached out and stroked Connie's hair. It felt soft as a baby's. All right, so now it was time to grow up. "Don't fret, you're not the first and you won't be the last. You'll do all right."

"That's what Pete said. He acts like we're sitting down to a game of checkers and I'm sitting here a nervous wreck."

Sarah chuckled. "Oh, I've seen him get plenty worked up about checkers. Maybe he's just trying to keep things evened out."

Connie flopped down on her back and folded her hands behind her head. "And that's only part of it. It's this damned wedding. We thought it would be so easy. Run into the town hall, say I do, get out. I don't know, Sarah."

"What don't you know? About the wedding or the marriage? Don't go mixing them up."

"Oh, it's not marrying Pete that worries me. That would have happened soon enough, I guess."

"Soon enough for whom?"

Connie's voice rose defiantly from the grass at Sarah's feet. "Soon enough for me. Don't you think I've made up my mind to give him my best shot? I don't see how some piece of paper can mean more than that. But you know Pete. Sooner or later he'd want us to get respectable. And the next thing you know you're dressed like Glinda the Good Witch, drinking champagne instead of beer and eating baby octopus on toast instead of pizza."

Sarah chuckled again, but not for long. It was true enough, some of what Connie had said, but still and all, it seemed to her something had been lost in the translation.

After some seconds Connie sat up. "Okay, what?"

"Nothing much. I'm just thinking about what my piece of paper meant. Arthur and I got married sixty-two years ago last April. I can still see him, standing in the front of the church, smiling at me fit to bust, me smiling back like some old Cheshire cat. Do you know, we never did stop smiling. At least not long enough to amount to much. Oh, we had our moments, everybody does. Those words best left unsaid. But we always managed to come out the other end smiling."

There followed an uncharacteristic silence. The next thing Sarah knew, Connie was on her feet, dusting off the seat of her shorts.

"Where are you off to?"

"I just thought of a few words I'd better un-say. So you'll come Saturday? Our house? Ten o'clock?"

"I'll be there at nine. And if you're one minute late, I'll marry him."

Connie leaned over and kissed her. "Over my dead body."

CHAPTER

23

The most formal beginning of a social letter is "My dear Mrs. Smith." The fact that in England "Dear Mrs. Smith" is more formal does not greatly concern us in America.

Hormones, thought Pete as he made himself a sandwich, doing the math in his head. Five weeks—no, almost six now—plus the other two, wasn't that how it worked? So eight weeks, subtract it from nine months, that left seven more months of this. Unless it wasn't hormones at all, but their own personal bad chemistry, in which case it would last for life.

Pete took his sandwich and a second beer out to the porch and he and the day seemed to cool off together. Eventually he regained enough composure to go back inside, pick up the phone, and call his parents. Polly had issued him an ultimatum. Tell Mom and Dad about the baby today or she would. But it made sense to tell them before they got here. They'd probably need a couple of days to adjust.

A couple of days? A couple of seconds was too much. That was how long it took for his mother to decide to move back to Nashtoba so she could babysit. Retirement was getting a little dull, she said, and this was just what she needed to put some purpose back in her life. Pete took down flight numbers and times. Fortunately, at least for the moment, there appeared to be a return flight.

When Connie came back he was in the bedroom, halfway out of his clothes on his way to the shower to wash off the day's sweat. She threw herself on the bed and exhaled. "I think this time around we should make up some new rules. Here's my first one. Every time we say something dumb, we get to take it back."

Pete crossed to the bed and sat. "Is this rule retroactive? If so, between the two of us, it could be a long night."

"It only goes back about an hour. To when I said you apparently weren't concerned with any of this. I take that back."

"And I take back whatever I said that made you think I wasn't. Concerned, that is. Now if there are some details that you think I should be more concerned with—"

"Yes. What are we going to wear? You wrecked your suit on Saturday."

"There's no rule that says I have to wear a suit. And there's no rule that says you have to wear those pearls. We can get married in blue jeans if we want."

Connie peered at him as if he'd just uncovered a new Rosetta stone. "We can, can't we?"

He leaned over and kissed her. "Strange how I seem to keep falling in love with you."

Connie reached up and hugged him hard. Pete kissed her again, this time in a spot she once said made queer things happen to her innards. Apparently, it was something good.

She pulled him down on top of her.

* * *

Connie lay awake afterward, staring at her usual spot on the ceiling, listening to her talking head. Clearing the air with Pete had helped. Maybe, just maybe, they were getting better at this. But Connie's visit to Sarah had also helped. What had Sarah said? Don't go mixing up the wedding with the marriage. Well, Connie wasn't going to. Unlike Aggie, Connie wanted to marry the man. No food or clothes or extraneous relatives were going to change that.

Unlike Aggie.

Suddenly Connie experienced a strange sensation, as if after weeks of running on old batteries she'd just been plugged into a wall outlet. Unlike Aggie? Who said she was unlike Aggie? Or, more to the point, that Aggie was unlike her? Not all that so-called evidence she'd collected. Here she'd thought she was proving Aggie's second thoughts about Walt. What if all she was proving was Aggie's second thoughts about her *wedding,* as Sarah had said. Don't go mixing up the wedding with the marriage. Maybe that was just what she'd done about Aggie. Aggie, happy at the jeweler's in March, bubbling all over the place at the doctor's. In March. *Before* her mother got here. And in April, after Alicia had arrived and begun to change the script, there was Aggie at the Whiteaker, enthusing about pizza and beer, maybe not for her mother's sake, or for Jack's sake, but for her own sake. Maybe Aggie, like Walt, had really wanted the beer and the pizza. And at the dressmaker's? She'd looked like a dream. Her mother had been on cloud nine. And Aggie had been . . . *subdued,* that's what Jeanine had said. Why subdued? Maybe because she'd fallen in love with a fifty-dollar blue dress that would never see the light of day. And by May, at the photographer's, when little if any of her own wedding plans remained, she'd acted like she'd had a gun to her head. By the time they'd hit the stationer's she'd begun to divorce herself from the proceedings. At the florist she hadn't even shown up.

And maybe, just maybe, Walt had known Aggie a whole lot better than he now thought he had. At least he had known that Aggie had been determined to please everyone. Who else would let the Reverend marry her just so she wouldn't hurt his feelings? Who else would toss her own dream wedding out the window just so her mother could finally live hers?

But suddenly, in the middle of this nice little road Connie's brain was traveling down, she came up against that old brick wall. Aggie's note. There was no discounting the note. Unless, of course, you were Ginny Turkle.

Ginny Turkle.

Connie tossed and turned and thought. Her head ached. Her back ached. But now, finally, it was Ginny Turkle's fairy-tale version of the Aggie-Walt romance that she knew was the true one. Not just because she wanted it to be the truth, the way Willy had said, but because of what she'd learned about Aggie and Walt.

Connie rolled over and gave Pete a gentle nudge in the ribs. "Hey. Are you awake?"

His eyes snapped open and he looked around wildly.

"It's just me," said Connie. "I've been thinking about that note."

Pete blinked and rubbed his face the way he did when he was trying to wake up. "Note?"

"Aggie's note. I think we should look at it again."

Pete groaned. "So go wake up Willy."

"The morning will be soon enough. But there's something else. About Saturday."

"Saturday."

"There's no rule that says we have to have a luncheon or a brunch. Why don't we do what we always do on Saturday?"

"Which is?"

"Coffee and donuts. From Mable's. Stick 'em out on the picnic table and be done with it."

As Connie watched Pete in the moonlight she felt that old familiar kick, almost like an adrenaline rush. Amazing, she thought. Still there, after all they'd done to almost kill it.

"I like it," said Pete finally. "Coffee and donuts. It sounds like us."

"Good. I'll stop at Mable's in the morning. I have only one more piece of news and then you may sleep in peace. I love you. Good night."

But after that Pete had a few things to say. And do.

And after Pete finally drifted off, Connie found she had a few more things to take up with the ceiling.

Pete woke in the morning feeling like he'd spent the last six hours on a trampoline. Connie had tossed and turned and pummeled him and here she was wide awake and hovering at the foot of the bed like a ghost of Christmas Past. And Future.

"You'd better hurry up," she said. "I called the station and Willy's waiting, but he can't wait long. He's on his way to Fulton. He's got a lead on Alicia Scott."

Pete rolled groggily to his feet and in twenty minutes he found himself shaved, showered, dressed, and standing in the police chief's office, trying to remember what they were doing there. Something about coffee and donuts?

The chief came around the desk and kissed Connie. "I didn't have a chance to offer my best wishes yesterday. Now what's this about Aggie's note?"

That was it, Aggie's note.

"We want to look at it," said Connie. Apparently it was enough of a reason. Either that or the chief really was in a rush. He opened the file cabinet, extracted a piece of blue paper encased in plastic, and laid it on his desk. Connie fished in her knapsack and pulled out one of the wedding invitations Aggie had handwritten. She opened the invitation and placed it beside the note on the desk.

Pete looked at the two papers and saw nothing new. It was the same handwriting. Same paper, even. Different ink, but so what? Most people had more than one pen in the house.

"Well?" asked Willy.

"I don't know," said Connie. "I had this idea."

"That Aggie didn't write it? You think we don't check?"

Connie didn't seem to hear him. She lined the two papers up side by side. Pete came closer and looked over her shoulder.

And there it was.

Aggie's note to Walt was written on paper that was an inch shorter. Even the chief noticed. He fished the letter out of its plastic and examined the top edge closely, first with the naked eye, then with a magnifier.

"Cut." The chief placed the letter on the desk so carefully that even before he said anything Pete knew he was steamed. "How could I miss this? No salutation. I admit it bothered me at first, that there was no salutation on this. But eventually I discounted it. There was no closing, either. It seemed obvious she was unsure how to address him, that under the circumstances the usual 'Dear' and 'Love' didn't feel right. But it bothered me. And when something bothers me, I follow up. Of course it would have helped if somebody had seen fit to show me this other piece of stationery."

"We are showing you," said Connie. "So now what? I'd say half your interest in Walt was provided by this letter. This was the motive, wasn't it? And now that motive is erased."

"Maybe."

"Probably. Admit at the very least this changes things a bit."

"Oh, it changes things," said Willy.

CHAPTER
24
<u></u>

It is even becoming the fashion for ushers at small country weddings not to wear gloves at all!

Just tell him," said Andy. "That's all I have to say. Just tell the chief about the gun. The defense rests."

"Sound more like the prosecution to me," said Walt.

Andy grinned. Then he yawned. He'd dragged out of bed early to try to catch Walt before his day got locked in and he still hadn't beaten Patrice. She'd been delivering breakfast, she'd said, just going out as Andy had come in. Well, now he'd made his speech. "Just think about it, will you?" he added.

"Yeah, I'll think about it. Some of it made sense."

Andy tried not to look surprised. "What'd you go buying a gun for, anyway? What was all that about sitting near doors?"

"I said I'd think. Now I'm going to work." Walt went to the sink, tossed a half a cup of coffee down the drain, and strode out.

Andy followed fast enough, but even so, by the time he got to his truck Walt was nowhere in sight. Patrice

Fielding was, though. She stood leaning against Andy's truck door, face tipped to the sun. "I've been waiting for you," she said.

"Oh, yeah? For what?"

"How is he? Is he doing all right?"

Andy shrugged.

"And you? Nobody gives a thought to the poor support troops. What do you suppose I could do to help out? I brought croissants for Walt. I could do better for you. A real breakfast, out someplace?"

"No," said Andy. He added, "No thanks." He didn't know just why, but he felt like Snow White being handed the poison apple. "I've gotta go." He turned to his truck, but a hand on his shoulder blade stopped him.

"Andy. Please."

When he turned around a layer seemed to have slid off Patrice's face. "You know him best. What do you think he needs most right now?"

That was easy. "Aggie," he said.

The minute they got home Connie left for Mable's. Pete decided what he needed most was to dislodge the night's cobwebs. He made a cup of coffee and hit the beach. It was early and the sand was cool and undisturbed. There was actually enough breeze off the water to lift Pete's cowlick and flip it east. He walked in long strides along the wrack line, trying to keep pace with his thoughts, but soon he found it easier to back up his thoughts, make them go step by step.

Why would somebody cut off the salutation to a letter? To conceal the name of the party to whom it was addressed. And why would somebody do that? To make it look like the letter had been written to somebody else, somebody like Walt Westerman. And why do that? To frame Walt. As Connie had said to the chief, the letter had provided them with Walt's big motive. If you took away the letter, if you took away the fact that Aggie had tried to leave Walt, you took away any reason Walt might have had for killing her.

So take away the motive and what was left? Pete knew better than to count the absence of an alibi for much, but there was still the small matter of Aggie's body in Walt's well, Walt's prints on the tarp. But why shouldn't his prints be on the tarp? It was his tarp. He'd identified it willingly enough as one of several he kept in the barn. Easy enough to take the tarp out of the barn, wrap Aggie in it, dump her in the well. If someone went to the trouble to try to frame Walt with the letter, the same someone could have framed him with the body. And if everything was a frame-up, Aggie's car being seen in the vicinity at three in the morning made perfect sense. She could have been killed elsewhere and driven to the farm in her own car. And then there was the dress. The killer must have heard rumors of the search for the dress. As the police chief dragged his feet arresting Walt, the wedding dress was added to the pot.

Which left the question, if the letter wasn't Walt's, whose was it?

Pete stopped walking and looked around. He'd gone almost as far as the point, long past the path that led through the scrub to the chief's house. The walk had heated him up—he pivoted in the sand and waded into the rustling water. He'd walk back the wet way. As he skirted a late-season horseshoe crab his thoughts turned to the Ides. This was something he could get to like— walking the beach with his kid, teaching it about ocean life. Assuming there was any time left after the swinging and braiding and golfing and trips with Aunt Polly to Walt Disney World. Hell, thought Pete. Not even born and look at the expectations already in place. And what about Pete's expectations? For a second Pete saw an image so real it almost stopped him in his tracks—a shadow of his younger self shagging fly balls in left field of Fenway Park. But that wasn't fair. That was his old dream. His kid would have dreams for itself.

And suddenly Pete was back to Aggie. People had placed enough expectations on her to sink a ship. To be the bride of her mother's dreams. To marry the man of her father's dreams. Connie's take on Gene Tilton had been interesting—that he must have cared for Aggie more than he'd cared to admit to Pete.

And thinking of people who cared for Aggie, Pete remembered Walt.

By the time Pete got back to the house, Rita was at her desk. She flagged him down as he attempted to stride past. "The Reverend Rydell just called. He said if you'd care to call him back he's just remembered something else about Friday night."

"All right. I'll call him. Is that it?"

"No, but it's all you're going to be any help about. How did Connie make out with the caterers? I included a half-dozen on that list, but it's such short notice, I've been worried sick."

"All taken care of," said Pete. "Mable's donuts on order as we speak."

"Donuts?" said Rita weakly.

"But we might want to borrow your coffeepot."

"Coffeepot."

"That's it. Coffee and donuts."

It was hard to describe Rita's expression, almost as if she'd just been told there was no Santa Claus, but apparently she wasn't about to give up without a fight. "I could bring a nice fruit salad. Maybe a spinach quiche. And Evan's sister has a wonderful cheese souffle dish."

"A coffeepot," said Pete firmly. "That would be great. Thanks."

He ran upstairs and dialed the parsonage, but no one answered. He ran downstairs, hopped into the truck, and headed for Walt's.

Connie left Mable's feeling more carefree than she had in weeks. At least she would feel carefree, she thought, if she could have gotten a little more sleep. After the mental, and other, gymnastics had come the backache, and it had kept her up half the night. She supposed she shouldn't complain. She hadn't felt sick in days, and according to the book she'd picked up at Jerry Beggs' book shop she'd expected to barf straight through the first three months. But somehow it had seemed more real, somehow it had been easier to believe that she and Pete were actually going to do this whole baby thing when she'd been vomiting her guts out.

As Connie drove along Shore Road and passed the church all thoughts of her own situation were supplanted as she remembered Aggie's note. Suddenly the whole Saturday picture had changed. It was no longer a matter of a jilted bridegroom, a bride too young to know her own mind. Aggie hadn't tried to leave Walt. He'd been framed with somebody else's note. So who *had* Aggie tried to leave? Connie knew of only one person Aggie had left Friday night, and that was Ginny Turkle. But there was no way Connie could make the rest of the pieces fit. Aggie writing Ginny that note? Ginny and Aggie not see eye to eye on something? Like what?

And still, here was Connie, heading for the Turkle house for what seemed like the tenth time this month.

As Connie pulled into the Turkle driveway she saw Duncan sitting at the picnic table, writing furiously in a notebook. When Connie approached he slammed the book shut and leaned on it with both freckled arms. Connie had had a notebook like that once, full of real and imagined things that had seemed at the time to be

matters of universal life and death and were actually of
no significance to anyone, even, taken in the long run,
herself. She smiled at Duncan, feeling suddenly connected. He didn't smile back.

"Got a minute?" she asked.

"For what?"

"I could use some help. It's sort of a favor to Walt.
We're trying to piece together the events of last Friday
night. You were at the church, right?"

Duncan nodded, eyes on the freckles on his hands.

"And then at Martelli's. And then what did you do?"

"I didn't do anything."

"I mean where did you go? Home? Out?"

Duncan blushed. "They wouldn't let me go out. I was
a member of the wedding party. They should've let me
go out."

"You're talking about the trip to Lupo's? So you came
home, is that it?"

Duncan shrugged. Connie pondered how to get him to
look up, but she remembered that about fifteen, too.
There must have been some unwritten rule—they see
your eyes and you're dead.

"So you came home, and your sister Ginny came
home, with Patrice. Were you here when Aggie arrived?"

Another shrug.

"Duncan, this part's important. It's important because of the dress. Did you see Aggie arrive with the
dress and the blue suitcase?"

He nodded.

"And later. Did you see her leave?"

Another nod.

"What time?"

Shrug.

"Did she have anything with her?"

"I didn't see *her*. I saw her car drive off. That was it."
He still hadn't looked up, but now something wet

splattered onto the cardboard cover of the notebook. Duncan snatched up the book and ran to the house.

He liked her, Walt had said.

Pete drove toward the farm with a sense of urgency that, taken in one light, was somewhat ridiculous, but taken in another, it made perfect sense. Aggie's note meant something to someone, but what it did not mean was a Dear John letter for Walt. And before Pete did anything else, he wanted to make sure Walt knew that much.

When Pete pulled into the farm he saw Ginny Turkle's car in the driveway. He found the two of them in the garden, picking horn worms off the tomato plants. There wasn't anything uglier than a horn worm, and it occurred to Pete it wasn't everybody who'd go for this kind of work. For example, he couldn't see Patrice Fielding offering to pick one of those things up.

"Could we have a word?" he said to Walt. He half-expected Ginny to jump at the excuse to quit, but it was Walt who stood up and Ginny who continued to pick as the two men walked toward the farmhouse.

"It's nothing conclusive, but it's important enough," said Pete. "It looks like that note you found in your door might not have been meant for you. The top of the paper had been cut off. Aside from the fact that it looks like you might have been framed, it means that it wasn't the Dear John letter you thought it was."

Pete had geared himself for a variety of reactions, but the one he got surprised him plenty. Walt turned around and looked in the direction of Ginny Turkle's red head.

"That's what she told me," he said.

CHAPTER
25

The bridesmaids are always dressed exactly alike as to texture of materials and model of making, but sometimes their dresses differ in color.

Connie gave Duncan Turkle a good two minutes head start before she followed him to the house. This time her previous good luck was reversed. Faye Turkle was home. Ginny wasn't. But for some reason Faye's attitude toward Connie also seemed to have reversed, possibly because there was no cub to protect. She invited Connie in and ushered her into the living room.

The first thing Connie noticed was that all the living room furniture matched. Pete and Connie's furniture never matched. For that matter, they'd never really had a living room, at least not since Factotum had taken over. Connie shifted uncomfortably in Faye's chair, trying to find a position that would ease her back.

"I don't know where Ginny is," said Faye. "Not that I couldn't make a guess. The one who's supposed to be over there making college money won't go, and the one who's supposed to be resting up to go waitressing tonight

is. But I told Duncan this morning at breakfast. By
lunchtime today I want him either at the farm or looking
for another job. I told him it won't get any easier the
longer he puts it off. I told him he can't leave that man
hanging this way. Let him hire somebody else."

"That man being Walt?"

Faye made a disapproving sort of a hmmph. "I could
wish it wasn't."

"I don't think you have to worry about Walt. The chief
is looking in other directions now."

"You think I care about that?"

Connie must have looked surprised.

Faye Turkle burst out in what was half-bark, half-
laughter. "Oh, I don't mean I want my daughter hanging
around some murderer's house. But I don't want her
hanging around with any brokenhearted semi-widower
either, if you see what I'm driving at."

Connie wasn't so sure she did. For one thing, she
thought they were talking about Duncan. "You think
Walt might—"

"I think Walt's out of his head over Aggie, that's what
I think, and I don't see him getting over it in any big
rush. In the meantime here's Ginny over there day and
night. Well, daytime, anyway. Oh, she won't admit it, not
even to herself. She's sorry for him, she says. He won't
eat and sleep, she says. He needs help with the farm, she
says. He's got nobody since Duncan got spooked, she
says. Well, Ginny, I said, he's got a family of his own.
He's got a cousin and an aunt and uncle. But Ginny says
he doesn't want to upset them, won't let them near him.
He lets Ginny come because they're just friends, or that's
what she says. Well, he never had a better one. From day
one she wouldn't hear of him being a murderer. 'He
loved her, he loved her,' that's all she'd say when I
asked."

"He has one other friend that he lets around. Patrice."

Faye's eyebrows shot up. "Oh he does, does he?" For a minute Faye seemed to brighten, but slowly she shook her head. "No, Patrice won't last long, she doesn't have the kind of patience Ginny does. Oh, if there's one thing I know, it's my daughter. She's got three brothers, two older, one younger. I can't for one minute make sense out of the way any of them thinks, but that Ginny, she's something else."

Connie rubbed the small of her back, trying to sort out Faye's oblique, and not so oblique, remarks. Finally she decided to go back to something more concrete. "The Friday night before Aggie Scott's wedding. Ginny says Aggie left here around ten-thirty, taking her dress and her bag with her. Did you see her?"

Connie watched Faye's face. Immediate dawning of suspicion, followed by puzzlement. She didn't much like the question, but she couldn't for the life of her figure out why not.

So she answered it. "I didn't see her. I was in bed, asleep. One teenager in the house and I'm through for the day by nine o'clock. As a matter of fact, I thought Aggie slept here and left first thing in the morning. But Ginny told me later she'd left the previous night."

"Maybe your husband or one of your older sons saw her?"

"On a Friday night? You think one of my boys is home by ten-thirty? Duncan was here, but not by choice. He was shut up in his room, sulking. And as for my husband, he works eight to midnight, hardly sees the kids, let alone his wife. Don't think he didn't plan it that way, either."

So there was nothing except Ginny's word to account for Aggie's leaving at ten-thirty, that and Duncan's sighting of the car as it drove off. Interesting, thought

Connie. And if Ginny and Aggie had some sort o fight . . . "Ginny and Aggie were good friends, wer they?"

Faye Turkle again surprised Connie by the sudden je of tears. She fished out a used tissue from the recesses o a Captain Kangaroo-style pocket and mopped her face "They were like sisters. Neither of them had one of thei own. I've lain awake five nights now, listening to Ginny cry herself to sleep." Suddenly Faye Turkle's head came up and her eyes hardened. "You never did tell me wha you want with my daughter."

Again, Connie shifted uncomfortably. "I came acros a letter Aggie wrote. The salutation was missing. wondered if it might be Ginny's. I was wondering i maybe Ginny was asleep when Aggie left on Friday, anc Aggie wrote her a note to tell her she was going."

"The night before the wedding? Ginny asleep with Aggie still awake? I doubt it. She'd be chattering he head off if I know Ginny."

Suddenly Connie's energy left her, her curiosity burned out. Her nausea seemed to be returning. The ache in her back was coming in waves now, each wave a little stronger than the first.

She thanked Faye Turkle and left.

Pete's mind wheeled crazily. Ginny Turkle? It made no sense. "Ginny Turkle told you it wasn't your letter?"

Walt nodded. "She said Aggie would never have written that to me. But I wouldn't listen. I didn't trust her. Didn't trust Aggie. Ginny was the only one whc did."

Suddenly Walt didn't look so hot. Pete pushed open the screen door and backed Walt into a chair. He crumpled over his knees as if he were in physical pain.

Pete bent over awkwardly and peered at him. "Are you okay, Walt?"

The screen door opened and Ginny Turkle stepped through it. Pete was never so glad to see anybody in his life. She kneeled in front of Walt, looked up at Pete. "What happened?"

"Aggie's note. It doesn't look like it was meant for Walt. I think it's sinking in that she—" That she what? That she'd loved him after all? That she was really dead? Pete supposed either, or both, would suffice.

Ginny took Walt's chin in her hand and pried his face toward the light. "Goddamn you, Walt Westerman. Why don't you just cry like everyone else?" But the tears streamed down Ginny's face, not Walt's. It occurred to Pete that this wasn't the first time he'd heard Ginny cuss out Walt. Ginny swearing at Walt. Patrice swearing at Aggie. Pete could only hope Walt had enough brains to see through all that.

But as Pete left the farm he felt like cussing out somebody himself. Killing Aggie was bad enough. Leaving that note on Walt's door had practically killed Walt. Maybe what he'd just told Walt would help in the long run. But there wasn't anything Pete could offer the other grieving party in all this, Ben Scott. Or was there?

The closer Pete got to Ben Scott's house, the more he began to think that a stop there might do some good. Most of Ben's bitterness seemed to be directed at Walt. Wouldn't Ben feel better once he was able to let go of that? If there was one thing Pete's own rocky past had taught him, it was that misdirected anger didn't do either the sender or the receiver much good.

Only Gene Tilton's Jag was in the drive. Pete debated whether or not to get out, but in the end he decided he was curious enough about Gene Tilton and Aggie to make good use of the wait and hopefully it would be short.

Gene opened the door. "Still here, I see," said Pete.

"Yes, but it won't be much longer. I was finally able to

get in touch with a brother-in-law. He's arriving late tonight."

"Are you expecting Ben back soon?"

"Since I don't know where he is, I can't speculate as to when he'll be back. You wanted him for something?"

"Not really. I was on my way by. Thought I'd see how he was managing. He looked in rough shape the other day."

Gene Tilton stepped aside and waved Pete in. "Nice of you to bother. You'd be surprised how many people haven't. The Reverend called earlier, but I can't honestly say it helped."

"I'm sorry I missed him," said Pete. "He left a message for me and I can't seem to connect. Did he say where he was headed from here?"

"Back to the parsonage, I believe." Gene Tilton turned and led them into the living room. He pointed to the phone. "If you'd like to call?"

"No, I'll stop by after I leave here."

Gene sat in a wing chair and waved Pete to another that, judging by the sag in the seat, must have been Ben's usual spot. Tilton removed a cigar from his pocket and offered it to Pete. Pete declined. Tilton lit up.

"So you'll be leaving once the brother-in-law arrives?"

"Yes," said Gene. He sounded relieved. And tired.

But what the hell, thought Pete. He was here, he might as well toss out a feeler, see where he got. "I guess you'll be glad enough to put this behind you. It seems like you've been put in a pretty rough spot from the start."

"Yes," said Gene again.

"That Aggie was a great kid. And not hard to look at. I couldn't help thinking about what Ben said the other day. You must have been tempted once or twice."

"Maybe. If I hadn't respected her so much."

"Or Walt Westerman so much?"

Gene Tilton's cigar snapped upward as his teeth bore down. "And what do you mean by that? You think I was afraid of what Walt Westerman would do to me, is that it?"

Pete shrugged.

"Don't let the evidence mislead you. I may not be much in a church brawl, but I'm not so spineless as to let some half-cocked young hood—" He broke off with a laugh. He sat back. "Listen to me. And I've been sitting here feeling so damned superior. I suppose we're all the same animal underneath."

"I take it you didn't much like Walt."

"I told you I didn't know Walt. Those were Ben's words I used just now, not mine."

"Still, you must have known enough about Walt's situation to see a few advantages for everyone if you took his place."

Gene studied his cigar. It must have been a good one—the ash was still hovering. "If you're asking could I understand how Ben felt, yes, I could. She was the apple of his eye. He only wanted what was best for her. I was here when Aggie left and I'll remember that morning as long as I live. When Ben found out she was gone I truly think his heart broke."

And this is what could lie ahead for me, thought Pete. His daughter running off with a younger version of Bert Barker, for instance. How in hell would Pete ever handle something like that? Well, he'd have to, that was all there was to it.

Pete decided it was time to go. He figured he'd heard enough to prove Connie right. Gene Tilton had been stuck enough on Aggie, Pete was pretty sure about that.

Those may have been Ben Scott's words he'd quoted, but it wasn't Ben Scott's venom he'd quoted them with. And that voice talking about the day Aggie left. *I'll remember that morning as long as I live.* That wasn't just a sympathetic ear talking. Gene Tilton had lost and lost big.

CHAPTER
26

In Protestant churches no fee is asked by the clergyman, ever, but those who would like to give something in appreciation of his services do so.

Rita Peck was flustered enough to see the Reverend Rydell standing in front of her. That he seemed to be in acute distress didn't help.

"Didn't Pete get my message?" he asked.

"He got it and he did try to phone. You weren't in."

"Ah. Yes, I see. I was paying a call."

"I'm sure he'll try again."

"Yes, but when? I'm sure I don't know what is the next best step. I suppose . . . the station, perhaps. No, no. I must try again. Just because I have not yet succeeded . . . All right. Would you be so kind as to tell him when he comes in that I would still appreciate a word. I do have one more call to make, but I expect to be back at the parsonage in an hour." He smiled ruefully. "And quite likely much sooner. Still, if he returns in the interim . . . Perhaps I should . . . No. I dare not wait."

I dare not wait. There was something so Romeo-and-

Juliet about it that Rita got flustered herself. "You say this is about Friday night?"

"Yes. About the young woman's whereabouts Friday night. If you tell Pete that, he'll know to what I'm referring. He specifically asked me about it. I suppose I should have realized sooner . . . But certainly one might be excused for thinking—" The Reverend straightened his countenance and wiped his face. "Heavens, listen to me making all this fuss. Please give Pete that message. Now, I have that call to make." He squared his shoulders and left.

When Connie came in Rita thought of giving her the Reverend's message, but Connie didn't stop long enough. As she stumbled up the stairs Rita caught something about a bad back and a bad night and taking the phone off the hook.

"Chief's not in," said the dispatcher, Jean Martell, the minute Pete came in sight of her desk. "Still trying to find that Alicia Scott. Just got back from Fulton. That's where she lives. Fulton. Chief got word she'd gone home, some neighbor saw her, but by the time he got there she'd gone again. Hardly took time enough to water the plants. Didn't know where she went to, though. Some neighbors, in Fulton. Not like this place. Around here, you came back and left again we'd know why you came and why you left and where you went."

"And what you had for breakfast," said Pete.

Jean Martell's eyes grew round. "She stopped for breakfast?"

"It was a joke. So where's the chief now?"

"Back at the hotel. Going through her things, looking for a hint."

Pete nodded. "I left something in the chief's office. I'll be right back."

"Now you hold it," said Jean, but for once Pete had a

bit of luck. The phone rang. Jean picked it up. Pete popped down the hall and into the chief's office, closing the door after him.

The Scott file had been in the top cabinet on the right, Pete remembered from the day he and Connie had come here to get a look at Aggie Scott's letter. It took him three seconds to find the file, one second to pull out the same letter, still in its plastic. He read it again. *It's finally sunk in we just plain don't see eye to eye on this. I've decided I have to go. I'm sorry if this hurts you, but I have to do what I think is best.* And there was the signature, complete with the mistake, that first *g* begun wrong, corrected.

"What do you think you're doing?"

Jean Martell stood in the doorway, bearing down on him with her finger raised as if she were ready to fence.

"All set," said Pete. "I talked to the chief earlier. Had to look something up." Pete shoved the file back in the cabinet, detoured around Jean's finger, and left.

When Pete walked through his front door Rita was on the phone. Something about somebody's awnings. She asked the party to wait and covered the receiver with her palm.

"Honestly, Pete, you'd better call that Reverend. He came by again and he's quite worked up. He said it's about Aggie's whereabouts Friday night. He had to make a second attempt at some call he's been trying to make, but he should be at the parsonage in—" She looked at her watch. "Fifteen minutes." She returned to the phone and the awnings. Pete headed for the stairs, but Rita rapped on the desk with a pencil. When he turned she pointed to the ceiling and pantomimed a sleeping person with hands folded and eyes closed. So Connie was asleep. Good.

Pete had just reached the door when it burst open and Maxine Peck reeled into him. Pete caught her by the shoulders, more to keep their feet under them than to stop her flight, but it stopped her quick enough. She looked up at him with eyes hot and black.

"I quit."

"Oh, no, you don't," said Rita.

"Oh, yes, she does," said Andy, coming through the door behind her. "And if she doesn't, I do."

Swell. Pete corralled Andy and herded him into the kitchen. Pete wanted to talk to Andy, anyway, but he decided to let him air out first. As best Pete could determine the problem seemed to be that just because Maxine knew a few more things about one certain subject it didn't mean she was the boss when Andy had been working at Factotum for at least half a century and was practically old enough to be her grandfather and he made a decent paycheck and was about to get his own apartment and he didn't want her lousing up this job for him or anybody else.

"You shouldn't be working together," said Pete. "I'll talk to Rita."

"Yeah, good." Andy opened the refrigerator and helped himself to a Coke. That seemed to de-steam him further. When he looked like he was room temperature again Pete said, "About Walt."

"Yeah, I did what you said. I talked to him about the gun. He said he'd think about it. He said it made some sense."

"Good," said Pete. "But I've got some more news." He told Andy about the altered note.

It didn't take long for the desired effect to register on Andy's face. "She didn't leave him?"

"No."

"And the chief's off his back?"

"Somewhat."

"So it doesn't matter about the gun."

"I'd say that would depend on a few other things."

"Yeah. Okay. I get your point." Andy drained the Coke, crushed the can, and tossed it in the sink. Pete never did get what crushing the can was supposed to accomplish. Sarah Abrew could crush a can, for Pete's sake. But it seemed to do something for Andy. He heaved a huge, satisfied sigh and wandered out.

Through the back.

Pete went out through the front, but Maxine was nowhere in sight. Rita was leafing through a pile of employment applications that she had collected once some years ago in a fit of pique.

"What are you doing?"

"Hiring someone. Preferably someone female. Or if absolutely necessary to hire a male, one with a disfiguring illness. Leprosy, perhaps."

"You figure Maxine's incapable of picking her own men?"

"Maxine is incapable of picking her own *lunch.*"

Maybe, thought Pete, but unless she got to try it once in a while, she'd never figure it out. He'd have to remember that. Maybe he should be making a list. To let his kid dream its own dreams, and once it grew up, to let it make its own mistakes. He was only just beginning to see how hard it was to do that. First of all, when had a kid grown up? At seventeen, like Maxine? Or at twenty-two, like Aggie Scott?

Aggie Scott. Pete looked at the clock. The hour was up. Time to see if he could find the Reverend and sort out those mystery hours on Friday night.

The Reverend's car was in the parsonage drive, but no one answered to Pete's knock. Remembering that the Reverend had been in the yard the last time Pete was here, he lifted the latch and followed the brick walk around back.

There was no one in the yard either—just the dogwood tree shivering in a welcome breeze, the empty iron furniture, the empty brick patio. Pete circled the furniture to the outside spigot where he'd found the Reverend last time, and there he was.

For a half-second Pete's brain went on the fritz. Why isn't he using the tap this time, too? he thought, not to clean the manure off his shoes, but to clean the blood off his head? The answer came soon enough.

Because this time the Reverend was dead.

CHAPTER

27

Nuts, candies, cinnamon, cloves, pickles, etc., do not belong on an afternoon tea table, which properly includes nothing except tea or fruit cup, breads, and cakes.

For some time after Pete left, Rita sat trapped at the desk. The phone seemed to ring incessantly. First it was Fergy Potts, wanting Pete to find her lost cat. Rita told her to look under the bed—that's where it usually was. Then Bert Barker and his awnings, again. Rita didn't know why the man couldn't put them up himself. But finally she promised to send Andy as soon as he reappeared. Next the Ardles over on Pond Street wanted their cottage opened before the thirty-first. Plenty of time for that. And Pete's sister Polly called. She was on her way now, she couldn't wait till Friday. She'd called upstairs, but the phone had apparently been off the hook.

After Rita hung up she tiptoed up the stairs. She found Connie sitting on the edge of the bed, looking frayed.

"How's the back?"

"Not good. I just can't get comfortable."

Rita looked at the disconnected phone. "Would you

like me to call Hardy, see if there's anything you can take?"

"No. It's just a backache."

Rita went to the bed and rearranged the pillows. "Here. Try that."

Connie lay down.

"Better?"

"I guess."

"I'll make some tea and bring it up." That was Rita's maxim. When in doubt, make tea. Tea *always* helped.

Pete figured it was plain enough what had happened. It was all there, right in front of his face. The Reverend, minus the upper rear quadrant of his head, slumped against the garage wall. The bloody shovel lying five feet away in the grass. Yes, the *what* was clear enough. But why? And who?

Pete phoned the station and waited for the chief. He hung around long enough to tell him everything he knew and left. At least he told him everything he knew he knew—there was something else, he was sure of it, something he couldn't sink his teeth into quite yet. But what?

Gene Tilton. Something Tilton had said. And something the Reverend had said. The message to Rita. The Reverend had remembered where Aggie had been headed Friday night. And today? Today he'd been on his way to make a call. He'd expected to be gone an hour at the most. Had he made the call? He'd had time. And if he had made the call, what had he done after that?

Gone home and got his head bashed in.

Okay, Pete said to himself, back up.

The Reverend Rydell had made a call. If Pete took what Rita had told him the right way, the Reverend was taking another shot at a call he'd so far failed to successfully complete. And who had he failed at? That was easy enough.

Walt.

The driveway in front of the farmhouse was so crowded Pete had trouble finding room to park. Ginny's car was still there. But so was Patrice Fielding's. And wasn't that Gene Tilton's Jag? And Ben Scott's Skylark? What the hell was this?

Pete decided not to let the fact that nobody answered his knock stop him. He could hear voices coming from the kitchen. He opened the door and called out.

The voices stopped. After some delay, he heard Walt's. "In here."

Pete rounded the kitchen door and froze. At least it put him in perfect keeping with everyone else in the place. They were grouped around the kitchen table, not sitting but standing—Walt, Patrice, Ginny and Duncan Turkle, Gene, Ben Scott. Everyone but Ben looked at Pete when he walked in, but no one moved. Pete couldn't blame them.

The shotgun in Ben Scott's hands was wavering all over the place.

Rita went down to the kitchen and put on the kettle. As she waited for it to boil she sat at the table and looked out over the marsh. She could see Andy out there, traipsing around with his head bowed like an ox, covering those brand-new sneakers in mud. Andy was a good kid. She supposed she should count herself lucky that Maxine hadn't latched onto the last few walking wounded she'd brought around the house. But she was so young. Too young. Sometimes Rita wished she could lock Maxine in her room and not let her out until she was twenty-one. Or maybe thirty-six. That was how old

Rita had been when she'd finally realized what it was she'd wanted in life—a divorce.

"What do you want?" said Walt.

"Um," said Pete.

"It seems," said Gene Tilton, "that we've got a bit of a situation."

"The situation being that Ben wants to blow my head off," said Walt.

"You killed her," said Ben.

"He did not!" Ginny Turkle shouted and took a step around the table. Or she would have if Walt hadn't reached out and thrust her back.

The shotgun wavered after her.

"Ginny," said Walt, "you stay put and shut up. Pete, why don't you get everybody out of here? This is between Ben and me, nobody else."

The shotgun traveled back to Walt.

Pete thought fast. Walt was right. There was no sense getting four other people shot. Five, if Pete counted himself. But once Pete got the bystanders out of there, Ben would kill Walt. Of course he might kill him anyway. He'd probably kill him anyway. But then again, he might not. Pete met Walt's eyes across the kitchen table. They were cold and calm. Walt jerked his head toward the door. *Out.* Okay, so maybe he had a plan. Maybe he figured he could handle Ben by himself. "Come on, Ginny," said Pete. "Duncan? Patrice? Why don't we—"

The next thing Pete knew he was looking into two barrels.

"No," said Ben Scott.

"All right, fine," said Pete. "No problem on my end. So. Now what?"

"We've been having a little chat," said Gene. "About who killed Aggie. Ben, here, seems to think it's now up to him to mete out the just deserts."

"Ah," said Pete. "That's tricky business, Ben. You've got to be sure you've got it right."

"I've got it right. He killed her. It was like I could feel him, feel his hands biting into her flesh, choking out her breath."

Walt whipped his head to the side. When he faced front again, he was facing the shotgun, of course.

Pete cleared his throat. "Actually, Ben, whoever it was, it probably wasn't Walt. You ask the police chief. He's after the person Aggie addressed in that note and that note was never addressed to Walt. It was cut off. It was written to somebody else and used to frame Walt."

"Note," said Ben. His eyes flicked for a split second to Gene Tilton.

Pete looked with him.

Gene Tilton closed his eyes.

And the light bulb went off over Pete's head.

Gene Tilton, who had cared for Aggie more than he'd cared to admit. He'd come weekend after weekend to Ben Scott's house, not to play in with Ben Scott's schemes, but to work on one of his own. To get Aggie away from Walt.

And suddenly the progression from there seemed to be nothing but one small step. What was the matter with Pete's brain that he hadn't seen it from the first? Okay, he'd been a bit distracted, but everywhere he'd gone he'd heard the same thing, time and again. Aggie, a young woman who wanted nothing but to please all parties at all times.

Back up, Pete cautioned himself. According to Connie, approximately a year ago Aggie and Walt had fought over Tilton's constant presence at the house. They'd broken up. So then what? What would a woman like that do once she and Walt had broken up? In the face of her father's wishes, in the face of Gene Tilton's desires, wouldn't she have tried to give it a shot? Yes. The Aggie

Scott who wanted to please everyone had then tried to please Gene and her father, at least long enough for Gene to raise his hopes. But it hadn't lasted long. Soon enough Aggie had realized there was only one person she would ever want and that person was Walt. So then what? So then she must have decided to get out and go back to Walt. And how had she extricated herself from the Gene situation? Obvious enough. She'd written Gene a note.

I was there when he found her gone, Gene had said. I'll never forget that morning as long as I live. Strong words for a casual observer. Not so strong for a rejected suitor. Gene Tilton had been there. Gene Tilton had gotten the note. A note that said they didn't see eye to eye, that she was leaving, that she was going back to Walt.

And then what? What if Gene Tilton, on the eve of Aggie's wedding to his rival, had finally snapped? What if he'd lain in wait for her that Friday night outside Walt's own house? When Aggie arrived home, just as Ginny had said, she'd taken her bag upstairs, found Walt asleep, set the bag down in the spare room, returned to the car for the dress. That's when Gene had intercepted her, before she'd collected the dress. They'd argued and he'd killed her. By accident, most likely, but still, that didn't change what he'd done after the fact. He'd panicked and fled. A few hours unaccounted for. Then he'd calmed down and begun to think. Aggie was dead outside Walt's house. How easy to blame it all on Walt. Gene had the old note Aggie had written him, and minus the salutation, every word could be made to fit the case. He'd dumped her in the well, jammed the note in the door, gone home to Ben Scott's, and when the news came out, he'd stuck around to comfort the grieving father as best he could.

Guilt, thought Pete. There it was, in Gene Tilton's own words. Why else would he have stayed around this long, taking abuse from a man twice his age, a man whom he admitted was at best a casual acquaintance? Or maybe there was another, even better reason. Maybe he had wanted to stick around to make sure Walt got picked up. And the dress. Pete himself had told Gene Tilton about the search for the dress, had told him that the investigation was swinging away from Walt.

So Gene had returned to the farm with the dress, the dress that he had removed from Aggie's car that Friday night.

But that was as far as Pete's thinking got him before the shotgun was back in his face. It was a tricky situation, all right. A murderer and a would-be murderer. Tough to decide which way to jump. Maybe Pete could negate the one with the other. Maybe he could draw Ben's attention to Tilton just enough to confuse him, just enough to throw him into doubt . . . even if it alerted Tilton, he wouldn't be able to do much with Ben Scott's shotgun aimed at his throat. It was risky, playing around with a loose screw like Ben Scott, but it was better than nothing.

Pete turned to Tilton. "What about you? What are you doing here? Come to visit your old pal Walt?"

"I came after Ben. The visit from the Reverend upset him quite a bit, I could see that. He drove off and after he failed to return in what seemed a reasonable amount of time I decided I'd better look for him. I gave some thought to his probable course and arrived here. To this."

"With a short detour to the Reverend's, is that it?"

Behind Walt, somebody moved. One of the Turkles, but Pete couldn't tell which. Ben took a step to the right. Walt took a step to the left. Blocked.

"The Reverend," said Ben, looking at Gene now. "You talked to the Reverend."

Yes, thought Pete. That was where the Reverend had

made his second call today—not to Walt's but to the Scott house again, this time in an effort to talk to Gene Tilton. Because that was where Aggie had gone Friday night, to make her peace with Tilton. And today the Reverend had figured it out, or remembered something Aggie had said in the parking lot. He'd realized Aggie had gone to see Tilton that night, and the fool had decided to approach Tilton directly, to reason with him, to do, most likely, what Pete and Andy had tried to do with Walt. To get him to fess up to the cops in person. But Gene Tilton wasn't about to confess anything. Instead, the minute Gene had learned the Reverend was planning to talk to Pete, he had gone to the parsonage and bashed in the Reverend's head.

So now what? Pete needed to say just enough to turn Ben's weapon away from Walt and onto Gene, but not so much that it would force the man to blow Gene's head off. Pete decided to take it step by step. "It might interest you to know, Ben," he began, "that the Reverend Rydell is dead."

Gene Tilton closed his eyes for a second time.

Walt Westerman gave Pete a good, sharp look.

Pete couldn't see the Turkles behind Walt, but Patrice Fielding opened her mouth and took a rasping breath.

Ben Scott's face never budged.

The kettle whistled. Rita poured the water over the bag in the mug, dunked it up and down a few times, and took it out. That was the way Connie liked it. When she walked into the bedroom Connie was in the bathroom with the door closed.

"Connie? Is everything all right?"

It took Connie a long time to answer. When she did she didn't sound like anyone Rita had ever heard in her life. "Please," she said. "Get Pete."

CHAPTER
28

No lady should ever sign a letter "Respectfully."

Ben Scott's shotgun drifted over to the general vicinity of Gene Tilton's spleen. "You," he said. "Much as you were worth. You were there and you did nothing. Found her gone and did nothing. If you were any kind of a man you would have gone and brought her back, made her see sense. But you didn't. And she's dead."

Okay, thought Pete. That confirms his previous theory. It was Gene who had found Aggie gone. So all Pete had to do now was to follow the thread.

"Was that it how it went, Gene?" asked Pete. "You were there. You got the note. The note saying you didn't see eye to eye, that she'd decided to go, to do what was best?"

Gene Tilton looked from Ben to Pete, his skin so white the veins showed through like the blue of skim milk. "A note? Why, yes, she left a note. And that's what it said. That she'd decided to go."

"You," said Walt. It was strange how much he sounded like Ben Scott.

Suddenly Gene Tilton looked so completely at sea that it baffled Pete. Was Gene that good? But dammit, the pieces fit. Or did they? Suddenly Pete remembered something else. Aggie's car being driven away from the farmhouse at three o'clock. How did his Gene Tilton theory account for that? But clearly, time was running out. Ben Scott looked more and more like he was losing his grip, not just on the conversation, but on the gun itself. "Apple," he said.

And there it was.

The second light bulb, a brighter one, one that completely washed out the first. Apple. Gene Tilton's face. The thing that had niggled, the thing that had two or three times now stared Pete in *his* face. Aggie's signature on that note, with the bobbled *g*. The backwards *g*. And what was a backwards *g*? A *p*. Aggie had started to write *Apple*. Her father had called the apple of his eye exactly that. But Aggie hadn't written *Apple*. She'd changed the *p* to a *g*. She knew she wasn't the apple of her father's eye anymore, or she knew she wouldn't be after he had read that note. Aggie had written the note to her father, not Gene. And the minute Ben Scott had read that note, he must have seen all his ill-gotten dreams go to dust.

A while ago Pete wouldn't have believed it. But that was a while ago, before he'd learned about the force of the dreams even an unborn child could set in place. *We don't see eye to eye,* Aggie's note had said. Of course they didn't. Not about Walt. *I've decided I have to go.* What else could she do in the face of her father's refusal to let her live her own life? So she had left her father's house, not last Friday night, but a night more than a year ago, and had moved in with Walt. And where had Aggie gone last Friday night? To try one final time to get someone to forgive her, to forgive that someone herself, at the Reverend Rydell's request. The job half-done. For all intents and purposes, at least to all appearances, Aggie and her mother had made up. Who was the remaining half? It was so obvious Pete was disgusted with himself. The remaining half was Aggie's father, Ben Scott.

Aggie had gone to see her father, to ask him to come to the wedding. Then what? Pete supposed they'd fought. Ben Scott wouldn't have given up that dream, that dream that wasn't his to keep, the dream of money or security or a name or whatever it was that he had wanted for his daughter in the form of Gene Tilton. And Aggie? All Aggie had dreamed about was Walt. As willing as she was to try to please the parents she'd always loved, the minister she'd always respected, the one thing she wouldn't sacrifice to them all was Walt.

It must have been an accident. It had to be an accident. In one second of blind fury Ben Scott must have reached out and grasped his daughter by the throat. One second was all it would have taken to clamp off the vagus nerve, to stop her heart. And afterward? How could a father live with such an act? He couldn't. Pete could see that. So Ben Scott had convinced himself it was someone else's fault, had convinced himself that it had been Walt's hands around Aggie's neck, whether he meant it metaphorically or not.

"Ben," said Pete softly. "Aggie left you that note?"

Six eyes and two shotgun barrels locked onto Pete.

"Notes," said Ben. "Nothing but notes. First her, then Apple. That's what the both of them did, walked out and left me with nothing but notes. I told the woman. I told her this was all her fault. If she'd stayed with me, if she'd raised her daughter as she should, it would have worked out. But no. My wife left me a note. Apple left me a note. But Apple's note should have been his. So I put it where it should have been left in the first place. And I put Apple where the blame should rest. Simple as that. But nobody did anything. Nobody arrested him. I heard they were looking for the dress. I went back and left the dress. Still nothing. The Reverend came and said he knew it was me, that he knew Apple must have come to see me that night. But it wasn't me that did it. It was him."

This time when Ben Scott swung the gun toward Walt it was different. Pete could smell it. This time the gun was steady, the eyes fixed with purpose. Oh, Pete should have known it would come to this. Now there was no time left. Or was there? Ben Scott shifted his fingers for a split second before squeezing the trigger, and Pete jumped.

And missed.

All he managed to do was to knock the shotgun out of Ben's hands. But as it skittered across the table and Walt Westerman grabbed it Pete exhaled, almost crying with relief. Good enough. Walt broke it to empty it. It was over. It was . . .

No, it wasn't. Walt wasn't emptying the gun, he was checking to make sure it was loaded. He snapped the barrel into place and raised it level with Ben Scott's chest. "You bastard," he said. "You sorry old bastard."

Walt was too far away. The table stretched between them. There was nothing Pete could do. Walt would kill Ben Scott and God only knew who else who happened to get in the way. More people would die and Walt would go to jail for life.

Pete's eyes, and everyone else's, were riveted on the shotgun when a freckled hand suddenly appeared from behind Walt. It dropped lightly onto the barrel of the gun, like a sparrow on a tree limb. "Put it down, Walt," said Ginny. "You're no murderer."

It took a light-year. Two. At least.

"No," said Walt finally. "I'm not."

He lowered the gun.

Ginny took it from him, rounded the table, and handed it to Pete.

Pete tried to look like he knew what he was doing with it. He stationed himself so that if he absolutely had to he could at least jam it into Ben Scott's ribs. He looked around the room. "Duncan," he said. "You seem to be good at it, why don't you call the police?"

The sun was just glazing the water when Pete pulled into the driveway. He saw the Renault without registering what it meant until he saw its owner, his sister Polly, sitting on the front stoop. He climbed out of the truck and dropped wearily down beside her.

"What are you doing here?"

"I decided to come up early. I called Rita. Didn't you—" She stopped. "No, I guess not."

"Christ, what a day this has been. Another murder. Almost two. Almost more than that, if you figure what could have happened with a bunch of shotgun shells flying all over the place."

"Pete," said Polly. "I've got more news and it's not good. It's Connie. She's at Bradford Hospital. She's had a miscarriage."

He went suddenly dyslexic. He heard it, heard the individual words, but couldn't seem to turn them into a sentence. "What?"

"I'm sorry. I'm sorry as anything."

Still, Pete sat, dumb.

"Rita called the ambulance. Connie didn't want to go, she wanted to wait for you. That's all she kept saying. Get Pete. Get Pete. But I think Rita got kind of nervous. There was a lot of . . . she said she didn't think they should wait. So finally Connie got in the ambulance.

Rita followed her in the car. She called a few minutes ago. Connie's all right. I mean, she's doing okay. We tried to find you. Andy went off looking."

Pete stood up. "She's in Bradford?"

"Yes. Here, I'll drive you."

"No, I'm all right."

"Wouldn't you like me to go with you?"

"No. Thanks."

He crossed the lawn, got into the truck, and headed for Bradford.

CHAPTER
29

First aid to the bereaved: ... A friend or a servant is always stationed in the hall to open the door, to receive notes and cards, and to take messages. In a big house the butler in his day clothes should answer the bell, with the parlor maid to assist him, until a footman can procure a black livery.

Polly waited in the kitchen until they got back. When they walked through the door she took one look at their faces, at whatever it was that had just been crushed out of them, and said, "I'll go. I just waited to see you. To say—"

"Don't," said Connie.

Polly couldn't tell if Connie meant *don't go* or *don't say.* She seemed to be struggling with either her breathing or her vocal chords. She turned to Pete. "I can't do it. Not Saturday. Not right now."

"Okay," said Pete.

"I don't want to do it feeling like this."

"I know. It's all right."

"I'll take care of it," said Polly. "If that's what you want. I'll call everybody."

Pete turned grateful eyes on her. "Will you, Pol? Just tell them it's postponed for a bit."

So she did. She called everybody and said what she

had to and listened to what they needed her to listen to.
When she was through she felt like she'd been put
through the wash on the heavy-duty cycle.

She saved Willy for last. Either he was sound asleep or,
more likely, considering the day's events, he'd just
walked in the door. He answered on the twelfth ring. She
told him where she was, but not why she was calling. He
lived a few hundred yards up the beach. "Meet me
halfway?" she asked.

"Sure. Yes." He sounded dog-tired on the first word,
partially revived on the second.

Polly left by the porch door and walked along the edge
of the marsh until she reached the beach. The creek was
ink black but the sand seemed to have nabbed some of
the moonglow. Long before she'd reached the halfway
point between their two houses she could see Willy's
dark silhouette against it. The minute he came close
enough she came out with it.

He said two words, one she'd never heard him use
before.

They sat in the sand. She talked. He listened. He asked
a few questions, but not many. She answered what she
could. When the silence fell he seemed in no rush to go
anywhere. He stretched out in the sand with his hands
behind his head. Polly lay down beside him and watched
the blinking lights of a small plane as it crossed under
the Big Dipper. After a while she was ready to talk about
something else.

"Tell me what happened at the farm," she said.

Willy told her. Then he backed up and told her the
events leading up to it. Pretty soon he was full circle to
the current day. Not just the events at the farm as he'd
managed to piece it together from the various eyewit-
nesses, but also events surrounding the Reverend Rydell
and Alicia Scott. They'd found her in a hospital not far
from Fulton. She'd gotten home only to realize she was

in worse shape than she'd thought, and had checked herself in. It was Ben Scott who had taken the chair to her, tried to blame her for what had happened to Aggie. Alicia had left Bradford Hospital because she'd been afraid he'd come after her, that this time he really would kill her. He'd apparently come close a few times in the past.

"How could she have left her daughter with a man like that?" asked Polly.

"People do a lot of things to survive."

Polly pondered. "I don't care, she sounds like a real idiot. And if you'll excuse me speaking ill of the dead, so does the Reverend. What in the world was he thinking of?"

"I admit it would have worked out better if he'd come to me instead of trying to reason with Ben Scott himself. Ben admitted everything at the station tonight. That was before he decided to take it all back. After the Reverend came to see him to ask about Aggie's visit that Friday night, Ben realized he was in trouble. He knew sooner or later the Reverend would have a talk with me, that I'd start digging, that he'd get picked up. I truly think in his mind it seemed a gross injustice. It wasn't his fault Aggie was dead. It was Walt's, and Alicia's, and Gene Tilton's, and the Reverend's, just about anybody's but his. That insane rage of his began to build. It started with his verbal attacks on Gene Tilton, then escalated to the actual physical attack on Alicia Scott. Then along came the Reverend, apparently ready and willing to put the noose around the wrong man's neck. Wrong neck, according to Ben Scott, that is. So he paid a call on the Reverend. Ben's account gets cloudy at this point, but it appears at some point Ben realized the Reverend was all that stood in the way of justice as he saw it. The end result was that he picked up a shovel and cracked the Reverend over the head."

Sally Gunning

"Odd that he used a shovel on the Reverend and a shotgun on Walt."

"Not really. I think Walt was the only one Ben really set out to see dead. He drove to the farm, took the shotgun out of his trunk, and charged the house. He didn't care that it was full of extraneous guests."

"But what about the dress? How was it Ben Scott had Aggie's wedding dress?"

"Ben said that was why she'd come to see him, to show him her dress. I figure it must have gone something like this. The Reverend talked to Aggie in the parking lot. He'd only just found out that night that her father wasn't going to be at the wedding. He probably suggested she try one more time to make peace with her father, to get him to give her away, or at the very least, to come to the wedding. Aggie must not have taken to the idea right off. She continued on with her plan to collect her dress and her bag and go to Ginny Turkle's house. At Ginny's she changed her mind and decided to go home to Walt. She probably carried the bag upstairs first, found Walt sound asleep, set the bag down in that spare room and returned to get the dress. Somewhere along the way she must have given more thought to what the Reverend had said and decided to give her father one more shot. I think either she didn't realize she had the dress with her, or she decided to use the dress as the excuse."

"You mean something like, 'look, Dad, I know you won't be there to see it tomorrow so I thought I'd show you my dress tonight'?"

"Something like that. I get the idea the dress is the big star, right?"

Polly twisted sideways, mouth open to protest, but on second thought she decided he might just be right.

"I figure the minute Ben Scott saw his daughter with the dress, the minute he realized she was going to go through with the marriage to Walt Westerman, he went

226

into his usual tirade. But still Aggie wouldn't budge. Ben says he doesn't remember reaching for his daughter's throat, all he remembers is that almost the very minute he felt her flesh under his fingers, she'd dropped out of his hands onto the rug, dead."

Polly shivered. Out of her peripheral vision she saw the police chief glance her way, unfold his hands from under his head, refold them across his chest.

"There followed a gap of some few hours," he continued. "But when the haze cleared Ben knew one thing and one thing only. It was Walt Westerman's fault that Aggie was dead. So he decided to put the blame where it really lay. He found the note she'd left him when she'd gone to live with Walt and he cut off the top. Then he took Aggie's body and threw it in Aggie's car. He drove it to the farm, found a plastic tarp in the barn that he hoped would further tie the thing to Walt, wrapped her up, and chucked her into the well, after removing her engagement ring and throwing that in first, of course. Nice touch. Then he walked home and waited for the idiot police chief to do his stuff."

"But the police chief was no idiot."

"Sure he was. There were a lot of things I should have seen, but didn't. The cut paper was only part of it. The note was in the screen door. If Aggie left that note for Walt she wouldn't stick it in the outside door, she'd leave it on the table or on the refrigerator or someplace safer than that. Ben stuck it in the door because he didn't want to go into the house and get caught in the act. And what about that bag? It wasn't me who realized Aggie had never packed a bag to leave Walt. Aggie hadn't been going anywhere except to Ginny's. Oh, I wasn't so smart. Connie was the one who was so smart. And Pete. Eventually."

"But you said Ben took his confession back."

"Oh, he tried, but by then it was too late. At least I did

that right. I may not have been too swift early on, but on the whole I know my job well enough. His confession will stick. And even if it doesn't we've got enough to convict. We found the dress bag stashed in the garbage at his house and his prints are all over the place—the note, the car, the tarp. And Tilton's been a big help."

A strung-out silence fell. Finally Willy said, "Connie's okay?"

"She will be," said Polly. "Eventually."

"You think they'll still get married?"

She thought of the two faces in the kitchen. "I don't know. If it were anybody else—"

"Yeah," said Willy.

More silence.

Finally the chief yawned and got to his feet. "I'd better get some sleep. Busy day tomorrow."

"Isn't it over?" asked Polly, surprised.

"No chance. The paperwork alone should take a month. You'll be around a while?"

"No. They'll want to be alone, I think."

"So this is good-bye, then." He stretched down a hand, pulled her to her feet. He sounded disappointed, thought Polly, but certainly not crushed. Definitely not crushed.

"Thanks for coming out," she said. "It helped." Her voice slipped alarmingly out of register on the *helped.*

He took a step toward her and suddenly she felt a tower of warm flesh against her, a moat of arms around her.

Then nothing but the cool of the night as he walked off down the beach.

CHAPTER
30

The bridegroom seldom receives any presents. . . .

The sun had just caught in the tops of the apple trees when Andy pulled up to the farm. He could see Walt washing off at the spigot. He walked across the field to meet him and without saying much they turned together toward the house. Walt grabbed two beers from the refrigerator and slid one across the kitchen table to Andy. For a while they sat in silence and drank.

"I guess you know I bought it from Frankie Reese," said Walt finally.

"Yeah," said Andy.

"It was a year or more ago. Things weren't working out with me and Aggie. Least it didn't seem so to me. Aggie was still at home, trying to keep her father happy. Everywhere I looked there was Tilton, staring into her eyes. Aggie wouldn't listen to me. Or she'd listen, but she wouldn't see sense. Not the way I saw it. I figured I knew where it was all going. And I knew I couldn't take it. So I went to see Frankie. That's it."

Andy waited, but Walt seemed to think he'd explained enough. Who had he planned to use it on, Andy wondered, Aggie or Tilton? And then it dawned on him.

Sitting near the exits.

Walt's way out.

"If you and Aggie busted up, you were going to blow your head off, is that it?"

Walt went back to that old not-answering trick of his.

"But you did bust up. A year ago, wasn't it? And you didn't do anything."

Something sheepish-looking happened to the corner of Walt's mouth. "Yeah. I started thinking about what Aggie kept telling me all along. That the only thing wrong with us was what was inside my own head. I went to see her. She said she'd talk to her father and make it all right. That's all she ever wanted, to make everything all right with everybody. Well, they might have talked, but how it ended up was, she moved out."

"And in with you. So you threw the gun in the well."

"Aggie did. She found it. Made me tell her where I got it, what I had it for. All she said was, 'you won't be needing this,' and out she went. Threw it after all those pennies she kept wishing on, trying to get everything to come out perfect. But it never does. It can't. Not with people like Ben Scott."

The words were just about as bitter as words got, but somehow something in them made Andy feel they were past the crisis. Best to make sure, of course. "You're not buying any more guns, are you?"

"No," said Walt. "Me and the chief, we had a talk about that. He's letting me off the hook. 'Seeing as how it wasn't in my desk drawer,' that's how he put it. And seeing as how he could see I wasn't planning to go get another one. I asked him how he could see that and he said, 'It's all happened. As bad as it can get. And you're still here. You took it. What can they do to you after this?' "

True, thought Andy, but it seemed like a pretty weird way to try to cheer somebody up. "And that doll? Aggie threw that in the well?"

"Yeah," said Walt. "It was the one her mother gave her when she was little. I've been talking to some people, thinking a lot. I'm starting to think Aggie didn't want that wedding her mother cooked up any more than I did. But she couldn't say anything to her face so she got mad behind her back. Chucked the doll out."

"I don't know," said Andy. "That doesn't sound much like Aggie. If she didn't get that mad at her mother for walking out, I don't think she'd get that mad at her over something like a dress, or the pizza, dumb stuff like that. Maybe she figured she just didn't need the doll anymore, once her mother came back."

Walt peered at Andy. After a minute he nodded.

They sat there a while longer. Finally Andy said, "Why don't you come home and eat dinner? I've been watching the folks like you said and I think you're wrong about that. I think they'd do better if they thought they were a help."

This time Walt peered at Andy so long he felt himself get his usual red. "You used to be a dumb kid. What happened?"

"I grew up. You just didn't notice."

Walt stood and put a hand on Andy's shoulder. "Okay, you win. Let's go eat."

CHAPTER
_31_

_How far may a girl run after a man? Catlike, she may do a
little stalking! But "run"? Not a step._

It got hot again August first. It was no day to be digging,
thought Pete, as he stripped off his T-shirt and turned
over another shovelful of earth. Weird thing to be doing
in August, starting a vegetable garden, but when Pete
had suggested it Connie had perked up, and that was all
it took.

A truck pulled into the driveway and Pete looked up.
Walt Westerman and Ginny Turkle got out and went
around to the back of the truck. When they reappeared
Walt was carrying two flats of plants and Ginny was
carrying a basket full of vegetables and fruit.

The screen door slammed and Connie came across the
lawn from the house. Even from this distance it seemed
to Pete he could see the shadows that draped her eyes.
They met up midway between house and garden and
reached for each other's hands. They'd been doing that a
lot these days.

"Thought you could use a head start," said Walt as he

came up. He pointed to the plants. "Cauliflower, Chinese cabbage, kale, these'll go into fall okay. The kale goes through to December if the weather holds out." He dropped the flats on the grass.

Ginny handed Connie the basket, out of which billowed corn, beans, eggplant, tomatoes, melons. "And while you're waiting for your own to sprout."

"Thank you," said Connie.

"Nah," said Walt. "It's me thanking you. You know. For what you did."

"We didn't do anything," said Pete. But as Connie and Walt wandered toward the garden talking about mulch Ginny Turkle said, "You're wrong about that. You did a lot, both of you did. Not just, like, getting him off the hook. You gave him Aggie back, for a little while, at least. Long enough to help. Long enough so he could feel, like, worth it."

Maybe so, thought Pete, but it seemed little enough. There were others who had done more. Ginny, for one. She was the one who had saved Walt from being the murderer they'd all thought he was up front. Or some of them had thought.

"She's really nuts about him, isn't she?" said Connie as they walked back to the house.

"Looks like it. Maybe someday he'll even notice."

"Maybe. Unless Patrice comes back from New York. She didn't stick around long, did she?"

"She's from New York, she's used to things moving faster than they do around this place. It must be all that caffeine. Besides, I got the definite sense her interests were strictly short-term. A weekend fling for old time's sake."

Connie gave him an amused look. "You don't have to sound so wistful."

"No? Maybe you'd better marry me before she shows up."

Connie dropped his hand like it was stove-hot and went into the house.

A month later Pete brought it up again. Ironically enough, it was on another day of collecting thanks, this time from Alicia Scott. She was sitting on the rattan couch in the Factotum office when Pete got back from removing a raccoon from Allie Bailey's chimney. He was tired and cross and more than half-covered in soot. But when she rose and came toward him with her hand out, Pete dusted his off as best he could and smiled and shook. Behind him he heard Rita leave discreetly, latching the door in her wake.

"I won't keep you long," said Alicia. "I'm sure you have enough on your plate. I've been arranging for some new shrubs for my daughter's grave. They let the first ones die out. I decided it was long past time I thanked you for coming to my aid."

"My—" He'd almost said "My pleasure," and only just caught himself. "I'm sorry it was needed," he amended. "You look better than the last time I saw you." Which was true, but not by much. Then he remembered the daughter's grave. Not a fun trip. But even so, there had never been much of the grieving mother about Alicia Scott. Maybe something of his thoughts had appeared in his face.

"People around here don't think much of me, do they?" she said.

"Oh, I don't know—"

"Because I left my daughter. Because I left her with someone like Ben. Because I left her and saved myself."

"I don't think—"

"You don't understand what it was like. You don't understand how he was. To me. That was the thing, you see. It was only to me. He never touched a single hair on that girl's head."

Until he killed her, thought Pete.

Alicia, too, must have had a similar thought. She closed her eyes and suddenly she looked just like she had in that hotel room when Ben Scott had caved in her chest with a piece of wood. And who the hell was Pete to judge?

"He never touched her," she repeated. "I knew he never would. If you knew how he idolized that child. And she him. I tried. Oh, I tried. I sent someone to the school. I knew I could never go myself. If Ben had found me he would have killed me. And I knew he'd never voluntarily let her come to me, even for a visit. So I sent someone, we had it all worked out. But she wouldn't go. She wouldn't leave her father. After a time I realized it was all for the best. I knew the most harm I could do her was to let her see us together. To let her see how it could be. I thought I'd saved her that much. And then the morning of the wedding, I found out."

Pete hadn't wanted to hear any of this. He hadn't wanted to listen. Until now. "What happened the morning of the wedding?"

"You see, all along he knew where I was. He'd hired someone to find me. I think if he'd found me right away he'd have killed me. But by the time he was handed my address some time had gone by. And he had Aggie. He must have realized how much he'd won, how little, after all, he'd actually lost. But he kept the address and one day Aggie found it. And when she was getting married, she wrote. I suppose it was what I'd been waiting for all that time. It was what I had never allowed myself to dream about. I came, of course. I forgot about Ben. I forgot about the fear. I didn't care about anything but seeing my daughter again, seeing what she'd turned out like. And she was wonderful. I thought I had saved her from it after all. She was a beautiful, beautiful child. She would be a beautiful bride, have a beautiful wedding, a beautiful life, nothing like mine. And then the morning of the wedding I went out to the farmhouse and discovered the truth."

"So you did go to the farmhouse."

"I thought she was at the Turkle girl's place. I went there, first. She told me Aggie had gone to the farmhouse the previous night. It had been arranged that I would arrive in time to help her dress. I supposed she forgot to tell me about the last minute change of plan. I went out to the farm and as I approached the house I saw all those broken windows. I saw him, sitting on the porch, his hands covered in blood. They say the cycle repeats itself. I saw with my own eyes what I never could have believed otherwise. My daughter had found another violent man to love. I ran from him and from that porch. I don't know where I went, into a field, I think. But he must not have seen me. He never followed me. After a while I collected myself as best I could and went to the church."

"Wait a minute," said Pete. "You saw blood. Didn't it occur to you it might have been Aggie's?"

Alicia shook her head vigorously back and forth. "No. No. I didn't think."

"And then you went to the church? As if nothing had happened?" It made no sense to Pete.

"I know. Looking back, I suppose it looks foolish. But at the time I couldn't think. It seemed to me the only thing to do was to proceed as planned. To move to the next step."

Like a robot, thought Pete. And suddenly he figured he understood what had happened well enough. Alicia couldn't think because she wouldn't let herself think. She must have had years of practice, after all, at blocking things out. And when you can't think, when you've denied yourself the luxury of rational thought, you act by rote. You return to some system of automatic responses or evasions that has kept you alive, or alive in the technical sense, at least.

"If you'd like, I'll keep an eye on the shrubs," said Pete.

"Thank you, that would be nice. In the spring it will be beautiful, absolutely beautiful. Rhododendron, mountain laurel, azaleas, just what she would have—" She stopped, again that one step short of giving in to what she felt. Maybe Pete could understand that better, now, too. Maybe she was afraid if she ever finally gave in she'd never come back out.

"Why don't you sit down?" he said gently. "I'll get you something to drink. I don't know what there is, I think our refrigerator has a hole in it someplace. But I'm sure I could scrounge up something wet."

The face in front of him seemed suddenly confused, almost hostile.

"Sit, please," said Pete. He bolted through the kitchen door. He wondered where Connie was. He grabbed a Coke from the refrigerator and returned to the outer room, but Alicia Scott was gone. He went to the door and saw her running for her car, still running from all the things she'd been running from all her life. Fear, guilt.

And now grief.

Pete found Connie on the balcony, watching the sky. "I think it's going to rain," she said.

"I think we should get married," said Pete.

A quick double take and back to the sky. "Is there some sort of big rush on this?"

"No," said Pete, thinking about the license that expired at the end of the month. Thinking of going through another one of those blood tests. Thinking about Alicia Scott. He didn't want them running from things. Running from this.

"Maybe some things aren't meant to be," she said.

Oh, Pete knew where that came from. She'd said it a few weeks ago. *That baby never did seem real. Maybe it wasn't meant.*

"Maybe some things aren't," said Pete. "But not this. What is it, Connie? Don't you want to marry me?"

She whirled on him. "Of course I do. I just don't see what's the big rush."

Again, he let it drop.

CHAPTER

32

But at every wedding, great or small, city or country, etiquette demands that high silk hats be worn with cutaway coats, and that the bridegroom carry a stick.

Connie woke to the half-remembered sensation that some words had just been said. She rolled over and saw Pete, leaning on one elbow, looking at her with one of those looks.

"What?" she said.

"I said it's September twentieth. Today's our last chance. Monday the license runs out."

Connie shivered. Why was it like someone was walking over her grave every time he brought this up? "You're telling me it's now or never?"

Pete leaned over and removed a loose eyelash from her cheek. "I'm telling you I'd like very much to marry you. Preferably today so I don't have to get stuck with a needle ever again in my life. But if you insist on these barbaric proofs of my love—"

Connie grinned. So that was it. A valid enough reason in its own right, but still, this feeling persisted. All right, so talk to him. She had to try to remember this. It was her silence that hurt him most. "I keep thinking about Aggie and Walt," she said.

Pete nodded, thoughtful. "Me, too. But isn't that just one more reason to do it? Who knows what will happen tomorrow. I say let's do it and—"

"Get it over with?"

"Let's do it and get on with our life," said Pete firmly. "Lay the ghosts to rest. Ours as well as everyone else's."

Yes, thought Connie. What the hell? Why not? "But we can't possibly do it today."

"Why not? I figure it will take three phone calls. Elsie McAllister, Willy, and if you still want Polly—"

Yes, she wanted Polly. It would only take her an hour and a half to get here if she pushed. And they *could* get married in blue jeans. And afterward? "We could go away," said Connie. "Couldn't we, Pete?"

She watched him thinking. They'd tried this once before. They'd actually tried to close down Factotum for two whole weeks. It had lasted, what, two hours? "Our mistake last time was we stayed here and everyone knew where to find us. It'll work if we just go away someplace."

"And if we don't try to close up shop," said Pete. "I should think Rita and Andy could hold things together for a couple of weeks."

"Sure they could. That's only one more phone call to Rita."

"If we pack now, we can leave straight from town hall."

"And drive up the coast. Oh, let's, Pete! We've always wanted to do that. Haven't we always wanted to do that? We can stop when we feel like stopping. Stop whenever we see someplace we like. It's off-season now, it shouldn't be hard to find a place."

And when they got back they could throw a party. It was, after all, something to celebrate. But not today. Today was for the two of them.

"Well?" said Pete.

"Yes," she said.

CHAPTER
33

*What you should say in congratulating a bridal couple
depends on how well you know one, or both of them. But
remember, it is a breach of good manners to congratulate
a bride on having secured a husband. If you know them
fairly well, you may say to him, "I hope your good luck
will stay with you always!" and to her "I hope your whole
life will be one long happiness . . .."*

*To all of the above, the groom and bride answer merely
"Thank you."*

The three men on the bench in front of Beston's Store
peered up at the September sky.

"Got some weather coming," said Evan.

"Yep," said Ed.

"Damn that Pete," said Bert. "I called over to Factotum to get him to take down my awnings and Rita said
he wasn't there. Away, she said. For two weeks, she said.
Right smack in the middle of hurricane season. She tried
to send that young clodhopper Andy and I told her you
keep him away from me. My awnings haven't hung
straight since the last time he touched them. I asked her
where Pete was and she says she had no idea."

"Pete away for two weeks," said Ed. "Now that's not
like him."

"No," said Bert. "And neither is drunk driving. But I
saw him getting caught in the act Saturday morning."

Ed and Evan looked at each other. "Pete? Drunk?"

"Right in front of town hall. His car and the chief's pulled up bumper-to-bumper. The two of them standing on the sidewalk. Pete was acting mighty queer, let me tell you. Had a sock in his hand, of all things, and he was arguing fit to kill with the police chief. 'If we rode together we'd be legal now.' That's what he said. The chief said something about it being bad luck and Pete needing all the luck he could get, and Pete near took his head off. Then he said something about this being his last chance because of his license expiring Monday, but it cut no ice with the chief."

"That's driving with an expired license," said Ed. "Not drunk driving."

"Open your ears, Ed. He said the license didn't expire till Monday. And I heard Pete refuse the breathalizer test."

"Now that's a fool thing to do," said Ed, who'd had some experience with this.

"Heard it plain as day. 'You won't get me taking that test again,' he said. Appears to have happened before, I'd guess."

"Could have fooled me," said Ed. "Then what happened?"

"Then Connie pulled up and Pete hollered out something like 'what'd you do, go by way of Duluth?' You know Connie, you can figure what she'd likely say to that, but she didn't toss back one single word. Looked like she was about to have a heart attack. Good thing Polly's visiting. She had Connie clenched by the elbow like she was afraid she'd fall in the street and Connie kept saying 'I can't believe this is happening, I can't believe this is happening.'"

"I don't know," said Ed. "Doesn't sound much like Pete. Or the chief. Figure he'd give him a break after what they've been through the past few months."

"Nah," said Bert. "Not the chief. Not when it comes to drunk driving. And how else do you explain Pete's being gone for two weeks? He's in whatjacallit, one of those programs."

"Must be," said Ed. "What do you think, Ev? You're quiet enough."

"Quieter than usual," said Bert. "Which comes as close as there is to dead." Bert guffawed loudly.

Evan Spender stood up and ambled down the steps of the porch in the direction of the Garret Gold Antique Shop.

"What are you doing?"

"Going to pick out a wedding present."

Ed Healey and Bert Barker looked at each other and shrugged. Then they looked back at the sky.

"Yep," said Ed. "I'd say we got some weather coming."

"Damn that Pete," said Bert.